W9-CCP-500

TERMINAL

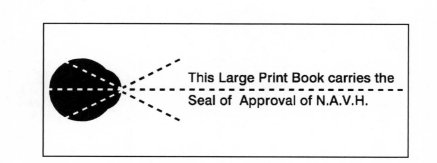

This Large Print Book carries the
Seal of Approval of N.A.V.H.

A BURKE NOVEL

TERMINAL

ANDREW VACHSS

THORNDIKE PRESS

An imprint of Thomson Gale, a part of The Thomson Corporation

EAST CHICAGO PUBLIC LIBRARY
EAST CHICAGO, INDIANA

Detroit • New York • San Francisco • New Haven, Conn. • Waterville, Maine • London

THOMSON
GALE

Copyright © 2007 by Andrew Vachss.

Thorndike Press, an imprint of The Gale Group.

Thomson and Star Logo and Thorndike are trademarks and Gale is a registered trademark used herein under license.

ALL RIGHTS RESERVED

This is a work of fiction. Names, characters, places, and incidents either are the product of the author's imagination or are used fictitiously. Any resemblance to actual persons, living or dead, events, or locales is entirely coincidental.

Thorndike Press® Large Print Core.

The text of this Large Print edition is unabridged.

Other aspects of the book may vary from the original edition.

Set in 16 pt. Plantin.

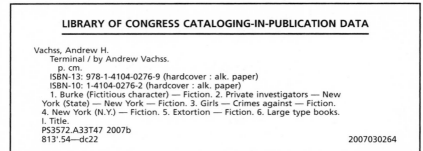

LIBRARY OF CONGRESS CATALOGING-IN-PUBLICATION DATA

Vachss, Andrew H.
   Terminal / by Andrew Vachss.
     p. cm.
   ISBN-13: 978-1-4104-0276-9 (hardcover : alk. paper)
   ISBN-10: 1-4104-0276-2 (hardcover : alk. paper)
   1. Burke (Fictitious character) — Fiction. 2. Private investigators — New York (State) — New York — Fiction. 3. Girls — Crimes against — Fiction. 4. New York (N.Y.) — Fiction. 5. Extortion — Fiction. 6. Large type books.
   I. Title.
   PS3572.A33T47 2007b
   813'.54—dc22   2007030264

Published in 2007 by arrangement with Pantheon Books, a division of Random House, Inc.

Printed in the United States of America on permanent paper

10 9 8 7 6 5 4 3 2 1

LP
F
V119t

for . . .

Judith Moore,
who used her sweet, soft heart to break
the cruelest of all chains.

You were never a fat girl to me,
beautiful.

I got to the job site a couple hours early. The kind of work I do, you show up too late, sometimes you don't get to go home when it's over.

Gigi was already planted in his spot, his enormous body mass taking up most of a wooden bench, a half-empty pitcher of beer on a little table to his right. The behemoth had a perfect sight-line on the front door, but his tiny eyes were too deeply flesh-pouched for me to tell where he was looking. Wrapped in a faded gray jersey pulled over drawstring pants of the same material, he looked like a moored battleship.

I found a stool at the far end of the bar. The guy behind the stick had a little slice of forehead and less chin. His eyes showed signs of life — I guessed somewhere around geranium level.

I ordered a shot — nobody does brand names in a joint like this. The inbred blinked

7

a couple of times, then brought me some brown liquid. I asked him for a glass of water. He stared at me for a minute. You could see his mind working — it wasn't a pretty sight. Finally, enough tumblers fell into place. He reached under the bar and came up with a glass the EPA wouldn't allow you to dump without a permit.

The TV set was suspended from the ceiling by cables at the opposite end of the bar from where I was sitting. Some baseball game was on. I was too far away to hear the sound, or even make out who was playing, but I watched the moving images. Reminded me of being Inside. They rig the TV in the dayroom the same way, probably for the same reason. Most guys want to be outdoors every chance they get, but there's cons who know their soaps better than any housewife.

Usually, I drink the water, slip the whiskey into the water glass, let the ice melt into it, and then ask for another. If I think anyone might be watching close, I transfer by mouth. I was raised in places where you learn to do that with meds you don't want, watched by "staff" who hoped you'd refuse — restraints and hypos were more fun for them.

Eventually, the bartender takes away both glasses, brings me a "same again," and everybody's happy. Any regular interested in the stranger sees a man drinking solo, dedicated to his work. In a place like this, you sit by yourself *not* drinking, it's like a red neon arrow pointing at you. *Down* at you.

But I watched how other guys at the bar had to practically scream to get the inbred's attention. He mostly just stood there, in the Zen state of just *being* the mouth-breathing genetic misfire that he was. So I nursed my drink the way a crack-addict mother nurses her kid — if it could figure out how to drink itself, fine.

Forty minutes later, a man in a bone-colored leather sports coat shoulder-rolled in and sat down in an empty booth. Late thirties, with a tanning-bed complexion. He sported a hundred-dollar short haircut — gelled, not spiked. His wristwatch was crusted with diamonds; a three-strand loop of eighteen-karat draped against a black silk collarless pullover.

The battleship slowly broke loose from its mooring and started across the room. From behind me, two torpedoes cut across his wake. As the first passed by where I was sitting, I slid the length of rebar out of my sleeve, gripped the taped end, and took out his knee from behind. The other whirled at his partner's scream, but I was already swinging. His collarbone snapped under the ridged steel whip.

The guy in the bone-colored jacket never made it out of his booth.

I was one of the men who flowed around Gigi like river water around a big rock, all of us heading for the door. The sidewalk was empty, except for a squat-bodied man in a wheelchair. He had a begging cap on the ground next to him, one hand under the army blanket spread across his lap. Nobody gave him a second glance.

◆

The battleship was docked at a pier overlooking the Brooklyn Navy Yard, behind the wheel of an ancient black Caddy. He covered more than half of the front seat; the steering wheel was hidden somewhere under his upper body. A thick skullcap of wiry black hair covered his bowling ball of a head. I was standing next to him, talking through the opened window. I'd done time with Gigi — keeping something solid between you and him is always a good play.

"Didn't expect you," Gigi said. "Never saw you before."

I shrugged, wasting fewer words than he had.

"I did time with your boss. Thought he'd be sending Herk to watch my back."

I shrugged again. "Herk" was short for "Hercules," named for his hyper-muscled physique. Everyone but Gigi called him "Big Herk," but Herk's 275 pounds of prison-sculptured, Dianabol-boosted chassis made him a middleweight in Gigi's league.

The man Gigi thought was my boss was me, the Burke he knew years ago. My face had changed — bullet wounds and trainee surgeons will do that for you — but the pay-phone that rang in the back of Mama's restaurant still took my calls. And my voice was still the same . . . when I wanted it to be.

"He still in your crew, Herk?"

I gave him the look.

"What?" he said, insulted. "You think I'm a fucking cop? They wanted to wire *me* up, they'd have to use a motherfucking bale of the stuff."

I shook my head.

"You're a dummy? You can't talk, that it? Look, pal, I can see you're not Herk, but I sure as fuck *know* you ain't Max, either."

Gigi meant Max the Silent, a Tibetan

11

combat dragon. Max can't speak, but that's not how he got his name.

"I'm not a dummy," I said, softly. "But I know when to dummy *up*."

"Not everyone does," he said, a tinge of nostalgia in his guttural voice. "Things ain't the same. These days, you got to pay a man to watch your back even when you get hired just to do a simple job like pounding on that mook. But with these punk kids taking over now, fucking *bosses* they are, you never know when they're gonna watch too much TV, start thinking all *plots* and shit."

"Those two guys, you don't think they were his?"

"Mario's? The guy in the pretty white coat? Yeah, they were his, all right. Even a fucking *stugotz* like him knows when he's been put on the spot, marked down for some serious pain. But he's still got to do business, got to make his rounds, show some face. It was just a matter of time. Wasn't me, it would have been someone else.

"Besides, if those guys you took out were from the . . . people who hired me, they would have been shooters. Those guys, they were just dumbass muscle."

I nodded agreement. If they'd been experienced bodyguards, one look at Gigi would have had them heading for the back exit. Probably a pair of strip-club bouncers, used to flexing their gym muscles at drunks.

"Mario could've got himself some shooters, but he'd have to go to the yoms, get someone to do that for the kind of chump-change money he's holding now. Can you imagine a nigger walking into that place? It'd be like one of them wandering onto our range, Inside."

I shook my head.

"You know what, pal? This is seriously fucked. I get paid to do some work on a guy, I got to pay a piece of that just to make sure my back don't get cold. Turns out, I wasted the money."

"You could have handled both of those guys, too?" I said, pretending mild surprise. I'd seen Gigi waddle up to whole *groups* of men Inside, then go through them like an enraged kid busting up balsa-wood model airplanes. He had all the speed of a fire hydrant, and about the same pain tolerance. Gigi wasn't any good at chasing you down, but that's the thing about prison . . . nowhere to run.

"Ask your boss," the battleship said.

I didn't say anything.

"Hey, fuck you, you don't want to talk. Here's the other half of your money. Tell

Burke I still owe him a glass of *vino*."

◆

Going back home to New York is like going back to an old girlfriend just because you remembered how great the sex had been. The minute you come, you remember all the reasons you'd decided to go the last time.

It wasn't that bad, not really. Being away from my family had hurt more than I'd ever imagined, but I had them back again. All the ones left, anyway.

I didn't have my old place, but the new one was better, once you got past the first couple of floors. I didn't have my dog, but I could go for days without thinking about her now.

What I didn't have was my old ways.

I couldn't go back to scamming-and-stinging. I had always specialized in fleecing the kind of humans who couldn't run to the Law, but the Internet boys had the freak market sewn up now. Promising kiddie porn I was never going to deliver was one of my bill-payers back in the day, but that's all done — Cyberville's full of places where freaks can sample the product for free before they buy.

14

Selling info on how to become a mercenary is another dry well. Worked fine back when "mercenary" meant government-funded, no-risk slaughter — machine guns against machetes, that kind of thing. Every master-race moron with heavy experience killing paper targets wanted to get in on the fun. That's a different game today, too. The real merc work is in overthrowing governments, and that takes specialists with track records, not fantasy-fueled freaks whose fetal alcoholism convinced them that they were the last hope of the White Race.

I used to middleman arms deals, selling ordnance to . . . whoever. But that's a no-touch ever since 9/11. The buyers could be Saudi-financed robots, or one of those neo-Nazi crews whose idea of "screening" is skin tone. And some of those are the kind of scum-sucking swine whose idea of a part-time job is being an informant for the *federales.*

One surefire sting had been offering kids for sale, then strong-arming the exchange — the old badger game, cranked up to big-number payoffs. Who were the ripped-off buyers going to complain to, the Better Business Bureau? But, today, the human-traffickers have so much genuine product in their pipelines that the price keeps dropping. What you could sell twenty years ago for a hundred grand wouldn't get you five today. Not worth the time and trouble to set up the mark, never mind the mess you sometimes make when they get all aggressive the second they find out what they *really* just bought.

I heard there was good money selling electromagnetic shields to poor souls who were sure they were being targeted by psychotronic weapons, but I couldn't make myself go there. Same reason I could never pluck the ripe alien-abductee fruit, even when it dangled so close to the ground.

Can't even rip off the dope men, anymore. They used to just truck the weight around, open for any hijacker with accurate info and the right skills. I'd done one of my stretches for a move like that. Had everything figured out: steal it, sell it back to the owners. Only thing is, they *did* call the cops. *Their* cops.

Anyway, that's all changed, too. Just read this whole frantic piece in the *News* about a new drug hitting the streets. Heroin cut with fentanyl. Supposed to have killed a few people already.

Reading stuff like that always makes me sad. Not because of a few dead dope fiends, but I can't figure out why anyone thinks that's news, or why it matters. This "new" stuff isn't new at all — it's been killing addicts in Chicago and Detroit for a long time now. What kind of chump thinks hard-core addicts read the papers for street news, like yuppies checking their mutual funds? For the dealers, a few deaths are good for business. Proves they've got the real thing, not some stepped-on lemonade that won't even buy you a mild buzz.

A junkie worries about only three things: finding the money to fix, finding a seller with righteous stuff, and finding a vein to slam it home. Death? You try *that* ride every time. Part of the deal. That's why the top dogs brand their stuff.

Maybe they'll make a movie about it.

◆

I used to find people. Kids mostly. I was good at it — the best tracker in the city, the whisper-stream said. But I'd finally learned that bringing kids back to the people who paid me didn't always make me a hero.

And the last job I'd done had changed that forever. The man who used to send me tracker work would never be calling me again, either.

I scratch around now. Helping people go and stay gone, that's something I know how to do. But there's not a lot of that kind of work around. And most of it just *vibrates* with danger, like the hum in an electric fence.

The thing about doing crime for a living is that you have to *keep* doing it. And, every time you do, the odds shift . . . in the wrong direction. I'm not going Inside again. Not for all the usual reasons — although every one of those is a good one — but because I can't play that hand anymore. At my age, with my record, any sentence would come with a lifetime guarantee. So when I do violence-for-money, like covering Gigi's back, I make sure I'm nowhere near the fallout zone.

Still, in my world, being "sure" is just another way of saying you had cut down the odds. Nobody was supposed to die in the job Gigi had hired me for, but accidents happen. What I *was* sure of was that nobody was going to talk. Not because of some bullshit "code," but because it was the smart play. The only play.

Nobody was even going to *call* the cops, much less talk to them. And if some passing citizen had a cell phone, good fucking luck interrogating that bartender — he wouldn't be *playing* dumb.

With all that, I still should have passed.

Anytime you cover Gigi while he's working, you could end up watching a homicide.

I've got some money. That last job had turned out to be worth a lot more than I'd thought it could be. Cost me a lot more than I thought I had, too.

No reason why I couldn't go the rest of the way on that one score. I live small. I have the whole top floor of a flophouse that's been scheduled for the wrecking ball for years, but the bribery they call "paperwork" in this town had prolonged the process through two administrations already. In the meantime, I don't pay rent. Or utilities.

I don't have a phone. For outgoing, I use an ever-changing batch of cloned cells the Mole puts together for me. For messages, there's the same number the underground has been using for years. The same one Gigi had called.

I've even got cable, a feeder line from the ground floor of the flophouse. I see whatever I want on the screen, but I never see a bill.

Thanks to my sister Michelle, I don't pay retail for clothing. Except when she gets in one of her "You need this *now!*" moods. Then I end up paying through both nostrils and a few assorted veins.

My car is as maintenance-free as an

I-beam, a '69 Roadrunner two-door post. It looks like a derelict from the outside but underneath is an all-new chassis, complete with a transplanted Viper IRS, and a bullet-proof, injected Mopar wedge, hand-assembled for torque. Purrs on pump gas, never uses a drop of synthetic between changes, and wouldn't overheat in a Saharan summer.

I shoot pool, but for nickels and dimes. I play cards, but only with my family — my brother Max is into me for over a couple hundred grand, but we agreed we'd settle up when we both reach the Other Side. He's my partner in our two-man betting syndicate, too, but we've never gone more than a few hundred plus-or-minus there.

I don't drink. Even when I did smoke, I only bought Dukes — meaning straight from North Carolina, without those pesky New York tax stamps. Later on, I used one of those hundred-foot Indian reservations they have on Long Island, the ones they built to display the government's deep respect for its favorite Native American tribe: the Casino Indians.

I don't use drugs for the same reason I don't drink. Some kids who come up the way I did use stuff like that to get numb. Others, the ones like me, take hypervigilance as a sacred vow.

No woman who ever loved me cost me money. But none of them are still with me. Some are dead; all are gone.

Max has his family. His wife, Immaculata; his daughter, Flower. The Prof, my only true father, has another child — a young gun he had picked up and lifted up, like he had done with me. I was way older than Clarence, but I'd never felt replaced; I felt added-to. He calls us both "son," but, to the Prof, I'd be "Schoolboy" forever.

He and Clarence had a crib together over in East New York. Michelle had the Mole; together they had Terry. I had snatched him from a pimp in Times Square years ago, before Giuliani cleared up midtown and left the boroughs to rot. Mama had all of us, but Flower, her granddaughter, was the pick of the litter, and none of us had a moment's doubt about that.

It wasn't so much that they all had one another — I had them, too, and they me. It was that they all had something to *do.*

◆

I walked in the glass door with the taped-over cracks, found myself facing a man in a wheelchair, sitting behind a wide wooden plank that holds a register nobody ever signs.

"Gateman," I said.

"Hey, boss. You had a call."

That meant someone had called me at Mama's and she had left word with Gateman. I wouldn't carry a cell on a job like the one I just did, and none of us would ever use an answering machine.

I nodded, then handed him an envelope.

"Thanks, boss."

"Count it."

"For what? We didn't set no exact price."

"Yeah, we did. Remember?"

"For real?"

"Count it."

"There's — fuck me! — five large here. What'd that humongoid pay?"

"Ten. Knowing Gigi, he probably got twenty-five, minimum."

"He's worth it," Gateman said, reluctantly respectful. "That monster motherfucker never misses. And he don't even know how to *spell* 'rat.' "

"True," I said, remembering a conversation I'd had with Gigi on the yard, a long time ago.

"I'm kind of like a whore," the monster said, *shocking me into silence. "I mean, we both rent our bodies, right? You know what makes*

22

me different?"

I made an "I wouldn't even guess" gesture, afraid to say anything out loud.

"We got different values," the monster said, solemnly. "There ain't a whore in the world you can trust to keep her mouth shut. And there ain't a thing on this earth that can make me open mine."

"Nobody rats *on* him, neither," Gateman said. "You know I was at a trial of his once, over in Brooklyn?"

"Yeah?"

"Square business. It was hilarious, bro. The whole courthouse was cracking up. See, Gigi rolled up these three jamokes who got behind in their payments. Probably three separate jobs, but you know that whale-scale bastard — he does them all at the same time, save himself a few steps maybe. So, anyway, while they're in the hospital, probably flying on morphine, they all give statements, and Gigi gets taken down.

"But comes time for trial, one by one, the three witnesses get up on the stand, point over at Gigi sitting there, and *swear* that he wasn't the one who did them.

"The DA, some kid probably a week out of law school, one of those Daddy's-got-connections clowns the DA's always hiring, he's fucking *screaming* at his own witnesses:

23

'Are you trying to tell this jury that you were beaten by *another* four-hundred-and-fifty-pound white male with a red lightning-bolt tattoo on his right forearm!? That *is* the exact description of your assailant that you gave the police, isn't it?' And the witness, *each* witness, mind you, stares him straight in the eye, says, 'That's right. All's I know, it wasn't him.' "

"Yeah. Gigi's a few hundred pounds over the ninja limit, but he can sure disappear right in front of your eyes."

Gateman high-fived that, said: "Five large, boss. Damn! So this is —"

"Half. Like we agreed."

"Ah, come on, man. I didn't think you was —"

"I said *partners,* Gate. Partners don't cut pieces, they split. Equal shares."

"You don't just *talk* it, man."

I tapped fists with one of the city's deadliest shooters, and headed up the stairs to my place.

"You know, when people say 'scared to death,' they don't mean it," the skinny brunette said. "Not for-real mean it. They're afraid of doing something, maybe. Or of get-

24

ting caught at it. A woman like me, if she said something like that, she might be talking about getting a beating. But not about dying. She's just being dramatic. You've seen that, right?"

I made a gesture that could mean anything.

"He'd do it," she swore, as fervently as a preacher selling lies.

I made another gesture.

"So I don't have any choice. Don't tell me about putting a restraining order out on him. He told me, I ever did that, they'd find it in my purse, lying next to my body."

I hadn't been going to say anything about restraining orders. I'm not a counselor. Or a citizen.

"I've got kids," she kept on, relentlessly trying to find another button to push. "Two kids. They're terrified of him. If I don't get away —"

She reacted to my raised eyebrows like I'd slapped her.

"Hey! I can't just *go*, all right? What am I going to do? This is real life, not TV. People don't just disappear. Specially people with kids. It costs a lot of money to do something like that."

I let the right corner of my mouth twitch, knowing her eyes were on me like prison searchlights when the escape alarm goes off.

"So where am I going to get the money for what I want *you* to do, right?"

I shrugged.

"He's got a life insurance policy. It comes with his job. I'm the beneficiary. You want to see it?" she said, reaching toward the purse where she probably also had the tape recorder.

I shook my head "no." The guy she wanted hit was a prison guard — a "CO" is what she'd called him. Even if I'd bought her story about the life insurance, no prison guard's union policy was going to buy her a sure-to-be-investigated murder.

How the live-in girlfriend of a prison guard got involved with a convict was more than I wanted to know. Why the convict wanted the guard dead probably had nothing to do with anything he was doing to the woman, but that didn't interest me, either. How the con got my name was no mystery — any one of a couple of dozen lifers up there could have dropped it.

Only thing was, not one of them had ever reached out to me himself, just to give me the heads-up.

"You've got the wrong man," I told the brunette.

Her dark eyes teared right up. "I can get

more —"

"No. I mean, you've got me confused with someone else. I don't do the kind of work you're talking about getting done."

"But I was *told* —"

"By who?"

"I'm not supposed to say. And when I give my word, that's it. I'd never give up someone who tried to do me a favor."

"I'm sure you're a righteous, stand-up woman. You sound way too good for the guy you talked about. I wish you the best of luck finding a solution to your problem."

"But —"

"I think whoever referred you to me — and I do respect you for not saying their name — was thinking about you going away. Disappearing. Starting over. There's a group I know that could help you with that. After they checked out your story, of course. That's all that happened, I think. Wires got crossed."

"I don't *want* to disappear. I want *him* to disappear."

"You should be careful who you say things like that to. You never know who's listening."

"I came a long way."

"Me, too," I lied. "That happens a lot, I think. People travel to meet their expecta-

27

tions, and they turn out to be disappointed when they arrive."

◆

If that woman had been telling the truth — and if she'd had the money — I could have helped her go and stay gone. I've got a whole stash of identities. Not ID, identities. Different planets. Today, any amateur can get photo ID — all you need is broadband, the right software, a color laser printer, and a laminator. But that's just pictures on documents, not an identity.

A real identity takes years to establish. You need credit cards, and you need to *use* them. Buy things, pay them off. Travel. Make a nice paper trail.

Driver's licenses get renewed. Taxes get paid. Phone numbers stay listed. Answering machines pick up.

If you're going to use a sham identity to work a score, it helps to have a Web presence, too. Not an actual site, just tracks — enough of a "trail" for chumps who think "Googling" makes them an investigator. Like a few posts to newsgroups, or even a blog. Faking a newspaper or magazine story is probably the safest — anything you plant on the Net will metastasize so quickly that tracing it back to the original becomes impossible for anyone less than a real pro.

All this costs money. An investment, the way I see it. Takes years to ripen on the vine, but when you harvest, it's a sweet crop. A cash crop.

I'd been stockpiling ID ever since I learned how to do it. Each new one is better than the last. Since 9/11, they're worth fifty times what they were, an inflation-proof asset. It isn't that I knew the government's license to invade privacy it has today was coming — but I always assume *something* bad is.

That's one bet I've never lost yet.

Today, my walk-around ID is Scott Thomas. Scott — or is it Thomas? Hard to tell with names like that — is a good citizen. He owns my car — that rust-bucket '69 Roadrunner with dog-dish hubcaps and a single, sorry exhaust pipe poking out the back — pays the insurance on time, keeps the registration up to date.

Scott pays his taxes, too. Of course, the poor guy doesn't make a lot of money, working as a kitchen helper. But he's lucky; the rent where he lives hasn't gone up in ten years. You could ask the landlord, but his building is owned under a corporate name it would take a team of forensic accountants a decade to unravel. They'd have to be fluent in Chinese as well.

Still, the brunette worried me. She'd called Burke's number, and she could have gotten it from anywhere. Some of those places are more reliable than others, so it was possible she'd been told Burke did contract jobs.

That rumor had been as much a part of the city as judgeships-for-sale since forever — but then Wesley had checked out so explosively that it made the front page of every tabloid in the city. He left behind a suicide note — being Wesley, it read like a threat — taking the weight for a whole string of killings that went back a long time. Some of those were mine. Wesley's suicide was anomic, but his confession was my inheritance. My brother, the iceman nobody could touch, still touching me.

Nobody doubted Wesley's note. Not the cops, not the people who live down here. That was what Wesley did, make people dead for money. He never asked why, just told you how much.

Years ago, my compadre Pablo told me about a contract Wesley had on a Puerto Rican dope dealer uptown. The dealer knew the contract was out. He went to a Santería priestess, begging for voodoo heat against the glacier coming for him. The priestess told him Chango, the warrior-god, would protect him. For a price.

The priestess was an evil old demon, feared throughout the barrio. Her crew was all Marielitos. Zombie-driven murderers. They set fires to watch the flames. Ate the charred flesh. Tattoos on their hands to tell you their specialty. Weapons, drugs, extortion, homicide. Their executioner's tattoo was an upside-down heart with an arrow through it. Cupid as a hit man.

The priestess called on her gods. Killed chickens and goats. Sprinkled virgin's blood on a knife. Loosed her death-dogs into the street looking for Wesley.

The dealer hid himself in her temple. Safe.

Blazing summer, but the kids stayed off the streets around her temple. They knew winter was coming.

A few days later, a UPS driver pulled up outside the temple. The Marielitos slammed him against his truck, pulling at his clothes. Eyes watched from beneath slitted shades. The killers took a small box from the driver, laughing when he insisted someone had to sign for it.

Experienced assassins, they held the box under an opened fire hydrant, soaking the paper off. Then one of them held the box to his ear, shaking it. Another pulled a butter-fly knife from his pocket, flashed it open in the street, grinning. They squatted, watching as the box was slit open. Looked inside. Saw a ghost.

They took the box inside to the priestess. A few minutes later, the dope dealer was thrown into the street, hands cuffed behind his back, duct tape sealing his mouth. He ran from the block. Never made it past the corner.

Nobody saw anything. His body was still there when the cops came.

The whisper-stream went mad with rumor. In the bodegas, in the after-hours joints, on the streets. It was said the priestess found the severed hand of her executioner inside the box, the tattoo mocking her. Chango was angry — she needed a better sacrifice than a chicken to appease him.

The Prof said it best: "Maybe that bitch *was* a witch, but Wesley just quelled her spell."

Everyone saw him die. Wesley's final moments were on live TV. Every channel in the city. But nobody ever found his body. The cluster of dynamite Wesley held aloft before he blew the screens into blackness hadn't left even a micro-fragment behind. So, every time a super-clean, no-trace kill goes down, some part of the whisper-stream questions whether the iceman is really, truly gone.

The more I thought about it, the more I was convinced that the brunette had just gotten bad info. Cons lose touch with the World; maybe her boyfriend was working off old rumors. Or just profiling, telling her he "knew people." If she'd been a plant, I couldn't see the cops doing it. Even if they somehow knew I was still alive, so what? I wasn't wanted for anything. Ever since I'd gone "missing and presumed" years ago, they hadn't even sniffed around.

No. Just a bad connection. My number's been the same since forever. You float a public offering, you can't choose who buys your stock.

"He was mad-dogging me, I mean right in my grille, so I fixed him up with a left hook," the light-skinned Latino with a coiled-cobra tattoo on his neck said to me. "And what does this punk-ass faggot do? Cocksucker runs down to the precinct like a slapped bitch, puts a case on me."

"And . . . ?"

"And *what,* man? What else I got to tell you?"

"I look like Legal Aid to you, *amigo?*"

"Yeah. All right, I get it. What are we talking about, then, make this go away?"

"You break anything?"

"Broke that punk's jaw," he said — proud, holding up the fist that had done the job.

"So it's a felony beef. Is that the problem?"

"Why you want to play me off like that, bro? I'm looking at strike fucking three, okay?"

"But you made bail."

He leaned forward, left shoulder dropping just a notch. "What you trying to say?"

"Me? I'm just listening."

"Yeah? Well, look here, the people who put up my bail, *they're* the ones who gave me your number to call. They said you had contacts, could take care of stuff like this."

"You got fifty?"

"Fifty what?"

He gave me a prison-yard stare for a long five seconds. I let my eyes go all soft and wet, so he'd know I knew. Every joint is full of murderers, but killers are a much rarer breed. All cons learn this, sometimes with their last breath.

"Not in my pocket, man," he said, giving it up. "But I can get it. Question is, what do I get *for* it?"

"A good lawyer."

"A lawyer? Fuck a bunch of lawyers, man. What I need is a judge."

"And the people who told you to call my number, they said I could get that done?"

"Nah. That was my idea."

"It's a bad one."

"So what *you* got?"

"I told you. A lawyer."

"What you been smoking, man? You talking about some self-defense thing, right? That won't —"

"Right. You can't take the stand, because then your priors come out. And your priors, they're for the same thing, same *kind* of thing, right?"

"I'm a collector," he said, crossing his arms to display his ropy biceps.

"Reason you want the lawyer is you need one to pull a Michael Jackson."

"A what?"

"The guy you clocked, he drops the case, okay? Then he sues you, like in civil court, for the damage you did to him. You settle the case for, say, thirty K. He gets twenty, his lawyer gets ten, *your* lawyer gets ten, and so do I. Nobody's mad, nobody goes to jail.

How's that?"

"I could just pay the motherfucker off myself."

"No, you can't," I said. Not arguing: telling. "You go anywhere near him, you're going back Inside. If *anyone* comes around with cash in an envelope, that's all kinds of hurt ready to be let loose. But if a *lawyer* approaches this guy, tells him he might have a good case . . ."

"How's *my* lawyer gonna approach *him?*"

"Not your lawyer. A barrio guy. *Abogado, comprende?* One of those vultures you see hanging around every night outside the Arraignment Part, looking to pick up some change. You know the kind I mean: got their office in their cell phone."

"Yeah. *Those* motherfuckers. So you're saying I need *two* lawyers?"

"Just hire the one I tell you to, everything else will take care of itself."

He nodded slowly.

My kind of score: low risk, low cash.

Big fucking deal.

◆

"Gigi? Never forget that two-ton, son," the Prof said. "Inside, you couldn't touch him.

They only got shanks in there, not har-poons."

"He sounds like a pig, mahn," Clarence said, fastidiously inspecting the line of demarcation between the edge of his butter-colored cashmere jacket and the protruding French cuff of a bronze silk shirt, anchored by glittering topaz links. "A gross, fat pig."

"There's all kinds of pigs, boy," the Prof said, seriously. "My man Gigi, he's a razor-back hog. Ain't got none of those down in the Islands, do they?"

Clarence's clean-featured face twisted into a grimace of disgust. "No, Father."

"Haven't seen one of those devil beasts since I was a boy. But once you see one coming your way, it's in your mind, perma-nent."

There was a tincture of pride in the old man's voice. I knew the Prof had been born in Louisiana, but he always swore the only good thing that ever came out of the place was Slim Harpo; didn't want to hear about Lazy Lester. I'd tried to interest him in Tab Benoit, but he said "Weary Time of Night" reminded him of Freddy Fender. Even Lon-nie Brooks didn't turn his crank. And he thought Zydeco was just plain wrong.

"He hasn't changed, Prof," I assured him.

"Who changes?" the noble-featured little

37

man said, challenge clear in the textured voice that gave him half the weight behind his name: "Prof" was either "Prophet" or "Professor," depending on how you knew him.

"Me. I've changed."

"Yeah? No offense, but your face wasn't exactly your case ace, son. The work they did on you in that hospital — so what?"

"I don't mean that. I'm just . . . bored, I guess."

"How you gonna be bored, boy? Hell, even Inside, we was never bored. Out here, there's a gazillion things to do."

"And if you already did them?"

"Look, fool, if everyone walked around with that attitude, nobody'd have more than one woman. And her only the one time. There's some things we *all* meant to be doing over and over again, get it?"

"You know what I mean."

The Prof took a long drag off his Kool, blew a harsh jet of smoke at the ceiling.

"You can't roll the dice —"

"— if you can't pay the price. Yeah, I know."

"So?"

"I'll come up with something," I promised him.

The Bowery station on the J line is what happens to a neighborhood once politicians realize the people who live there don't vote. Caveman paintings lined the dingy walls. Like all artists who can't afford new canvas, the taggers just painted over the ones they already had. The structural columns were so encrusted with layer after layer of graffiti that they were an inch thicker than when they started.

One tagger had blazed **NOFEAR 13!** just past the third rail. Kid wasn't lying. He must have stood on his toes, bent at the waist, his sneakers in puddled filth, leather-lined socks to protect him from the river of rats that made short work of all the fast-food containers tossed onto the tracks. Making his statement in hyper-drive, every nerve ending exposed, tuned to catch the sound that could mean he'd just run out of time. . . .

The tag had been sprayed in yellow-outlined orange fire. Looked pretty fresh. Maybe the kid himself was still alive, somewhere.

In this station, women don't wait on the platform for the train to arrive. They stand huddled on the stairs, not moving until they hear the rumble of an incoming.

I didn't make eye contact with any of them.

I was on my fourth cup of Mama's hot-and-sour soup when she left her register to sit across from me in my booth.

"You working?"

"Looking."

"Look hard?"

"I am, Mama."

"Good."

I expected more. Usually, no matter what I say, Mama berates me for lack of effort. In her mind, you look for work, you find work, period.

But she just nodded. Didn't even ask me if the soup had been good.

I could feel the city shifting all around me. Under my feet, too. Like an earthquake rising up to meet a hurricane.

Slums being torn down to build high-rent high-rises — urban renewal, New York style. Maybe they'll build a tent city on Welfare Island to house all the "service personnel."

Ferry them over every day to wash the hallways and clean the toilets, take them back to where they belong before it gets dark.

The Fulton Fish Market is closed down now, all the action relocated to the cheaper real estate in the Bronx. The subways may be underground, but any strong rain takes them out of service. The average cabdriver won't leave Manhattan, and most of them won't take a black man north of Ninety-sixth.

It isn't even news anymore that some restaurants are selling hundred-dollar ham-burgers, or that reciting a list of brand names is enough to make some girls wet. The evangelicals don't have a chance in this town. Consumerism always trumps Chris-tianity in a city where pieces of red string for your wrist are going for a C-note.

Celebrities need causes — it's an image thing. And you can't have a cause without a gala. Ice-sculpture swans, caviar canapés, and enough jewelry to cure MS if you pawned it. They always announce how much money they brought in, but never how much they actually paid out.

Who's supposed to give a damn? The pa-parazzi?

They do TV specials on human-trafficking. You know what that means: beautiful European women tricked into coming here to be "models" who end up in brutal whorehouses. Just say "sex slaves" and you've got a guaranteed audience. The truth — that every child victim of incest is the very definition of "sex slave" — just doesn't make for good cheesecake. Not in public, anyway. But you can't walk into a porn shop without finding an "incest" section. I guess it's true: if you build it, they *will* come.

Hobbyists troll the Internet pretending to be children to attract pedophiles. Some pathetic first-timers actually show up at the "girl's" house, looking for the hot underage action they've been promised. Naturally, the camera crews are waiting. Nobody ever goes to jail, but it makes for nice low-budget TV. Another public service, brought to you by the network.

Sex offenders are being disgorged from prison like toxic waste into drinking water. Profiteers are selling Megan's Law snake oil to morons who think a human that would rape a baby would never lie about his home address.

Some other geniuses are pushing GPS cuffs for the freaks. Won't stop them from doing what they do, but it'll save a lot of money on cadaver dogs.

It's just a matter of time before some marketing degenerate wires up a halfway house for sex offenders and makes a reality-TV show out of it.

On *Law and Order,* everybody's taking the "Man One and he does the max!" deals. In the streets, they just deal out the manslaughter.

Borough racism is back in style, from Bensonhurst to Howard Beach. Street gangs are making a comeback. If you melted down all the illegal handguns in the city, you'd have enough steel to put the Twin Towers back up.

The Albanians are moving in on the Italians. The Vietnamese are making things tight for the Chinese. The Puerto Ricans are getting tired of the Dominicans having all the fun. The Jakes are looking to take back the turf they lost to home-grown blacks.

The mayor spent the gross national product of most third-world countries just to beat out a party hack who had all the charisma of a poorly embalmed corpse. Pocket change for a sheik who has his eyes on a bigger throne.

In this city, the politicians tax everything except the bribes they live on. The former

Commissioner of Corrections was such a model of "tough on crime" that they named a jail after him. Bush was going to make him head of Homeland Security when the "favors" he took from companies who did business with the city started to surface. So he pleads guilty to the usual "no jail" deal, they take his name off a building, he doesn't get the public job. Maybe he'll write a book about how he *would* have gone about being corrupt . . . *if* he'd actually done it.

Judges buy their way onto the bench, then sell their judgments. When they get caught, they roll faster than a greased ball bearing down a Teflon slide. Can't wait to put on the wires and help nail the same lawyers they used to take money from.

It's never over, not really. Hell, you can get disbarred here and still get licensed to practice in Florida. Just like one of those pedophile priests they used to recycle.

Everybody takes the pills, but nobody reads the labels.

◆

The letter took a long time to get to me. There was no date on it, but the postmark on the envelope was six weeks old. I recognized the name on the return address. And couldn't miss the NEW YORK STATE DE-PARTMENT OF CORRECTIONAL SER-VICES — INMATE CORRESPONDENCE PROGRAM printed on the back, never mind the CORRECTIONAL FACILITY stamped in red.

The man who wrote knows I don't person-ally check the mail drop I use. He knows the pickups over in Jersey are made once a month, at most. And take even more time to find their way into my hands.

There's a lot of names on that drop. All of them belong to me, but nobody who uses it knows more than one of them. This was ad-dressed to "Gustav Erchdorf." The prison censors run a random scan on outgoing mail, but known gang members get special scrutiny. And if a ranking member of the tightest white-supremacist crew in New York sent a letter to any of my other covers, from Rubinowitz to Rodriguez, it would trip even the low-voltage wires that pass for a "secu-rity squad" Inside.

Of course, even if one of those ace code-crackers opened this one, all they'd find is what I read:

Gus, my <u>main</u> man!
I bet you didn't know I've been trying my hand at poetry. Got to kill this time

45

somehow, right? What do you think?

My pain banishes
White window, filmy shallowness.
Clearest, fairest, willfulness. Telling:
Universe is eternity.
Not fate, common comedy.
Truth's lethal Taxation.
   14 Words
   44 Twice
   30 Pieces

The closing was the authenticator.

"14 Words" is a standard signature for neo-Nazis: "We must secure the existence of our people and a future for white children." Written by David Lane, former member of The Order, doing life-plus in supermax for his part in the assassination of a radio talk-show host. A Jewish one.

"44 Twice" comes out to "88." The eighth letter of the alphabet, so "HH." As in "Heil Hitler!"

And the "30 Pieces" wasn't about Judas; it was about what they paid him with.

Silver was an old friend. Better, an old comrade. Inside, I'd never run with his crew. Given a choice, I don't think he would have, either. But his destiny changed the day he killed a black convict for stealing his wife's picture from his cell.

Must have taken Silver a long time to put that message together. Just the right touch of could-mean-anything, bullshit-mystical "poetry" to give off that authentic aura to any mailroom cop who sees the same kind of crap every day.

But there's no single "convict culture," no matter what Hollywood tells you. There's only one thing all prisoners have in common: time. Some do it; some use it. And there's all kinds of ways to do that, from learning to be a better person to learning to be a better predator.

The letter code works like this: if you see an exclamation point, you throw out every word before the last question mark. The whole thing's written in ultra-fancy, "artistic" script. You see this from convicts a lot, so the watchers are used to it: laboriously hand-printed words, each letter as individually detailed as a piece of netsuke. To decode, you take the first letter of the first word, second letter of the second, and so on, making one word per line, starting each line with the first letter of the first word.

I did that. Came up with:

Man will call. Use name Tex.

It was another couple of weeks before that happened.

I hadn't been there the first time he'd called.

"He say, no phone to call him at; he call you. What time? I say, 'I just answer phones. Answer lot of phones. Business, answer phones, okay?' "

The number the underground has for me rings different places — the Mole reroutes them all the time — but it's always forwarded to Mama's. Only a few people know about me and Mama's place, and nobody was guaranteed I'd be around at any given time. But Mama always was.

"He say, tell you his name Tex. You expect his call. I say, 'Sure, sure. Tex. You call couple of days, Tex. Maybe Mr. Burke check messages by then, leave number for you call him at, okay?' "

"How'd he take that?" I asked her.

"Very polite man."

"Sound nervous? Angry?"

"Very calm man. Quiet voice. Not soft, quiet, okay? White man. Not young."

"Smell bad to you?"

She shrugged, her ceramic face expressionless. "Maybe bad man," she said. "But not police. Not police, not this one."

When he called again — forty-eight hours to the minute from when he had first tried — Mama gave him a number for me . . . a cloned-and-clipped Mole special, way past untraceable. Besides, it was only going to be used once.

"What?" I answered when it rang.

"A brother of yours told me to call you. Said to use the name Tex. Said you'd recognize it."

"Enough to listen."

"I have something big. Huge. Enough for everyone. No bang-bang, no B-and-E, nothing but talk. My brother said you were the man for this. He said I could trust you, down the line. I want to pitch the job —"

"Go ahead."

"Not on the phone." His voice was exactly as Mama had described. Quiet, not soft, with the absolutely neutral hardness of a blue-white diamond. The real thing. With plenty of miles on his odometer. No "you know better than that" speeches from this one. No flexibility, either.

"I don't make dates."

"Any way you want to do it, it's done. Point-blank."

"That could mean —"

"It doesn't matter," he said. "My brother told me I could trust you with my life. I'm ready to do that. You name your terms, I say yes, and we do it. If that's not enough, you want me to prove in first, just say what you want and it's done."

◆

I was watching from behind the second-story kitchen window of a Chinatown apartment, invisible through glass a trompe-l'oeil master had turned into translucent orchids on a white frost background.

A man entered the small park. Difficult to guess his height from my angle of observation; impossible to guess his weight inside the thigh-length denim coat. White man, red knit watch cap on his head, some kind of work gloves on his hands.

All of the battered benches were occupied except for one. Every time a local wino had tried to stretch himself out on it, a couple of young Chinese with glossy pompadours and high-sheen silk shirts under fingertip black-leather jackets would detach themselves from a clot at the entrance, stroll over, and explain that the bench was reserved.

Most just moved along, but one guy, who had approached the bench while having an animated, angry conversation with himself, swung a clenched fist at the first Chinese kid who approached. They took him down like wolves cutting a cripple from the herd.

Those kids were all shooters, but I never saw a gun, much less heard a shot. I guess they were learning more from Max than humility and respect.

The white man walked over to the empty bench. Sat down. Lit a cigarette. Stared straight ahead, as if the smoke held secrets he needed to know.

Five of the Chinese kids approached. Two behind him, one at each side, the other squared up, hands empty but ready to draw.

I'm not a lip-reader, and I didn't have binoculars anyway. But I didn't need any of that to know what the Chinese kid said as he carefully removed a small, bronze-colored glass bottle out of his jacket and handed it to the man.

"You drink this now."

The man never hesitated. He opened the bottle, tilted it to his lips, swallowed. He held the bottle upside down, shook it a few times, showing them he had emptied it.

The Chinese kids took the bottle and walked away from the bench, back to their posts.

Nobody bothered the white man when he

stretched out on his back and closed his eyes.

◆

Four hours later, the man opened his eyes.

"Don't sit up too fast," I told him. "Just ease into it, or it's gonna hit you like an ice pick in the spine."

If waking up in an abandoned warehouse with holes in the roof and rats running the rafters bothered him, he didn't show it.

"You" — he glanced at his wristwatch, taking care to move slowly — "had plenty of time to make sure. Right?"

"Right," I agreed. Whoever he was, he'd been searched as deeply as you could search a human. By the best in the business, men and machines both. He hadn't been carrying a weapon, or anything that could be used as one. He hadn't been wired. He wasn't GPS'ed.

And nobody could have followed the pony-express handoffs we'd used to finally get him here.

He gingerly patted his pockets. We'd put everything back where we'd found it. He'd been carrying a current California driver's license. Claude Davis Dremdell. Brown/blue. Six feet one, 212. DOB: 1/9/44. His photo matched all the info except that this guy was bald. Not skinhead-shaved, hairless as a teardrop. And not just his head, his whole body. He didn't even have eyebrows.

When his clothes had been removed, I could see his upper body had been covered in White Power ink, prison-issue. Some of it pretty artistic, some just blue blobs of hate messages, down to the thick swastika on the back of his left hand.

"Anything else you want me to do?" he said, slowly pulling himself into a sitting position, patting his pockets again until he found his cigarettes.

"Yeah," I said. "Talk."

◆

"You know how the niggers call each other 'dog,' like they invented the concept? Well, they didn't. Niggers never invented —"

I raised my hand like a traffic cop.

"Yeah, that's right. Silver said you run with —"

"What he would have told you is there's only one color I care about. You went to a lot of trouble to get this meet. Took a lot of risk, too. Silver vouched for you with me, same way he did me with you. There's nothing about you that smells cop. Fair enough.

But you've been around enough to under-stand we're not alone here. You wanted it this way: nothing on the phone, nothing in writing. When this is over, you're going to have another drink. We'll leave you some-where safe, make sure nobody bothers you until you wake up.

"So there's only one question left," I said to him. "When do you want to take that drink?"

"Can I tell my story?"

"Not if it's going to be the one you started with. I heard that one already."

"But that's the only way to set the —"

"You're an intelligent man. I can see that. Feel it. And you must be a righteous one, too, if Silver has your trust. But me, I'm a money man, period. You want to tell me a story with a big-money ending, I got all the time you need. You want to tell me some mud-people/ice-people story, you might as well drink up now, pal."

He got his smoke going, closed his eyes for a second, then nodded, like he was agreeing with himself.

"You got other references, you know," he said, giving me a skull's smile. "Guy named Bobby says you did a deep solid for us, way back."

I picked up the sound of a slowly ap-

54

proaching car. Nothing necessarily bad —
there wasn't ever much traffic out where we
had him stashed, and the unlit roads were
busted concrete, so nobody went *too* fast,
but . . . I raised my left finger to my lips in
a "ssssh" gesture, giving me the half-second
I needed to slide my short-barreled .357
Mag out and center it on his chest.

He didn't move. Neither did I. Not my
body, anyway. My mind searched for what
he'd meant by the "us" I'd done a major
favor for. Then I remembered. Went back.
Long time ago.

Bobby took a seat on the hood of my car. "You
calling in the marker?"

"There is no marker, Bobby. I'm asking an
old friend for a favor, that's all."

"The guys you want to meet — you know
who they are?"

"Yeah," I told him. My eyes were on his
hand. The hand with the crossed lightning
bolts that looked like a swastika.

"Say the name," Bobby shot at me, cold-
eyed.

I put it on the table. "The Real Brotherhood,"
I said, my voice quiet in the empty garage.

"You didn't say it right, Burke. It's the *Real*
Brotherhood."

"That's how you say it, Bobby."

"That *is* how I say it. And that's how it is."

"I told you on the phone. I got no beef with them. I just want to talk."

I let it hang there — it was his play. He reached into my pocket and helped himself to a smoke. I saw the pack of Marlboros in the side pocket of his coveralls — he was showing me we were still friends.

Bobby took the blazing wooden match I handed him, lit up. He slid off the fender until he was sitting on the garage floor, his back against the steel of my car door. The way you sit on the yard.

He blew smoke at the ceiling, waiting. I hunkered down next to him, lit a smoke of my own.

When Bobby started to talk his voice was hushed, like in church. He bent one leg, resting his elbow on his knee, his chin in his hands. He looked straight ahead.

"I got out of the joint way before you did. Remember I left all my stuff for you and Virgil when they cut me loose? I got a job in a machine shop, did my parole, just waiting, you know? A couple of guys I know were going to the Coast. See the sights, nail some of those beach blondes out there, check out the motors, right?

"I get out there and everybody's doing weed — like it's legal or something. I fall in with these hippies. Nice folks — easygoing, sweet music. Better than this shit here. You see it, Burke?"

"I see it." It was true — convicts see all kinds of things, always going over the Wall in their minds.

"I get busted with a vanful of weed. Two hundred keys. Hawaiian. And a pistol. I was making a run down to L.A., and the cops stopped me. Some bullshit about a busted tail-light."

He took a drag of the smoke, let it out with a sigh. "I never made a statement, never copped a plea. The hippies got me a good lawyer, but he lost the motion to suppress the weed, and they found me guilty. Possession with intent. Ex-con with a handgun. Worse, I wouldn't give anybody up.

"They dropped me for one-to-fucking-ever. Knew I'd have to do a pound before I even see the Board."

Bobby locked his hands behind his head, resting from the pain. "When I hit the yard I knew what to do — not like the first time, when you and Virgil had to pull me up. I remembered what you told me. When the niggers rolled up on me, I acted like I didn't know what they were talking about. They told me to draw my commissary the next day and turn it over."

Bobby smiled, thinking about it. The smile

would have scared a homicide cop. "I turn over my commissary, I might as well turn myself over at the same time — so they could fuck me in the ass. I get myself a shank for two cartons — just a file with some tape on the end for a grip. I work on the thing all night long, getting it sharp.

"In the morning, I draw my commissary. I put the shank in the paper bag with the tape sticking up. I walk out to the yard with the bag against my chest, like a broad with the groceries. The same niggers move on me, tell me to hand it over. I pull the shank and plant it in the first guy's chest, trying for his heart.

"The spike comes out of him when he goes down. I back up to get room to finish him. Turn around and . . . I'm alone — the niggers took off. I hear a shot, and the dirt flies up right near me. I drop the shank, and the goon squad comes for me."

"You should've dropped the shank and run," I said.

"I know that now. I wasn't expecting them to shoot so quick. Things are different there."

Bobby ground out his cigarette on the garage floor, took one of his own, and lit it. "They put me in the hole. Expected that. Fucking solitary out there, it's as big as a regular prison; guys spend fucking *years* in there. Only they call it the 'Adjustment Center.' Nice name, huh? There's three tiers on each side. Little tiny dark cells.

"The noise was unbelievable — screaming all the time. Not from the guards' beating on anyone — crazy assholes screaming just to be screaming. Half of them were stone fucking nuts . . . maybe from being locked up there for so long.

"I was sitting in my cell, thinking about how much more time I'd get behind this, even if the guy I stuck didn't rat me out. I mean, they'd caught me with the shank and all. Then it started.

"The niggers. 'You a dead white motherfucker!' 'You gonna suck every black dick in the joint, pussy-boy!' All that shit. I yelled back at the first one, but they kept it up, like they were working in shifts or something. And then one of them yelled out that the guy I stabbed was his main man, so he was personally gonna cut off my balls and make me eat them.

"They were fucking animals, Burke. They never stopped. Day and night, calling my name, telling me they were gonna throw gasoline in my cell and fire me up, put glass in my food, gang-fuck me until I was dead."

Bobby was quiet for a minute. His voice was solid, but his hands were shaking. He looked, curled them into fists. "After a couple of days,

I didn't have the strength to yell back at them. It sounded like there were hundreds of them. Even the trusty — the nigger scumbag who brought the food cart around — he spit in my coffee, dared me to kite the warden.

"Finally, they pulled me out to see the Disciplinary Committee. They knew the score — even asked me if the niggers had hit on me. I didn't say a word.

"The lieutenant told me the shank itself was no big deal — the other guy was going to make it, claimed he'd never seen who stuck him. But I'd have to take a lockup — go into PC for the rest of my bit. You know what that means?"

"Yeah," I said. PC is supposed to stand for "protective custody." For guys who can't be on the mainline: informers, obvious femmes, guys who didn't pay a gambling debt . . . targets. To cons, PC means Punk City. You go in, you never get to walk the yard. And you carry that jacket the rest of your bit.

"They kept me locked down two weeks — no cigarettes, nothing to read, no radio, nothing. Just those niggers working on me every day. They never got tired, Burke, like they fucking *loved* that evil shit. Screaming about cutting pregnant white women open and pulling out the babies, stuff like that.

"Then, one day, it got real quiet. I couldn't

60

figure it out. That fucking trusty came around. He didn't have coffee that time; he had a note for me — a folded piece of paper. I opened it up. There was a big thick glob of white stuff inside. Nigger cum.

"I got sick, but I was afraid to throw up — afraid they'd hear me.

"That's when one of them whispered to me — it was so quiet it sounded like it was coming from the next cell — 'Lick it up, white boy! Lick it all up, pussy! We got yard tomorrow, punk. The Man letting us all out, you know what that means. You lick it all up, tell me how good it was!' He's saying all this to me, and all I could think of was, there was no way to kill myself in that lousy little cell. All I wanted was to die. I pissed on myself — I was sure they could all smell it."

Bobby was shaking hard now. I put my hand on his shoulder, but he was lost in the fear. "I got on my knees. I prayed with everything I had. I prayed for Jesus — stuff I hadn't thought of since I was a kid.

"If I didn't say anything, I was dead. Worse than dead. I looked at that paper with that nigger's cum on it. I went into myself — and then I saw how it had to be. I found a way to get the only thing I still wanted . . . to die like a man.

"I got to my feet. My voice was all messed

61

up from not saying anything for so long, but it came out good and steady. It was still quiet; everybody heard me. 'Tell me your name, cocksucker!' I yelled at him. 'I don't want to kill the wrong nigger when we go on the yard, and you monkeys all look alike to me.'

"As soon as the words came out of my mouth, I felt different — like God came into me — just like I'd been praying for.

"Then they went fucking crazy! Like a pack of raving maniacs. But it was like they were screaming on some upper register . . . and underneath it was this heavy bass line, like in music. A chant, something. It was from the white guys in the other cells — some of them right near me. They hadn't made a sound through all this shit — just waiting to see how I'd handle myself, I found out later. I couldn't hear them too good at first, just this heavy, low rumbling. But then it came through all the other stuff. 'R *B!* R *B!* R *B!*' "

Bobby was chanting the way he'd heard it back in his cell, hitting the second letter for emphasis, pumping strength back into himself, squeezing the pus out of the wound again.

"They kept it up. I couldn't see them, but I knew they were there. There for me. They didn't say anything else. I started to say it, too. First to myself. Then out loud. Real loud. Like prayer words.

62

"When they racked the bars for us to hit the exercise yard — one at a time — I walked out. After so long, the second the sunlight hit me in the face, I almost couldn't see.

"I heard a voice. 'Stand with us, brother,' it said."

Bobby looked at me. His eyes were wet, but his hands were steady, and his voice was cold. "I've been standing with them ever since, Burke," he said in the quiet garage. "If you got a beef with them, you got one with me."

I stood up. Bobby stayed where he was. "I already told you — I got no beef with your brothers. I want to ask some questions, that's all. I'll pay my own way."

Bobby pushed himself off the floor. "You think you could find the Brotherhood without me?"

"Yeah," I told him, "I could. And you know I could. If I was looking for them like you think, I wouldn't have come here, would I?"

He was thinking it over, leaning against the car, making up his mind.

Bobby made a circuit around my Plymouth — the one I'd had back then — peering into the engine compartment, bouncing the rear end like he was checking the shocks.

"When's the last time this beast got a real tune-up, Burke?"

"A year ago, maybe a year and a half, I don't

know," I said.

"Tell you what," he said, his voice soft and friendly, "you leave the car here, okay? I'll put in some new plugs, time the engine for you. Change the fluids and filters, align the front end. Take about a week or so, okay? No charge."

"I need a car for my work," I said, my voice as soft and even as his.

"So I'll lend you one, all right? You come back in a few days — a week at the most — your car will be like new."

I didn't say anything, watching him. "And while I'm working on your car, I'll make some phone calls. Check some things out, see what's happening with my brothers . . ."

I got the picture. My old Plymouth could be a lot of things — a gypsy cab, an anonymous fish in the city's slimy streets — whatever I needed. This was the first time it would be a hostage.

"You won't know your own car when you come back, Burke," Bobby said, his hand on my shoulder, leading me out to the front garage.

"I always know what's mine," I reminded him.

Bobby had done his checking. And when he called, I'd been ready for his questions:

"All I got is this, Bobby. One of them, big guy, he did some work. Delivering money."

"For her?"

"With *her. Bodyguard work.*"

"We do that . . ." he mused, thinking.

I waited.

"You never joined us," he said. Not an accusation; a fact.

"I joined *you,*" I reminded him. Again.

When I pulled into the shop a few days later, Bobby was waiting. "The other guys are out back, Burke. Okay?"

"Okay. You want me to leave Pansy out here?"

"Fuck, no! She might eat one of the cars."

Bobby led the way, me following, Pansy on my left, just slightly in front of each stride.

There was only one car in the back — a Mustang. And three men — two a few years older than Bobby, the other more like my age.

They all had prison faces. The older guy had a regular haircut and was wearing a dark jacket over a white shirt, sunglasses hiding his eyes. The other two were much bigger men, flanking the guy in the sunglasses like they were used to standing that way. One was blond, the other dark, both with kind of long hair, wearing white T-shirts over jeans and boots.

The blond had tattoos on both arms. In case anyone could miss where he got them, he had chains tattooed on both wrists. Black leather gloves on his hands. The dark one had calm eyes; he stood with his hands in front of him, right hand holding his left wrist. On the back of his right hand were the crossed lightning bolts.

I stopped a few feet short of the triangle. Pansy immediately came to a sitting position just in front of me. Her eyes pinned the blond — she knew.

Bobby stepped into the space between us, speaking to the older guy in the middle.

"This is Burke. The guy I told you about."

The older guy nodded to me. I nodded back. He made a "come closer" gesture. I stepped forward. So did Pansy.

The blond rolled his shoulders, watching Pansy. "The dog do any tricks?" he asked.

The hair on the back of Pansy's neck stood up. I patted her head to keep her calm.

"Like what?" I asked him.

The blond's voice was half snarl, half sneer. "I don't fucking know. Like shake hands?"

"She'll shake anything she gets in her

66

mouth," I told him, a smile on my face to say I wasn't threatening him.

The older guy laughed. "Bobby vouches for you. That's enough. If we can help you, we will."

"I appreciate it," I said. "And I'm willing to pay my way."

"Good enough," he said. "What do you need?"

"I know you," the blond suddenly blurted out.

I looked at his face — I'd never seen him before. "I don't know you," I said, my voice neutral.

"You were in Auburn, right?" he said, as if daring me to deny it. "I saw you on the yard."

I shrugged — Auburn was a big place.

"You mixed with niggers," the blond said.

"I mixed with my friends," I said. "Same as you did."

"I said *niggers!*"

"I heard you. You hear me?" I said, knowing the price of showing weakness to one of his kind.

The blond rolled his shoulders again, cracking the knuckles of one gloved fist.

"B.T., I told you what Burke did for me," Bobby put in. No anxiety in his voice, just setting the record straight.

"Maybe you like niggers?" the blond said, a step away from chesting me.

No point keeping my voice neutral any longer — he'd take it for fear. "What's your problem, pal?"

The blond looked at me, watching my face. "I lost money on you."

"What?" I said, honestly confused.

"I fucking lost money on you. I remember now. You was a fighter, right? You fought that nigger. I forget his name . . . the one that was a pro light-heavy?"

Ah. *That* nonsense. The black guy had been a for-real contender before he beat a guy to death over a traffic accident. I don't remember how it got started — although I still figure the Prof for the culprit — but it ended up with a bet that I couldn't go three rounds with him.

I remember sitting on the stool in my corner waiting for the bell to start the first round, the Prof whispering in my ear. "Send the fool to school, Burke," reminding me how we had it scripted.

I was a good fifteen pounds lighter than the black guy, and quite a bit faster. Everybody betting on me to last the three rounds was expecting me to keep a jab in his face, bicycle backward, use the whole ring. Make him catch me. That's what he expected, too.

When the bell sounded, he came off his stool like he was jet-propelled. I threw a pillow-soft jab in his general direction and started backpedaling to the ropes. The black guy didn't waste any time countering. He walked through my jab and pulled his right hand all the way down to his hip, trying for one killer punch that would end it all.

That was when I stepped forward and fired a left hook. Caught him flush on the chin as he was coming in, and down he went.

But then the plan came unglued. He took an eight-count, shaking his head to clear it. He got to his feet so smoothly that I knew I hadn't really hurt him. The black guy waved me in, grinning. I took him up on the offer and pinned him to the ropes, firing shot after shot. But he wasn't just a tough guy — he was a pro. He blocked almost everything with his forearms, picking off my punches until I realized I was running out of gas.

I leaned against him to get a breath. He buried his head in my chest, loading up an uppercut. I collapsed all my weight on his neck, stepping on his toes, not giving him an inch of room to punch. The guard in charge of the bell rang it early — he'd bet on me, too.

I let him chase me through the second round, still an easy step faster than he was. He wasn't going to bull-rush me again, so he just took his time, taking what I gave him, pounding my shoulder, my forearm, whatever I blocked with, waiting for my hands to come down. He hit like a hammer. My arms ached so much from blocking I could hardly lift them.

He caught me good at the beginning of the third round — I felt a rib go from a right hook. He doubled up, catching me on the bridge of the nose with the same hand.

"Grab him!" I heard the Prof scream. I brought my gloves up over his elbows, pulling his hands under my armpits, until the referee finally forced us apart. He butted me on the break, aiming for my bloody nose. I staggered back, letting my knees wobble to get closer to the ground.

When he came over to finish me, I threw a Mexican left hook — so far south of the border that I connected squarely with his cup.

The black guy dropped both hands to his crotch, and I launched a haymaker at his exposed head — missed by a foot and fell down from the effort. The referee wiped off my gloves, calling it a slip, killing time.

He came at me again. I couldn't breathe through my nose, so I spit out the mouthpiece, catching a sharp right-hand lead a second later. I heard the Prof yell, "Thirty seconds!," just before another shot dropped me to the canvas.

I was on my feet by the count of six, with just enough left in my tank to dodge his wild lunge. He went sailing past me into the ropes.

I drove a rabbit punch to the back of his head and slammed my shoulder into him at the same time, pinning him to the ropes with his back to me. He whipped an elbow into my stomach and spun around, hooking with both hands, knowing he was almost out of time.

I grabbed his upper body. He blasted at my ribs. I drove my forehead hard into his eyes, not giving him room to punch. If I'd let go of him, I would have fallen for good.

I was out on my feet when I heard the bell. It took four men to pull him off me. We won almost six hundred cartons of cigarettes that day. The State even threw in a free bridge for my missing teeth — I'd have to wait for my go-home to have the deviated septum repaired.

"If you lost money that day, you bet on the other guy," I told the blond. "The bet was that I couldn't last the three rounds."

"I bet on you to win," the idiot said. Fucking sucker had gone for the fifty-to-one shot.

I shrugged my shoulders.

"You didn't even try and beat that nigger," the blond said, like he was accusing me of treason.

"I was trying to survive," I told him reasonably. "Look, pal, it's not a big deal. How much did you lose?"

"Three fucking cartons," he said. Like it was

his sister's virginity.

"Tell you what I'll do. That was a few years ago, right? Figure the price has gone up a bit — how about a half-yard for each carton? A hundred and fifty bucks, and we'll call it square?"

The blond stared at me, still not sure if I was laughing at him.

"You serious?"

"Dead serious," I told him, slipping my hand into my coat pocket.

The blond couldn't make up his mind, his eyes shifting from Pansy to me. The guy with the sunglasses finally closed the books. "Let it go, B.T.," he said. The blond let out a breath.

"Sure," he said as he walked over to me, hand open for the money.

Pansy went rigid. Her teeth ground together with a sound like a cement truck shifting into gear.

"I'll give it to you when I leave," I told the blond. Even a genius like him got the message. He stepped back against the fence, still flexing the muscles in his arms. Pansy was real impressed.

"Can we do business?" I asked the guy with the sunglasses.

He waved me over to the side, against the fence by the Mustang. I flattened my hand against Pansy's snout, telling her to stay where she was, and followed him over. I lit a cigarette, feeling Bobby against my back.

"One of your guys did some bodyguard work. Delivered some money to a day-care center. Money was in a little satchel, like a doctor's bag."

I couldn't see his eyes behind the sunglasses; he had his hands in his pockets — waiting for me to finish.

"There was a woman with the bodyguard. Maybe he was protecting her, maybe he was guarding the cash, I don't know."

"Anything else?" he asked.

"The woman, she's no youngster. Maybe my age, maybe older. And she has a house somewhere outside the city. Big house, nice grounds. Has a guy who works with her: a big fat guy. And maybe a school-bus-type vehicle."

"That's it?"

"That's it," I told him.

"And you want to know what?"

"All I want to know is who this woman is. And where I can find her."

"You got a contract for her?"

I thought about it — didn't know if the bodyguard work was a one-shot deal, or if the Brotherhood was part of the operation.

"She has something I want," I told him, measuring out the words as carefully as a dealer dropping cocaine on a scale.

73

He didn't say anything.

"If you've got something working with her . . . then I'd like to ask you to get this thing I want from her. I'll pay for it."

"And if we don't?"

"Then I just want her name and address."

He smiled. It might have made a citizen relax; I kept my hands in my pockets. "And for us to get out of the way?" he asked.

"Yeah," I told him. "Exactly."

The blond moved away from the guy in the sunglasses, his back to the fence. Pansy's huge head tracked his movement as if she was the center of a big clock and he was the second hand.

"B.T.!" Bobby said, a warning in his voice. The blond stopped where he was. He'd be a slow learner to the grave.

"What is this thing you want?" the leader asked.

"It's nothing you'd want."

"I don't know where her stash is."

"It's not dope I'm after," I told him.

The leader took off his sunglasses, looked at them in his hands as though they held the answer to something. He looked up at me. "You're a hijacker, right? That's what you do?"

I held my hands together and turned my palms out to him, putting my cards on the table. "I'm looking for a picture — a photograph."

"Who's in the picture?"

"A kid," I told him.

He looked a question at me.

"A little kid — a sex picture, okay?"

The leader looked at the dark-haired guy standing next to him. "I thought it was powder," he said. "I never asked."

The leader nodded absently, thinking it through. "Yeah," he said, "who asks?"

I lit a cigarette, cupping my hands around the flame, watching the leader from the corner of my eye. He was scratching at his face with one finger, his eyes behind the sunglasses again.

"Bobby, you mind taking your friend inside for a couple of minutes? We've got something to talk over out here, okay?"

Bobby put his hand on my shoulder, gently tugging me toward the garage. I slapped my hand against my side, telling Pansy to come along. She didn't move, still watching the blond, memorizing his body. "Pansy!" I snapped at her. She gave the blond one last look and trotted over to my side.

Back in the garage, I opened both front doors of the Plymouth and signaled Pansy to climb in.

"B.T.'s okay, Burke," Bobby said. "He's just

a little nuts on the subject of niggers, you know?"

"No big deal," I assured him.

We waited in silence. Pansy's dark-gray fur merged into the dim interior of the Plymouth. Only her eyes glowed — she missed the blond. I closed the door, but didn't click it.

The garage door opened, and they came inside. The leader sat on the Plymouth's hood, leaving his boys standing off to one side.

"The woman told us she had to deliver money to various places. Serious cash, okay? She was worried about somebody moving on the money. Victor" — he nodded his head in the direction of the dark-haired guy — "he picked up a couple of grand for every delivery. He carried the bag. We thought it was a regular series of payoffs — she never took anything back when she turned over the money."

I didn't say anything. I had a lot of questions, but it wasn't my turn to talk.

"She told Victor no weapons. If someone made a move on them with a gun, he was supposed to turn over the bag he was carrying. He was just muscle, okay?"

I nodded. The woman hadn't been worried about being hijacked — Victor was there to intimidate the people who supplied the kids. One look at him would get that job done.

"You're sure she has this picture?" the leader asked.

"No question," I told him.

"This means she has others? That she does this all the time?"

"It's what she does," I said, flat.

The leader was wearing his sunglasses even inside the garage, but I could feel his eyes burn behind the dark lenses. "I'm a thief," he said, "just like you are. We don't fuck kids."

"I know that," I said.

"Some of our guys, they're a little crazy. Like B.T. He'd stab a nigger just to stay in practice, you know?"

"I know."

"But none of us would do little kids. Our brotherhood . . ."

I bowed my head slightly. "You have everyone's respect," I told him.

"We do *now,*" he said, his voice soft. "If word got out that we were involved with stuff like that . . ."

"It won't," I said.

He went on like he hadn't heard me. "If that word got out, we'd have to do something serious, you understand? We can't have anything hurt our name — people would get stupid with us."

I kept quiet, waiting.

"If we give you the information you want,

are you going to try and buy this picture from her?"

"If she'll sell it."

"And if she won't?"

I shrugged.

"Victor made a lot of those cash runs for her," he said. "A couple of day-care centers, private houses . . . even a church. There has to be a fucking lot of those pictures around."

"Like I said, she's in the business."

The leader put his hand over his heart — I could see the tattoo on his hand. His voice was still very soft. "Her name is Bonnie. The house is on Cheshire Drive in Little Neck, just this side of the Nassau County border. A big white house at the end of a dead-end street. There's a white wall all around the property — electronic gate to the driveway. Big, deep backyard, trees and shrubs all around. Two stories, full basement, maybe some room in the attic, too."

"Anything else?" I asked him.

"She has that school bus you talked about — a little one, maybe a dozen seats in the back. She uses the big fat guy as the driver."

"Any security in the house?"

"I don't know," he said. "When we work, we play it straight. We weren't even thinking about taking her off."

I handed him five grand, all in hundreds.

"That square us?" I asked. "And you take care of B.T.?"

He nodded, and we were done.

They stepped away. Later, I stepped in.

It made the papers.

The perpetrators were never caught.

Bobby had spent a lot of time trying to get me to spray my old Plymouth. The guy I'd gotten it from had been trying to build the ultimate New York taxicab, until the wheels came off his life. Bobby passionately believed I could get the two-ton beast into the twelves if I went nitrous.

I knew he'd love the Roadrunner I drive today. Kept telling myself I'd bring it over, show it off, take him out for a ride.

Someday.

The car I'd heard was well past us by the time I came back to the present. I pocketed the .357, nodded at the man I'd been holding it on, telling him we were back in business.

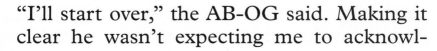

"I'll start over," the AB-OG said. Making it clear he wasn't expecting me to acknowledge what he'd called my "references." He just wanted me to understand that he knew I'd been certified, measured up to the real convict's standard. Time-tested. "The . . . other stuff, it has to come in. But just a stage-setter, no soap-box. Work for you?"

"Your dice," I told him.

◆

"People think prisons were always mixed, but that's wrong. It wasn't until Lyndon Johnson was making all his moves that they started desegregating the joints. I was in Q in '64. Already been through the whole Youth Authority. Soon as I turned seventeen, they decided I was all grown up.

"It sounds like it would have been bad there. But I'd been schooled, spent more time locked up than I had on the streets. If they'd just kicked me to the street, I would have been lost. But a prison — even a much bigger prison, full of older guys — I knew how to get along there.

"I found a little car to ride in — that's what we called crews back then, cars — and I was just jailing. You know: lifting on the yard, playing cards, moving slow, doing a little of whatever was around, jawing, TV, even some reading. Time, you know how it is.

"But the minute they made us mix, the niggers took over. They grabbed *everything.* I don't just mean they ran the place; I mean it wasn't safe to be a white man in there anymore.

"They didn't try to *ease* in — negotiate, make deals, split things up. Fucking animals wanted the drugs, they wanted the cash-queens, they wanted the gambling, they wanted the home-brew. They wanted *any-thing* that was yours, they just took it. You know what I'm saying?

"So that's where we sprung from," he said, tapping a crude "AB" tattooed in Prussian script over his heart. " 'Cause it wasn't just the colored gangsters coming at us, it was the fucking 'revolutionaries,' too. White trash like me, bad-to-the-bone outlaw peckerwoods. Born someplace else, it always seems like. Our people came to the Coast one step ahead of the law, and raised us to be worse than them. No education, no hopes. A whole breed of winos and check-collectors, and *we* were the fucking 'oppressor'?! The 'ruling class,' if you believed those stupid fucking apes."

He lit a smoke, showed some teeth. "You know what's funny? The only ones who ever

81

did believe them were the same rich mother-fuckers *we* hated."

He blew out a long exhale, giving me a chance to talk if I wanted it. I didn't.

"And then you had the beaners," he said. "Specially EME then. Flexing their muscles, starting to get strong, too. It was like it had been up in Tracy. 'Get in the car,' that's all you heard if you were white in there. 'Ride with us, or ride alone.'

"You ride alone, you don't ride long. So we rode together. But we didn't have anything to *hold* us together. That's where the Aryan thing came from. Blood. Pure white blood. Same thing our grandfathers got bought off with, understand?"

"No," I said. This wasn't a man you ever wanted to pretend you understood if you didn't. I sat back. He lit another smoke from the butt of his last one, settled in.

"You're living in shacks and trailers, eating off food stamps, got nothing, never going to *have* nothing, but at least you're not a nigger. You get conned, tricked, put down, spit on, you're not welcome in the good parts of town. That's what 'trash' means, right? After you're done with it, you throw it away. But at least you're not a nigger," he said, self-mockingly. "So you beat the crap out of a man for looking at some pig of a slut you wouldn't fuck if you were drunk *and* blind, and you call it protecting the race."

I said nothing, waiting.

"Yeah," he rolled on, grim-faced. "Got that beautiful, pure white blood beating in your veins. Remember, your ancestors *owned* those fucking niggers once.

"Well, that wasn't what we were about. I don't mean any of us were liberals, but hating niggers, that's an attitude, not a job. When *we* went out to work, we wore ski masks, not punk-ass white sheets over our heads, like faggot ghosts.

"Didn't matter what you did so long as it was work, am I right? We were robbers, burglars, dope-dealers, muscle for hire, safe-crackers . . . in that class. The Life, the *outlaw* life, that was our identity then. *That's* what set us apart.

"So, when we got locked up, we were somebody. Convicts, not inmates. And what we cared about wasn't white supremacy, it was supremacy, period — see? Being in charge. Running things.

"You know what? Quiet as it's kept, some of us, we worked with colored guys. In the World, I mean. When you're working, you want the best. Turns out the best wheelman out there's a different color than you, who

83

gives a fuck? Work, that's the thing. You know the two tests, right?"

"What'd you go down for? And did you come alone?"

"Yep. Same as it is everywhere. I worked with black guys who'd walk into the fucking Death House alone — rather die like a man than live as a rat. But a diddler? Sicko like that, he could never be with us, no matter what kind of skills he had. Because a baby-raper, he'll give you up before they get the second bracelet on his wrists.

"Inside, sure, we stayed to ourselves, color-wise. But when we *thought* of ourselves, we didn't think of 'Aryan,' that never came into the picture. Way before we got started, you had bikers wearing Nazi crap, you know, like Kaiser helmets and stuff like that. Plenty of them even wore big-ass swastikas on their jackets. But that wasn't about anything but blowing minds. Making a show. All they wanted to do was ride, fuck, and fight. Took *them* a long time to get the picture, too.

"Anyway," he said, with the air of a man who knew he'd digressed, "when things changed Inside, we saw right away that we needed something more than being stand-up thieves to keep us together. You got niggers who'd stab each other in the back walking around calling each other 'brother.' What's *that* tell you?

"Right," he said as if I'd actually responded to his speech. "All of a sudden you got the black-liberation guys. They didn't want nothing to do with nigger pimps, but they're not trying to knock them out of the way, they're trying to *recruit* them. Just like those Muslims. They got their religion shuck, but they were a gang, for real. Good *tight* gang, I'll give them that. So now you got George Jackson spades who want to ice guards; and you got Elijah jungle bunnies who say, 'When you in the Man's house, you live by the Man's rules.' And, naturally, you *always* got niggers who just want to take over the rackets, like in the streets. You see what I'm saying? Color's never enough.

"And I'm not just talking about niggers, either. Say you're a Mex, it matters if you're from south or north. California, I mean. Their Mason-Dixon Line was Bakersfield, I heard. I mean, EME and Nuestra Familia, they're both brown, right? But could they ever get together? Fuck, no."

I shook my head in agreement. I hadn't come up with Mexicans, but Puerto Ricans have gone the same route here — they won't mix Latin Kings and Netas on the same tier at Rikers unless they *want* a war.

85

"And *those* motherfuckers are all born blade-men," he went on. "Turned the joint into Shank City. But you know what they all had in common? If you were with one of the crews, any of them, you were safe. Not safe when race war jumped — anyone can die then, you know that. But say you were a seventeen-year-old black kid. Light-skinned, sweet face, skinny little body. You walk the yard alone, you've got a daddy by nightfall. Or you get busted up so bad that, next time the wolf barks, you turn right over. But you claim Black Muslim, that's not going to happen. A lot did, for just that reason.

"So we knew we had to stand together, or we'd all be plucking our eyebrows, putting on lipstick, and cutting the back pockets off our jeans. We had to *consolidate,* because there weren't enough of us to split into separate crews, like the niggers had. So we needed something else. Something the niggers had. And the spics, too. *Brotherhood.* We had to be the same. Shared blood. Heritage.

"That's where this started. And now it's full-circle. We were a gang, threatened by bigger ones, so we all came together for protection. Way it always happens, you think about it. Then we got this . . . ideology. The

86

key word in AB isn't 'Aryan,' it's 'Brotherhood.' And we still use it, for the same reasons. We use it to recruit, to hold us together. But the last part of the circle is where we are now. All of us. We all know it's a lie.

"You listen to some of us, you listen to Elijah's boys — I guess they're Foghorn's now — you'd hear the exact same thing: It's the fucking Jews. They're the ones who cause all the misery we suffer. They're the reason we're *in* the joint to begin with: Jew laws, Jew lawyers, Jew judges.

"But's that a mountain of bullshit. And when you're *serious* about your work, bullshit gets in the way. We got some dumbass 'Aryans' who can tell you all about the Vikings. Odin. Valhalla. All that crap. Always reading. Big students of history. Assholes are as lame as the Christers who they used to send around from outside. The only history a good thief should care about is history he can *use.*" He laughed, sweet as cyanide.

He lit another smoke, asked: "Did you know that Al Capone only committed one murder himself in his whole life? I mean, he must have ordered a couple of hundred hits, but he only did one himself. You know who he whacked?"

"Some punk who beat up his best friend," I said.

He gave me a look, said nothing.

"Guy named Jake Guzik," I went on, making it clear I could go on a lot longer if he wanted.

"Yeah," he said, slowly, shifting his tone, not his posture, but it was enough of a tell that I'd surprised him. "And when he did that Valentine's Day Massacre, it was the Purple Gang he called in for the work. Kikes, every one of them."

"Dumb ones, too," I said.

This time, his laugh was chestier. "Yeah, there goes another rumor down the toilet. But that boat still floats. You got Italian guys saying they're 'Aryans.' You got skinners thinking they're part of the 'Master Race.' They go around quoting Nietzsche, got their spiderweb tattoos, all that crap. But here's the joke: any real con with half a brain knows it's all a hose job. Just like those Black Muslim bosses — you think they really believe some mad scientist on a secret island created the whole white race in a test tube? Sure.

"What we are now is a gang. Same as the bikers. May have started out different, but now we're about money. Most of the race stuff, it never makes it to the streets. Look at the white kids we should be recruiting. But what do you find in the trailer parks, now? Dumb-fuck skinheads who just want to get wasted and go out and whack somebody with a baseball bat. Or punk-ass 'Nazis' who have to hide behind the goddamn *police* when they go on one of their little marches. And white kids are turning into stone whiggahs — they want to be fucking 'rappers' or play in the NBA.

"Look, this is about *business,* okay? There's even . . . You ever hear of the Nazi Lowriders?"

"No," I lied. More to keep in practice than for any other reason.

"They started out like an . . . auxiliary, I guess you'd call them. We were in; they were out. So they got things done for us, specially the drug stuff. Worked out good for everyone. Only thing, some of them are spics. I don't mean no half-and-halves, either."

"Nazis, huh?"

"Yeah," he said, dry-laughing. "Heil fucking Hitler."

"I get it," I said. Not lying, then.

"As long as you have prisons, you'll have gangs," he went on, like I hadn't spoken. "They got them in Australia, they got them in Thailand, they got them in Russia. And when members get out — and most do —

they just keep on trucking. Back to business. It works for us, and it works for them, too."

"Them?" I asked, keeping anything resembling a challenge out of my voice.

"You think, if all the gangs Inside got together, the guards could hold the joints against us? Not for a minute. Long as they can keep us killing each other, they're pretty safe. Sure, every blue moon, they put an ultra-hard-core like Tom Silverstein in a unit with a guard that just *has* to fuck with him, and then . . . But most of the time, the cops Inside just stay out of the way, let us do what we need to do, so long as we don't do it to them."

He fired another cigarette. "Ever notice how often you hear 'blood' in this? Niggers call each other 'blood' — even named one of their gangs that way — the one that kills another nigger gang on sight. It's *all* a trick, and we *all* get played.

"Now, listen for another minute, 'cause I'm coming to what *really* counts. You know what every AB man Inside fears most today?"

"The same thing they experiment on in labs."

"Huh?"

"White rats."

"That's it," he said, grimly. "There's *dozens* of our men looking at the Death House right now because they got snitched off. Not infiltrated — those movies where they put undercovers in prison, never happen. *Couldn't* happen — we've got that acid test for new members. Cops kill people all the time — blow away a bunch of dealers, keep their stash, and get medals for it. Fuck, some of them hire *out* as killers. But there's no way their bosses give them *permission* to take someone out just so they could work undercover. That kind of thing, there has to be a record of it. I met some dumb motherfuckers who carry a badge, but never one *that* pure-grade stupid.

"No, it's always one of our own that turns. Some pure white Aryan warrior, one hundred percent man, ready for Valhalla when his time comes, *that's* who gets on the stand and fingers us.

"That's why all the Brand bosses got their California life sentences commuted by the governor a while back — so they could start on their federal time. That was supposed to be to spread out the leadership, but it was really about setting us up for one big takedown.

"And it worked. By now, there's so much paranoia running wild that you got guys checking in because they think they're about to be put on knock-off, see? If you're going to be iced for ratting when you're innocent, why not make yourself guilty, and score all the rewards that go along with it?"

I shrugged at the perfect cross he was describing. It was true enough — every gang put out hits on *suspected* rats, so it had to happen. You start suspecting you've *been* suspected, and . . .

He dragged deep enough on his cigarette to reduce it by half — guy had lungs like bellows. "Few years ago, there's this guy — Felton, I think his name was. Anyway, he's East Coast, *big* player in one of the max joints in Jersey. Second-in-command. He gets out, ready to kick it off. 'Rahowa' — know what that is?"

"Racial Holy War."

"Yeah. This guy, he's not going out to work, he's going to start blowing things up, bring on the revolution. Naturally, being an amateur, he screws up. All that time Inside, he never learns anything about crime? Fucking amazing. Anyway, he gets caught passing some funny money — I mean, real *silly* shit that he made on a Xerox machine or something.

"So back Inside he goes. And that's when it hits the fan. This guy, he's half mud. And his mother, the white half, she's a dyke. Probably got some Jew in her, too. So, naturally, the *real* white guys put him on the KOS list.

"But he never turned rat!" the AB man said, pride overruling everything else in his voice. "He never rolled, and he could have given them a *lot.* So who's more old-school? Who's more real? Who's more loyal? A nigger passing for white, or a white passing for a man?"

"That's not a question."

"Right. I'm not telling you anything you don't already know. But I had to say it, because otherwise nothing I'm going to say now is going to make sense, all right?"

"You're still talking."

◆

He stubbed out his cigarette. Reached toward his shirt pocket, then stopped, as if he was trying to prove something to himself.

"You're at the bottom of a long steep hill. There's an enemy waiting for you at the top. He holds the high ground, and he's comfortable up there. If you stay where you are, you starve to death. But you can't rush him. You can't charge up that hill. You'll be out of breath, your muscles will lock up on you.

Even if you make it to the top, you're easy pickings. So what do you do?"

"Depends on what you've got," I said. Emotionless as a mathematician reciting a theorem.

"Give me some examples."

"Trick him into coming down off that hill. Blow the whole thing up. Get a sniper to pick him off."

"No," he said. Not disrespectfully, just giving me more facts.

"Sneak up the hill, then. Take your time — more important that he doesn't see you coming," I said, reciting my ghost brother's mantra. "So, when you make your move, you're as close to ready as you can be."

I didn't bother to say, "Don't fight fair." In the world we share, that's the air we breathe.

"That's right. That's the only way. And you know what *gets* me up that hill? What gets me close enough to make a fight of it?"

"Money."

He nodded.

"And you know where there's a lot of that, but you can't put your hands on it yourself," I said.

"You're asking, or telling?"

"Guessing."

"I went to Silver for a reason. I'm not go-

ing anywhere near a Brand for this one —
not one on the street, I mean. You never
know who'll turn. Not anymore. Silver, he
knows this, too. So — remember what I said
about 'references'? There's only one I care
about: can you be trusted? You know what
Silver told me about that. But he told me
something else, too. He told me you were
the smartest guy he ever met."

I didn't react.

"I'm dying," he said. "Doctors told me I
got a year, maybe a year and a half."

I watched him, waiting.

"I'm not just rolling over for it. I spent
what I had, used up a lot of favors. There's
a place over in Switzerland where they're
supposed to have been doing stuff with stem
cells for a *long* time. Years and years before
that asshole we got running this country
said it was illegal. Anyway, supposedly, *supposedly,* they've got a way to beat this . . .
thing I got."

"For money."

"I need a million and a half, cash," he
said. "That's for everything. Getting over
there — I got no passport — getting fixed,
few months in their clinic, then coming
home."

I kept my face expressionless. All this for
another ex-con with some dream heist he

95

conjured up in the darkness of his cell. Now all he needs is for someone to put the right string together, take all the risks, and, if it actually works, give him his piece. If the poor bastard was looking at me for it, he was rolling a pair of one-dot dice.

"I know what you're thinking," he said. And he probably did.

He tapped another smoke out of his pack, lit up. "It's *not* that. This is as real as steel. Got enough patience left to hear the rest?"

"Ask Silver."

◆

"When we started, the Brotherhood was . . . rotating. We'd have guys Inside, guys on the bricks, guys making the return trip. Outside, race war was just yak-yak. But Inside, once it moved from the occasional flare-up to . . . to the way we lived *all* the time . . . we had to change the rules. The rules about getting in, I mean. It wasn't enough to say you'd *die* for the race — that was something you *could* do, not something you *did* do. Acid test, like I said before."

"Blood in, blood out."

"Yeah. No more 'get in the car.' The car was too big. More like a bus; even a convoy of buses. Only one driver, just a few in the

96

front seats. The rest were passengers. And passengers, they have to buy tickets. If you came to us for protection, you paid for it. If you came to us to *be* us, you had to pass the test.

"What that meant — sooner or later, what it *had* to mean — is that we had some guys who were never going to rotate. Killing a man Inside, it used to be you got some A.C. time. But the worse it got, the harder they came down. Turned cases over to prosecutors out in the World, not the kangaroo court they run behind the Walls.

"So, instead of just losing some good time, you got actual charges. Which means, all of a sudden, the Man was holding a lot more cards. You with me?"

"Sure. Anyone with the power to add to one sentence has the power to cut another one."

"Right. So some of us ended up with a string of Life-Withouts on top of what they were already doing. The shot-callers now are the guys who're *never* going home, see?"

He got a nod out of me, nothing more.

"Mercy is always a symptom of weakness," the dying man said. "It's just another form of fear — you're secretly afraid that if you don't spare your enemy, someday your enemy might not spare you."

His eyes, so light a brown they were almost colorless, held all the empathy of an alligator waiting in shallow water for something — anything — to walk too close to the riverbank.

"I was one of those on rotation. Got out before it went crazy. By the time I came back, I was already one of the Originals — nobody thought to even *ask* me to prove in. I kept going . . . in and out . . . always affiliated, though.

"I met Silver when the feds had us both — him short, me a little longer. He went on — you know his story — and now he's got two life sentences. He owes one to the State, and one to us."

He took a deep drag of his cigarette, giving me a chance to ask him a question without interrupting. I signaled him to keep talking.

"No matter what we called ourselves in the World, Inside we went back to being together. It was when the feds had me that I met this guy — the one who's the key to everything. He was in for business stuff. Not the kind of stuff you'd expect to see a Level Six joint for. So, the way I saw it at first, he must have been a stand-up guy, because they *always* offer those business boys some soft ride if they give people up.

"He needed us. No chance he was going to prove in — that wasn't him. And he could pay for protection. So we did business. Nothing special. We did it for a lot of guys, even Mafia bosses.

"One day, out of nowhere, this guy, he gets me alone on the yard. And he tells me why he kept his mouth shut when the feds dropped him. He had something to trade, all right. Something so big he probably could have walked away with probation — maybe even immunity and relocation. But he didn't want that. He wanted the money. The money these other guys — three other guys — owed him. At least the way he saw it they owed him. He'd been waiting years — I mean, a *lot* of years — to collect what he thought was coming to him. But he knew it had to be done just right, and he wasn't man enough for the job."

"So he came to prison to find the right guys?"

"No," he said, giving me a look I couldn't interpret. "What he did was, he fucked up his life. Tapped these other guys for 'loans,' started businesses, went belly-up every time. So he started stealing. Cooking the books, skimming, that kind of bullshit. The tax guys nailed him first, then the locals piled on.

"That's when he realized the truth. He was born to fail at anything he ever tried. That was his destiny. It didn't matter how many chances he got, he'd mess them all up. What he needed was one T-rex score, so he could live in the Philippines — he never explained *that* one to me — for the rest of his life, live like a god."

I shrugged my shoulders. We'd both heard this one before. Hell, I thought I'd been about to hear it again a few minutes earlier.

"What he had was some information. Three guys — three *rich* guys, from the best families — had committed a real ugly murder. Gang rape, torture, you name it. Then they killed the girl — and I *mean* a girl; she was, like, twelve, thirteen years old. When they did it, two of them were fifteen, the other was sixteen. This was in 1975. Today, they'd be in their forties."

"He wanted you to get them to buy the proof he was holding?"

"Yeah. He knew he couldn't pull it off himself. You need a whole crew for something that complicated. Besides, he was scared of them. Or at least of the muscle their kind of money can buy."

"But you never did it?"

"No. One, it isn't the kind of job you farm out; you've got to be in control yourself.

Two, even if it worked, the money would get whacked up so many ways before I saw any myself, it wasn't worth the risk."

"So?"

"So he never tried it, either."

"How do you know?"

"This guy, he found me. Just a couple of months ago. He's been out for years. Now he's just a pathetic little piece of shit, owns some kind of two-bit strip club, kicks back to everyone who says 'Boo!' to him, drives an old Caddy, wears cheap jewelry, gets a free blow job whenever he wants one."

"Not the paradise in the Philippines, huh?"

"No. I guess whatever scheme he had didn't play out. But he still wants it to happen. That whole life, I mean. Says he can do it on a half-mil. I collect that, whatever's left is mine."

"So you want me to get it done, and I get to keep whatever's over two million?"

If he thought I was being sarcastic, he let it slide. "These guys — check them out for yourself first, be as sure as you need to be; I got the names — could come up with a couple of mil *apiece.* Wouldn't even make a dent."

"That's if this guy — the one who came to you — is for real."

"What's he get out of making it up? He's pretty sure I can get the job done on these three guys, but he *knows* I can get it done on him, this easy," he said, snapping his fingers. "Plus, he'll *show* the proof . . . provided I say I'm ready to make the move."

"So how's he know you won't just move in, get the other three to pay you, and walk away with it all? Leave him with nothing?"

"He's one of those guys — you know the kind I'm talking about — he *wants* something to be true so bad, he *needs* it to be true so bad, that it turns into truth in his mind. He needs me to be an Aryan of Honor — my word is my bond. In his mind, I'd never cheat him."

" 'Cause he's *with* you," I said, letting the AB man know I understood the difference.

"Yeah," he said, his voice as cold and unyielding as an iceberg. "He knows what I am; his kind is always studying mine. I let him tell me everything he knows, make a ton of money out of it, and walk away without giving him his cut, that wouldn't be honorable. Wouldn't be merciful, either."

"That door you talked about, it swings both ways."

"You mean, what's to prevent *you* from burning *me?*" he asked.

"Yeah."

"What do you care? What should it matter?"

"If you were to cross this guy, what could he do about it? Nothing, right?"

"Right," he agreed.

"So?"

"Ah, I get it. You want to know what I think I'm holding that I could use if you crossed *me.*"

"You were me, wouldn't you want to know?"

"I would. But I wouldn't want you to take the answer the wrong way."

I made a "come on with it" gesture.

"Silver."

"Silver? You're saying you got plenty of soldiers on the streets? And if I walked away with the money, you could find me. Or . . . ?"

Not saying it aloud — the one threat that could change everything. If this guy was what he said he was — and he must be something close to it, for Silver to have reached out for me, and vouched for him in the bargain — and any threat to my family came out of his mouth, he wasn't going to die of cancer.

"No, no. Not that," he said, raising his hands as if he was warding off evil spirits. "Do I know bad guys? Absolute fucking psychos who'd take a week to kill you, and come a thousand times while they were doing it? Sure. But they're not . . . they're not *with* me any more than this other piece of shit is.

"That's what I was telling you. That long story I made you listen to. Silver's my ace. Not because he's down with the Brotherhood — the old-school Brotherhood, when our honor *was* our life — but because he says your word — your real word, the one you give to your own people — makes one of those girders holding up a bridge look shaky."

I cocked my head at an "I'm listening" angle.

"Look, you got a guy with you," he said. "Black guy. Silver says people Inside call him the Prof. Used to be a preacher or something? Little guy, always talks in rhyme? Silver told me he heard him say this: 'Lying to a sucker is just playing a role. But lying to your own is giving up your soul.' "

"I'm listening," I said, out loud this time.

"No, you're not, man. You're not tuning in. See, Silver says this Prof, he's got everyone's respect: all the time he put in, he always walked it righteous. So, when he talks, everybody listens. But *you,* it's much more than that. It's like he was your father or something."

I didn't say a word. Just watched. Watched a man walking across a tightrope in a high wind, suspended over a shark tank.

"Silver, he says you and him, you're brothers. For real, brothers. One of your own, see? You'd never lie to him. It just wouldn't be you."

"And?"

"And it's not me you'd be giving your word to, it's him. Silver."

"*If* I did that, what's in it for him?"

"He doesn't want anything," the AB man answered, knowing I'd check for myself. "Silver said you already did things for him he wouldn't trust another man on earth to do. He says you know things about him that could get him done in a heartbeat. And you never would. He says you already fixed him up with a great lawyer. And, if he ever needed anything, you'd take care of it for him. He knows he's risking all that by saying you can trust me.

"Now, me, I figure a man doesn't get to be your brother behind what he says, or some silly-ass tattoo, or just hating the same people you do. A man gets to be your

105

brother because of what he *does.* Am I right?"

"By me you are."

"And Silver, he's your brother?"

"He is."

"And that's my insurance. I want to be able to get a message to him — my own way — and tell him you gave your word. To him, I mean. Nothing cute: so long as I play it laser-straight with you, I get my cut. Can I do that?"

"Yeah. You can do that."

"I've got a satchel with me. I know you already went through it. Nothing in there but paper, and a cassette tape. I'm leaving it here when I go. All you need to check out everything I told you. Everything except the guy himself, of course. You go through it. Decide if the peach is as ripe as I say it is. You think it is, you think it's worth climbing the tree to get it, you call me, and I'll do whatever you say after that. You don't think so, just call and say one word, and I'm out of your life forever. Your name will never come out of my mouth again."

Meaning: no matter what I decided, he was going to take the shot, play the only cards he was holding. And if he couldn't pull it off, so be it. He was going out the same way he came in. Because there's one thing you *do* take with you when you go: your rep.

I walked over, shook his hand.

"Close your eyes," I told him. "Your drink will be here in a minute."

◆

"He *worked* on this," Michelle said, standing with her hands on her hips, looking down at the Kong-sized table we had made out of rough planks laid across seven thick sawhorses. It took up just about all the space in what used to be my living room. No easy feat: the living room had been constructed by knocking down non-load-bearing walls that had separated all five of the flophouse "rooms" on that floor.

"He had plenty of time, little sister," Clarence said, pointing with a shooter's index finger at the array of brightly colored file folders. Each was labeled in block printing as anonymous as the pasted-up words in a ransom note.

"Time ain't worth a dime," the Prof said. "He was Inside, son. Ain't no kind of space in that place."

I nodded. Looked up to see Max doing the same thing. That "satchel" was more like a small suitcase. "Forty-point-nine kilos," the Mole said, after he was done putting it through his machines.

Inside, it's not space that's the biggest problem; it's privacy. The hacks — that's what we called them in New York, back when I was locked up; they call them "cops" in Jersey, "screws" in Massachusetts — who knows what they called them where the cancer-ridden man had done his time — could turn your house upside down just for the fun of it. They liked doing things like that, but they were always careful who they did it to.

If you were someone they hated — and it never took a lot to get on *that* list — they didn't just search, they destroyed. Tore up precious photographs, letters you would never see again, an art project you'd been working on. Just because they could. Those "soldiers" who played torture-power games with Iraqi prisoners, you think they were from one of the elite fighting forces, like the Rangers, or the Green Berets? Forget that: former prison guards is what they were. They'd had their own off-the-books training, spent their days in a subculture the World never sees. They're not allowed to bullwhip prisoners anymore, so they learned new tricks.

All the power-boys do it. They don't

change their attitudes, they just adapt them to fit the times. Ever notice how the cops always scream "Stop resisting!" while they're gang-beating some poor bastard into permanent paralysis, just in case there's some good citizen with a videocam lurking nearby?

A convict can spend years, decades even, planning a job. But he's not going to draw diagrams of it, not while he's a captive. Unless he wants to stay one.

"He's not an impatient man," I told them. "Even with that cancer clock ticking inside him, he wasn't going to panic. He talked tough in that warehouse, but we're his last chance. His last *real* chance, I mean. He could put together another crew, but where would he find one he could trust? Not in the time he's got left."

"It's only a plan, man," the Prof said. "You got the time to make one, you got the time to fake one." Not arguing for one side or the other, just saying it like it was. He and Silver had a friendship of sorts — shared respect, more, actually — but even if it had been Silver himself pushing the score, the Prof would have wanted his own look first. Trusting a man doesn't mean you trust his judgment.

Max reached over, tapped the face of my

wristwatch, held up one finger.

"First thing," I answered him, and everybody else, "is we check out everything that's got an independent source. So, for openers —"

"I can do all the newspaper stuff, mahn," Clarence volunteered, his Island voice expressing pride in his recently acquired computer skills. "There is a database — LexisNexis, it is called — that I could look through. Very quickly, too. If all those articles he collected are true — not true in what they say; true copies of what was in the papers, or the magazines — I can tell you."

"Perfect," I told him, as the Prof nodded approvingly. "Remember, though: this case was never solved. So there's no court proceedings. And there's a lot of stuff in the police files we're never going to get a look at."

Michelle exchanged a look with the Prof.

"Forget it," I told them. I wasn't going back to Wolfe's network, not after the last time. Wolfe. An angel's face, and eyes that matched her name. She'd walk through hell wearing a gasoline dress to put a freak down for the count, but she never considered ass-kissing part of that job. Or looking the other way, either. Because she hadn't come up through the clubhouse — in Queens, the Democratic machine doesn't just control judgeships, it runs the whole show — she never participated in the "voluntary" fundraisers, or tacked up campaign posters, or kept a photo of the DA in her office. The only mistake I'd ever known her to make was thinking that being the best sex-crimes prosecutor the city had ever seen would be enough to let her keep her job as head of the Special Victims Bureau.

She never understood the "go along to get along" mentality of the political appointee, so she was probably the only one in the city who was surprised when they finally fired her. After that, she'd gone outlaw. Not committing crimes, but going places she wasn't supposed to go. She ran the best info-trafficking cell in the city. And she still had a *lot* of friends on the force.

I thought I had a chance with her once, but I waited too long. Crossed too many borders, too many times.

"You and me, it's not going to be." That's how she'd ended it between us.

Last year, I'd taken some risks to show her I was back to myself — the man who . . . well, the man who she once . . . Hell, I didn't know, but I wanted to be that man again, if only in her eyes.

I'd sworn to her that I was doing the right thing, for the right reasons. That wasn't a lie, but it wasn't all of the truth. The whole job had reeked of money, and I was looking for some of that, too. So she'd used up a big favor, gotten me some stuff from inside police files.

But she'd made it clear I couldn't go there again. I kept hoping word of the last thing I'd done would get back to her. Kept hearing Johnny Adams wailing "Reconsider Me" in my head, hoping she was tuned to the same station.

If she'd reach out to me, any excuse would do. But she hadn't, and I wasn't going to break my word not to contact her again. Sure, I could get to her crew, buy some information, like anyone else. But police files, only Wolfe herself could get *that* kind of thing done. Not an option.

"We're not trying to solve a case here," I told everyone. "If the guy Silver sent is telling the truth, the case is already solved . . . only nobody ever paid for it."

"Writing a check won't clear *that* deck."

"I know, Prof. Look, I'm not saying we should do this. We're family for real, not some fucking TV show. So, straight up, this is an extortion job, okay? If — *if* — this guy is telling the stone truth, there's guilty people — *rich* guilty people — who'll pay major bucks to get their hands on something that proves they killed a little girl. *That's* the job. The girl herself, she's been in the ground for thirty-some years. There's nothing we can do for her. Thing is, do we want to do this for ourselves?"

"I . . . don't think I do," Michelle said, softly.

"How come, sis? It's not like we never —"

"Just stop it!" She whirled on me. "You know perfectly well what those . . . degenerates who killed her want. There's only one way they can ever be *sure* whoever has the goods on them never comes around again, no matter how much they pay."

"That's Silver's pal's problem, not ours."

"We'd *still* be helping them get away with it."

"They *got* away with it, honeygirl. You think there's still an investigation going on? This case is as buried as that little girl's body."

"Look at me!" my sister commanded.

I held her eyes as best as I could — my eyes don't work together anymore, not since that gunshot wound a few years back, and the learning-on-the-job surgery that followed. The two eyes aren't even the same color anymore. But Michelle had been read-

113

ing the truth in them since we were street children together.

"I see," she finally said.

Everybody looked at her, waiting.

"And I'm in," Michelle said.

"The copies were authentic," Clarence said, "every single one." It was four days later, all of us in the war room. Like before, the makeshift table was covered with paper, but none of it had come out of the satchel that the AB man had handed me.

The walls were now plastered with white oaktag, fastened with pieces of duct tape, covered with writing in different-colored Sharpies. Everyone had their own color, so you could tell at a glance who made the comment. I don't know where Michelle had found a lilac one.

Clarence's voice was deliberately flat, showing us he could be professional about . . . even this: "On August 17, 1975, the body of Melissa Welterson Turnbridge was found in the woods north of the Merry Meadows Country Club golf course. The child" — Clarence stumbled a little over the word, but didn't look up from his computer screen — "was thirteen years old.

Born August 27, 1961. She would have turned fourteen in a few days. Reported missing by her parents when she had not come home by ten at night on August 4. The police had been looking for her ever since."

"Teenage girl breaks curfew and the parents call in the police?" I said.

"And they rush right out and start looking for her?" Michelle put in, laying her suspicions over mine.

"Different schools, different rules," the Prof said, sweeping away our doubts. "Walk into a big-city precinct, tell that same story, parents get the brush-off. Up there, the cops *rush* off. You call from the Projects, say your little girl hasn't come home, the blue boys think she's probably up on a roof somewhere, giving blow jobs to gangbangers. But when you call from a town where being a millionaire puts you on the wrong side of the tracks, they call out the SWAT team if you tell 'em there's a possum in your backyard."

"There had been a big storm the night before," Clarence went on as if nobody had said a word, his voice still as impersonal as the screen he was reading from. "One of the men who works for one of the owners — the Shelton Estate, the papers called it

— was out checking for damage. From knocked-down trees and things like that. It was that man who found her. Just her leg, sticking up. The storm had uncovered her."

"So she wasn't buried?" I asked.

"No, mahn. It was like someone rolled a big log over her, then covered it with whatever they could find. She was never actually under the ground."

"Huh!" the Prof said.

Everybody waited, but he didn't say anything more.

Finally, Clarence picked up the thread: "She had been dead for days, the coroner said. Probably killed the same night she hadn't come home."

Max tapped the table to get Clarence to look up, then made the sign of a pointed gun.

"No," the West Indian said, his Island voice so hard and tight that the lilt had been squeezed out of it. "She wasn't shot, and she wasn't stabbed. Beaten to death. Strangled, too. 'Multi-sexual assault,' they also said."

"Before or after?" I asked.

"It does not say," he answered. "There is a lot more. It was the biggest story in the local papers for *months*. A lot of national coverage, too. All I am saying is — the clippings this man brought to you? — he did not make them up. Or change them. Even the pictures — there are lots of those, mostly from her junior-high school; she was supposed to start the ninth grade in a couple of weeks — those are the same. Not Photoshopped or —"

"Photo— ?"

The Mole waved away whatever ignorant question I was going to waste his time with.

"You started at the other end?" I said to Max, gesturing as I spoke. He can read lips as easy as he reads print, but the sign language we'd taught each other was ours, and I was never giving up that part of our bond.

The Mongolian nodded.

"They ever get specific about the cause of death?"

He shook his head. Shrugged his shoulders. Then slammed one steel chunk of a fist into an open palm. Over and over again. As we watched, he mimed a beating. A vicious, systematic beating. And the kind of rape maggots do with a broomstick or a beer bottle. The mute Mongol pointed at the pile of paper, and shook his head. Then he pointed to his own temple, held up a "number one" gesture.

We all nodded, following along. The

papers had never said so, not out loud, but the little girl had been strangled *after* the kind of beating that might have killed her anyway.

Some freak had pain and sex twisted together into a single wire, a wire he had wrapped around that little girl's neck. The actual cause of death didn't matter. We didn't know who, not for certain-sure, but we all knew why.

And a white supremacist with no reason to lie said he had a man who could tell us the part we didn't know.

"We have to —"

The Mole doesn't interrupt, unless he needs to get the train back on the track. This time, he pointed to a large, flat piece of equipment, with four VU meters on the front.

We all turned to watch as he stood up and pushed a button.

◆

"This is 'pause,' " the man with the subterranean complexion and Coke-bottle glasses said. "When I activate it, what you will hear is not the original. The signal-to-noise ratio was very poor — probably just a cassette recorder in the pocket of one of the people talking. There are only two voices. I put them on separate tracks" — he pointed at a pair of cone-shaped speakers, placed equidistant from the thing with the meters on the front — "so there will never be a doubt as to which one is talking. Here is a transcript my son made." His pale-blue eyes met Michelle's lilac contact lenses; the pride of parenthood lanced between them, so clear you could actually see the beam.

He handed Max a thick sheaf of paper, bound along the left side and coated in heavy, transparent plastic.

Then he pushed a button.

◆

"How come you give me the full search, and I don't get to do the same to you?"

I didn't recognize the Tootsie Pop voice — hard around the edges, soft in the core — but I put the speaker's age around fifty.

"You think I'm working for the Law, walk out." The cancer-man's voice: low in volume, too self-assured to waste effort on threats.

"It's not that," the other voice said, whining with resentment. "It's just . . . well, you know, I haven't had a finger-wave since I got out."

"You think that was a thrill for me?"

"No. You know I didn't mean that. Only . . ."

Nothing but a throbbing silence for several seconds.

"Okay, forget it. But something like this, a man has to be careful."

"I was."

"Not you. Me."

"You said a man," the AB old-timer said, his voice the opposite of the other guy's. "There's only one of those here, in this room. You asked for me. There had to be a reason. Whatever it is, I know it's not Brotherhood business. So it better be money. Lots of money. Something you want done, but you don't have the stones to do on your own, maybe. Or, maybe, something you need a crew for, and you don't have one. So you're going to say something. Something you don't want anyone else to hear."

"If it was, you could understand why I'd want to check for —"

"You don't need to check for what you already know. You know me. You know my name. You know my pedigree. You know I don't talk."

"Sometimes, when people get . . . desperate, they —"

"Look at me," the AB man commanded. "Look at me the way you looked at me Inside. What do you see, *punk?* I'm the man who stood between you and a ram job from every nigger in the joint. Right? *Right?!*"

The tape was silent for a few seconds. Long enough for the other man to nod, I was guessing.

"You were supposed to be some kind of long-con guy," the AB boss said. "A paper man. So you must have done your homework. Before you got word out to me, I mean. You know I don't have paper on me. No wants, no warrants. No parole, no probation. No arrests, no charges. You could confess to more killings than that sack of shit Henry Lee Lucas, what could I use it for? The Law's got nothing I want. And I sure as fuck wouldn't waste my time blackmailing *you.*

"I searched you to make sure you're not here working for the Feebles, trying to get Brotherhood info, make some kind of deal for yourself. *Me,* I got no deal to make. So now we're done with this. Talk, or walk."

The sound of a cigarette being lit. Exhalation.

"I've got something," the stranger's voice said.

Another exhalation.

"A murder."

"Call 911," the AB man said. I could hear the dismissive shoulder-shrug in his voice.

"This is an old murder. More than thirty years old. Three men — boys they were then, but that doesn't matter — did it. Rich boys. Rich boys who got richer."

"The ones you told me about when we were Inside? They're still alive?"

"Yes! All three of them. I've got *everything* on them. And every single one could pull millions in cash out of safe-deposit boxes alone."

"So what changed since you first told me? You've got some suspicions —"

"Proof," the stranger said, confidence adding strength to his voice. "Absolute, rock-solid, stand-up-in-court proof. What's changed is that *now* I realize that I can't turn it into the kind of money it's worth, not by myself."

"This proof — you saw it for yourself?"

"I . . . Yeah, I guess you could say that."

"This murder's never been solved?"

"Never. And the girl they killed was no throwaway, either. Her family was rich, too. They still have muscle. Thirteen years old. Raped to death. You think they forgot? I'm telling you, this is worth a fortune. Millions."

"So you say."

"No. I mean, I *will* say, if it comes to that. But I've got a lot more than that."

"What? DNA? Fingerprints?"

"Not DNA . . . probably. It was a long time ago, like I said. Fingerprints? They probably left some, but how could they still be around now? It doesn't matter. Even without any of that, I've got something that nails their coffin."

Sound of another cigarette being lit.

"I got pictures. I got one of the bats they used on her. And the kicker: a piece of paper. An *old* piece of paper — they've got all kinds of ways now to prove how old it is — with them all but admitting it. This club they had, they kept a journal. I made them give it to me, to protect myself, from what they asked me to do. Plus, for all they know, I got them on tape, too. I always had a lot of that recording stuff in my place back then . . . and that's where we were when they told me about it."

"So you want to give them what you have in exchange for — ?"

"A million apiece. That's three. And all I need is a half."

"Half of — ?"

"No, no. Half a million. The rest is yours, all yours. I know there's expenses with something like this."

"How come *you* never just — ?"

"These are rich men," the stranger's voice said, fear threatening to break through the thin membrane of his voice. "*Really* rich. Who knows how they might react if I was to —"

"So you want me —"

"The Brotherhood. I want the Brotherhood. That kind of . . . operation, it's not part of their world. If they even *saw* some of the men you've —"

"They might just call the cops."

"Not a chance," the stranger said, confidently. "Not when you put certain stuff — stuff I'm going to give you — on the table."

Another exhale.

"Then it's done," the stranger said. "Done for everyone. They're not coming after *you* guys, not people like them. And me, I'll be in a place where they could never find me.

"See how sweet? You get paid. I get paid. And they get the Sword of Damocles removed from hanging over their heads all these years. Everybody wins."

Sound of another cigarette being lit.

Exhale.

"I'll listen," the cancer-ridden man said. "If you're playing straight, there might be a move here. If you're not, I can find you a lot easier than you found me."

"It happened in 1975," the other man's voice said. "It was late summer. Maybe two-thirty, three in the morning. I hear a car pull up. I figured it was probably one of the local rich boys, looking to score some weed. My light was on, so —"

"Your light? Outside your house? Meaning you were open for business?"

"Exactly! Everyone in town knew that signal."

"Which means the cops did, too."

"Sure. And so what? The kind of kids I sold to, you think the cops would've done themselves any favors busting *them?*"

Silence on the tape. I could see the AB man on the screen in my head, making a "keep talking" gesture.

"There were three of them. I knew them all. From dealing. But they weren't there to score weed — they were scared. Scared to death. You know how some people get so scared they actually *stink* from it?"

On that screen in my head, I could see the AB man. Just sitting there. Staring at the sniveler, not saying the obvious.

"I got them calmed down. Best I could,

anyway — one of them, he couldn't stop crying like a baby. What they told me was this: There was this girl in their neighborhood. A little younger than them, but *way* filled out, and she knew it. The oldest one, he had his own car. You know what that kind of thing means to kids. And this girl, she wasn't even fourteen, okay? But when he asked her to go someplace with him — the movies, I think it was — she just laughed in his face.

"It wasn't like she had a boyfriend or anything. She was just one of those natural-born cock-teasers. You know the kind I mean. She let one of the other two — the one who couldn't stop crying, in fact — hold her tit once. In the backyard of her own house — *big* house, with a gazebo — you know what that is . . . ?"

Sound of a match scraping. Flame. Cigarette being lit. Exhale. Figuring that was all the response he was going to get, the stranger picked up his story:

"Well, anyway, here's the thing. He had to kiss her ass first. I don't mean be nice to her; I mean, get down on his knees like a bitch and actually kiss her ass. And he did it. Me, I would have —"

"It doesn't matter."

"Yeah, it does. I'm trying to show you

what kind of —"

"It doesn't matter what *you* would have done."

"Oh. Yeah, that's . . . Anyway, she was — to hear them tell it — like some kind of devil-bitch. She gave the other one — not the crying one, not the guy with the car, the third one — a hand job once. But she stopped before he got off. And *then* she told him, if he ever wanted another one from her, he had to finish that one himself . . . and let her watch. You see what kind of cunt she was?"

Sound of a cigarette exhale.

"They spent a lot of time on her. Like they had some sort of club. Sick bastards. They took pictures of her. One even broke into her room, took a pair of her panties. Next day, the cunt sees him, tells him he should have taken a pair from the hamper — they'd smell better.

"All they could do was think about what they wanted to do to her. Tie her upside down and whip her until she begged. Begged for everything, I mean. The guy with the car, he kept talking about how he wanted to fuck her in the ass, make her *scream,* you know?"

Exhale.

"They followed her everywhere. She knew

it, but she wasn't afraid of them. She wasn't afraid of anything, the way they told it. One night — the night they came to my house — they caught her alone. They decided they were going to do it. All of them. One after the other, then all at the same time. Teach the dirty little whore a lesson she'd never forget.

"They took her to this place they had all set up. A house that was empty for the summer. One of them had the keys — he was supposed to water the plants or something. They even had this old rug they were going to lay down on the floor. When they were done, they were just going to roll her up in it, and unroll it on her front lawn.

"They had cameras. Polaroids. If she ever opened her mouth, the whole school would see them. See her on her hands and knees, one cock in her mouth, another up her ass.

"It worked just like they thought it would. They grabbed her, took her to the place. And they all did her. She wasn't such a mouthy bitch then. Even posed for the pictures. Only . . . only she died."

Exhale.

"That's when they went nuts. They never figured on . . . something like that. She just stopped breathing. They knew it was all over then."

"Why come to you?"

"I was a little older than them."

"How little?"

"What difference does that — ?"

Silence.

Cigarette exhale.

"Twenty-two," the stranger said, just the faintest hint of defensiveness in his tone. "They knew I was a man — they were boys, just little punks — they knew I could get things done. I told them, yeah, I could take care of it. Take care of everything. But it would cost them. Cost them big."

"How much?"

"I didn't say. They didn't ask. They just said, 'Do it, Thorn. *Please* do it.' And I did."

"Did what?"

"Just what they planned, only in a different spot. I rolled her body up in the rug, carried her out to this place in the woods I knew. I pushed a big log over her, covered the body with stuff from the ground. Didn't take long."

"They never found the body?"

"Oh, they found it," the stranger said, bitterness almost overpowering his voice. "Assholes didn't give me enough time to do a professional job. I would have put her through a woodchipper or in a furnace. Or gutted her and dumped her in the lake. But it didn't matter. The cops never had a suspect. Never made an arrest."

"Her parents had money?"

"A *lot* of money. Everybody there had money. Even *my* parents had money . . . not that you'd know it from the way I had to live. They — the cunt's parents — they hired private detectives, even got the FBI involved, I heard. But there was nothing."

"That big a case, maybe they still have tissue samples, hair, fingernail scrapings. . . ."

"The kids were all wearing rubber gloves. Masks, too — I don't know why — they told me she knew it was them from the moment they snatched her. Condoms. Like I said, they were planning this for a long time. Now, the rug — that I *did* burn. But they don't know that. If I still did have it, the forensics guys might get enough stuff off it to bury them all."

"What'd they end up paying you?"

"A 1976 Corvette Stingray," the stranger said, reverently. "Brand-new. I ordered it with *everything*. All white, inside and out. Man, if I still had that car today, it'd be worth —"

It'd be worth crap, I thought to myself. Maybe ten thousand, tops. The Vettes of the Gas Crisis era were sad little weaklings, about as "collectible" as Edsels. I filed the thought away: either this guy knew nothing about cars, or he was someone who kept his lifelong bitterness derma-close, hating the rest of the world for the opportunities he fucked him*self* out of.

"That was it?" the AB-OG said, in his machine voice.

"Well, yeah. I mean, later on I tapped them for little loans. That was *much* later, when things went bad for me. They were always happy to help out an old friend who fell on hard times."

"You *don't* have a tape, do you?"

"No. But they don't know that. And they *sure* don't know I don't have that rug."

"What *do* you have?"

"The Polaroids. Nice clean, sharp copies. And something else. Something special."

◆

I didn't know what the Mole had done to the cassette tapes the AB man had left with me — probably wouldn't have understood if he had explained it, either — but the audio quality was like being in the room. I caught the Prof's eye. His slight nod told me he was thinking the same thing I was. Max was buried in the transcript, still reading.

131

"You're not from out here," the stranger on the tape said, a little bit of confidence seeping into his voice. "New York, it's got a set of laws you wouldn't believe. Back then, anyway. Here's the way it worked: you're under age sixteen, you could walk into a church with an Uzi, mow down a few dozen people, and the worst you could get was juvie time."

"Until you were twenty-one, right? Then they'd just put you —"

"Then they had to cut you loose!" the stranger's voice said, proud to out-knowledge the man he feared. "There was this kid, I forget his name, but I know he was a mud; he killed a whole lot of different people, just because he liked doing it or whatever. He was the one that got the law changed. A reporter did this big story on him — for *New York* magazine, it was, I remember — about how kids could get away with murder. *That's* what got the law changed."

"So?"

"So that law, it was like standing between heaven and hell. Because, if you were under sixteen, no matter what you'd done, you'd never see a real penitentiary. But on your sixteenth birthday, you're a man. None of this 'transfer hearing' stuff you read about in other states. You know, where the court gets to decide if you should be tried as a juvenile or as an adult. In New York, you turn sixteen, you go straight to criminal court. No social workers, no 'best interests of the child,' none of that crap. Trial by jury. And if you lose, you go down the same as any other adult."

Exhaled cigarette.

"Don't you see what I'm telling you, br— ?"

I could *feel* the stranger stop himself before he slipped and called the cancer-ridden man "brother." He was tiptoeing as it was — that deep of an insult could cost him a lot more than a refused offer. "Look," he said, quickly, "two kids commit the *same* murder. I mean, they do the exact same things . . . say, shoot a guy in the head, using two different guns, and the coroner said either shot would have been fatal. Only difference between the kids is they were born twenty-four hours apart. One turns sixteen the next day; the other turned sixteen a few hours before the murder. It's 1975, remember? The younger one gets kiddie camp; the older one gets life. Sixteen in this state makes you a man; and a man's crime means a man's time."

"That's the trick in this?" the AB man

said. Not challenging, just making sure he understood what he was being told. "The fifteen-year-olds, they don't have that much to worry about, but the one who's sixteen, he gets The Book?"

"Right! So, if you go to one of the fifteen-year-olds — right now, today, I mean — he *knows* the one who was sixteen at the time is going to confess, cut a deal for himself. He *has* to. And if you go to the one who was sixteen, he knows the other two will talk — what would there be to stop them?"

"That law — that was then."

"I know. But it still works. Look at that guy from Connecticut. He commits a murder, what, twenty years ago? He was just a kid when he did it. But when they finally bring him to trial, he goes down as an adult."

Exhale.

"But before they did that, they had to give him a hearing, see? Like he was still a kid. To find out if he was a good candidate for rehabilitation. It was just a farce, sure, but they still had to do it. In New York, for the sixteen-year-old, they wouldn't even have to go through that dance."

"What's the difference?"

"Between a few years and forever?" the stranger said, only fear keeping the sarcasm from his voice. "Are you kidding?"

"It's really the same risk for all of them," the AB man explained, patiently. "Whether they go down for five minutes or five hundred years, they're done. Even if they beat the rap on some technicality, once the family of the murdered girl finds the right lawyer, they'll all end up on Welfare."

"Oh," the stranger said. "I see what you mean. But that makes it even better, then, don't you see?"

Exhale.

"I mean, now that I think about it, you're right. What they did to that girl . . . I mean, they were stone fucking skinners. When I found the body, I almost threw up. I don't go for stuff like that. I'm a thief, not a —"

Silence. Dead silence. The stranger had come perilously close to claiming in. To call yourself a thief in front of a real convict, especially a high-status one like an AB-OG, you were saying you were a righteous man. Trustworthy. Committed to The Life. Holding the values sacred. And this guy, he was just a low-grade scam artist who couldn't even make a living at it. For some clubs, just *claiming* you're a member could get you seriously dead.

"Look," the stranger said, hastily. "I've got *everything* you need. You — well, anybody you sent — they wouldn't be bluffing. It *did* happen. They *did* do it. They're *all* guilty. And they're all rich."

Silence. Sound of a cigarette being lit. Exhale. Then: "I'll get back to you."

"Better make it soon," the stranger said. "There's other people who'd —"

"Don't play that with me," the AB-OG said. "Don't *ever* do that."

◆

"Maggot," Michelle said, as quiet as acid in a beaker.

"Doesn't mean it's not all true."

"Oh, I think it *is,* baby," she told me. "They knew who to go to, the ones who did that little girl."

"Being scum don't make him dumb."

"My father is correct," Clarence said instantly. "I did a public-records search on some of the paper that man gave to you, Burke."

"And?"

Clarence cleared his throat. "We have the names. The names this . . . person gave, anyway. Here:

"Donald A. Henricks, born February 7, 1960. He would have been fifteen at the time of the murder.

"Reginald William Bender, born July 31, 1960. He also would have been fifteen.

"Carlton John Reedy, born May 17, 1959. He would have been sixteen that night.

"And this . . . person. The one who wants to shake them down. *His* name is Percival K. Thornton. Born April 5, 1953. He would have been twenty-two — just as he said — on the night the child was killed."

"Okay. You already checked — ?"

"Do the three he named have money, mahn? The . . . informant was not lying there, either. Henricks owns so much real estate, through so many corporations, it is impossible to tell how much exactly, but —"

"Maybe he's cash-poor?" Michelle said, looking over from where she had been copying all Clarence's information onto more blank pieces of oaktag — one per name. She didn't use the lilac marker for any of them.

"No, little sister. His house alone is worth several millions, and there is no mortgage. He owns two other homes: one in Montana, one in the Bahamas. No mortgages there, either."

"Ah."

"Yes. Now, Bender is an owner, too. Shopping centers, hotels — small ones, independent, very high-end — a horse ranch . . .

137

too much to list, but he is wealthy, beyond dispute.

"And Reedy, he *declared* an income of thirty-one-plus million dollars last year alone. He is an 'investor,' which could mean anything."

"That's nice work," I told him.

"Oh, there is something more, mahn. Terry and I" — if he caught the Arctic blast from Michelle's eyes, he ignored it — "we ran that pattern-recognition software. You know, the one we designed when you were looking for that —"

"Yeah. And?"

"They were all born on a Sunday, mahn."

"They? All three of the killers?"

"Them *and* the others. The man who wants to blackmail them. Even the little girl they killed. It was on a Sunday that they found her body, too."

"Damn *that* church," the Prof said.

◆

We all went silent. Except for Max.

He stood up, pointed at Clarence's computer, at the Mole's recording rig, at the paper spread out on the table, the walls covered with our writing. Then he walked to the wall himself, and drew a hollow rectangle on a blank spot. Max swept his arms, indicating he was including everything he had pointed to originally.

Using rapid broad strokes, he blacked in the rectangle. When he stopped, more than half of it was still white. Empty. He filled the space with a huge question mark.

We all watched, as attentive as yuppies getting an insider tip on a stock.

Max tapped his own chest. He flowed into a kata so perfect that it was like watching vapor crush bone.

He pointed at the Mole. Tapped his temple. Bowed.

Pointed at the Prof. Spread his arms wide. Bowed again.

He went through all of us. Everyone got their recognition. Their respect for what they did best.

Except me.

Max stepped to the chart with THORN-TON at the top. Made the gestures of a man, talking, as if in conversation with another. Then he pointed to the question mark inside the rectangle again. And then at me. He covered his right fist with his left hand, bowed. Couldn't be clearer.

"Max has it straight," the Prof said. "Ain't but one of us that can throw *that* hard eight."

"I do not —" Clarence started to say.

But the Prof cut him off: "This ain't about the gun, son. Burke, he's got the touch to open them up. You want a freak to speak, Burke's the best there is."

"Because you taught —"

"Listen to me, boy," the Prof said. "You can only train a man so much. Like with fighters. You can teach a man to *deliver* a punch, but real power, that's something you born with. And that's never enough. See, being a puncher don't make you a *fighter,* son. You got to have this" — touching his heart — "or you got nothing. If you can't take it, sooner or later, you stop giving it. And you start giving it *up* — am I telling the truth?"

"Yes, Father," Clarence said. Getting it. Getting it now. The man he worshiped wanted only the respect he earned; he wasn't some half-ass guru who snatched credit he didn't deserve.

The Prof turned and gave me a hard, deliberate look, meaning: "I know what you're thinking, but stay out of this."

And he *did* know what I was thinking, as if he was inside my head. The second the Prof put "heart" and "fighter" together, my mind flashed on boxers who'd rather die in the ring than quit. Mike Quarry didn't have his brother Jerry's punch, but he had his heart. They're both gone now, way before their time. Dementia from subdural hematomas. Too many punches to the head. "Boxer's brain," they call it, without a trace of sarcasm. Michael Watson, Gerald McClellan, Greg Page . . . a long list.

But there's another kind of heart some fighters have — the one you don't see inside the ring. Wife-beaters, rapists, child-molesters. If they can make some promoter money inside the ring, who cares what they do outside it?

Davey Hilton had been one of the three Hilton brothers, Canadians who followed their father into the pro ranks. They were all top-ten guys, real bangers, willing to take two to land one. Matthew was the best, but it was Alex who stopped Shawn O'Sullivan, a fast *and* tough Irishman I was sure would win a welterweight belt when I watched him get jobbed at the Olympics. Davey was holding one of the minor belts as a fifty-four-pounder when he was convicted of holding his two daughters in sexual bondage over a period of several years.

They were the ones with heart — it took a lot to get on that witness stand and tell the truth. Rape was the least of it, and the jury dropped him for enough crimes to bury

141

him. But the judge didn't count him out. Not even a standing eight. The "champ" was out in less than five.

Maybe his prison psychologist will quit and become his manager, like Tony Ayala's had. Rehabilitation, it's a wonderful thing.

The Prof took my slight nod for what it was, turned back to Clarence: "Now, Burke here, you should have seen *him* in the ring. Slippery? My man made an eel look like sandpaper. And fast? He could put four on you before you could blink. But that one-punch knockout power? Not there. Just not there. Understand?"

"But what does that have to do with — ?"

"Burke's got the magic," Michelle confirmed. "He can . . . I don't know how to say it. . . . He can *be* them. They'll say things to him. . . ."

"I have seen this for myself," the Mole agreed.

Max swept the room with his eyes — he'd seen it, too. Satisfied, he sat down.

◆

"This AB guy — the one who made that tape — he was just there to listen," the Prof said, thoughtfully.

"And you think the guy who told the story

was lying?"

"Is Clarence Thomas black?" the Prof countered.

"If you mean his color —"

"*Now* you driving the nail, son!"

"It *sounds* right," Michelle explained. "But that doesn't *make* it right."

"So this . . . all of this; *none* of this . . . is enough?" Clarence said.

"Scamming — *pro* scamming — is a special art," the Prof explained. "Once you figure out the stupidity level of the mark, you adjust your game, see? You think this AB guy, he'd answer an ad in the papers about earning five grand a week for stuffing envelopes? This is a hard man. Been around. Even if he *wants* to believe — and Lord knows he does; he *has* to — he's not going for any quick-fix trick. But, against *this* boy" — pointing at the THORNTON chart — "he's so overmatched they shouldn't let him in the ring."

"He's lying," Michelle said, as certain as the Prof. "We just don't know about what . . . and how much."

"And if this AB boy wants us to get down, he's got to come around," the Prof said.

"I'll put it to him," I said.

143

When you talk about a fighter's class, you're not talking about his weight. There's bantams with hearts strong enough to pump out a flooded basement, and heavyweights who can *beat* a man okay, but turn to jelly if the other guy takes it . . . and hits back.

Life is a fight, but not everyone's a fighter. Otherwise, bullies would be an endangered species.

I sat alone that night and worked on a plan. On a whole bunch of plans. Wolfe's crew could get me a complete breakdown on all three targets in a finger-snap. No way Clarence is as good as they are for that. Wolfe's people use special tools to unearth ancient bones, an artist's brush to clean them off, and, when they finally put the pieces together, they always fit.

But computers have their uses, and none of the three rich boys — grown men now — were underground. Sure, maybe they had *assets* hidden. Probably did, considering the kind of money they got to play with. But we didn't care where they got their money, we just wanted some of it. According to Thornton, what we were after was such a small chunk the marks wouldn't even miss it.

I'd asked Clarence what he found out for me. And got this:

"I am . . . I am still a student, mahn. Terry, now, *he* knows how to do things I could never —"

"So bring him in. What's the problem?"

"Well, even Terry, he is not the *very* best. He would be the first to say so himself."

"You're saying we *need* the very best? Just to do a simple scan on these three guys?"

"When you are fighting a mind war, the more you know —"

"The harder you throw," I finished one of the Prof's adages for him. "So?"

"Well, we could ask —"

Stepped in that one, didn't you, sucker? I mentally kicked myself. Clarence's unrequited love for the cyber-slinger we all called the Dragon Lady was no secret. "Yeah, fine. Ask your girl to show you some more tricks," I said, surrendering. "But whatever it costs, that's coming out of your share."

The Islander tried to keep from grinning, but he couldn't pull it off.

◆

I told myself I didn't want to go to Wolfe's crew because the fewer people who knew, the better — the urban survivalist's version of the Golden Rule. But once you start lying to yourself, the danger is that you'll get too good at it.

So I just faced it. Faced it and took it: The last time I'd asked Wolfe's cell to do a job, I'd ended up seeing Wolfe in person. That's when I told her I was back to being myself. To being the man she first knew. The one she . . . I never finished that part: she'd drained my tank before I could get out of first gear.

But this thing, it was all about money. And no matter what story I might try to tell Wolfe about bringing a little girl's killers to justice, no matter how many layers of lead I wrapped around it, she'd see through it.

That last time, I hadn't been lying when I'd told Wolfe I was doing the right thing, for the right reasons. But, like always, I'd left things out.

I'd done a lot of thinking ever since that last job. A lot of thinking about myself. About how I saw things. Why I did them. Who I was.

Now I knew. And I wasn't going anywhere near Wolfe. Not because I had crossed some borders that she wouldn't; because I lived on the other side of hers.

"I *did* learn some things," Clarence reported, happily. "The only reason those newspaper clippings were in the database was because they were *added.* The database itself was not even in existence when —"

"And we care about this because . . . ?" Michelle said, just short of sarcastic.

"It is a small town," Clarence said. "With its own newspapers. It would be quite an undertaking —"

"All it takes is coin to join," the Prof cut him off. "Look, son, we already knew this was a rich ville. That computer thing of yours, it's real nice and all, but Burke used to get that same stuff out of libraries all the time. They got it on . . . what, Schoolboy?"

"Microfiche," I said. "Sometimes, if the town is small enough, they actually keep a copy of every issue they ever printed. Old-time newspaper guys called it the morgue. The Internet may get it quicker sometimes, but it's not any better than —"

"With all respect," Clarence said, "the Internet is a tool. Like you are always saying, what good is something you don't know how to use? What I *learned* was that there is a way to locate old Web sites, ones that used to be available but have been taken down. You will not find such things in any library."

"I *still* don't see —"

"Little sister, please," the young man said, the Island sweetness sugaring his voice. "Just take a look."

◆

The now-dead Web site had been **<Who KilledMelissa.com>.** The screen of Clarence's laptop filled with a photo that looked as if it had been scanned from a yearbook, with **HELP US FIND HER KILLER!** scrolling across the bottom of the screen in a blood-red font. At the top were icons of various weapons: pistol, knife, strangler's rope. . . . Clarence demonstrated how playing the cursor over each icon showed what they would open into, stuff like:

Contact Us • The Crime • Help! • Suspects?

There were a lot of those links. We patiently watched as Clarence opened "Suspects?" but it held nothing except mug shots of convicted sex killers. All they had in common was that they weren't in custody at the time of the girl's murder, and that the killing "fit their known pattern."

Total crap. TV "profiler" bullshit.

I spent an hour clicking links before I realized what I was really looking at. So I asked Clarence to run a certain name, just to be sure my nose was working. Sure enough, the site had been set up by one of those "true crime" quickie-paperback specialists. Apparently, this "journalist" couldn't crank out her usual couple of hundred pages of cribbed newspaper accounts — plus the obligatory photos and autopsy reports — as fast as the market demanded anymore. So she had decided to ride the "Unsolved Mysteries" train, panning for gold.

Since she was nothing resembling an investigator — excuse me, "criminal investigative reporter" — she had thrown up the Web site. Probably hoping someone from the girl's past would give her enough to cobble together another piece of porn that would have Jack Olsen spinning in his grave.

That old site was now as dead as Melissa Turnbridge. I even looked at its message board, but it was just the usual collection: from ghouls salivating over "More details, please!" to conspiracy theorists — the Monarch Program just barely edging out the Illuminati — to suggestions for casting when this all got turned into a movie. Not a hint of contact by anyone we were interested in. Still, I had to ask:

"Was the site hacked down, or just — ?"

"The domain name lapsed," Clarence said. "And there were no new buyers. That means the person who put it up just let it die a natural death."

"That's worth something right there," I said, aiming it at Michelle's caustic comments about Clarence consulting the Dragon Lady, but feeling it inside my heart, where the beast-killer always lurks.

◆

"Is this going to mean another milkshake?"

"No," I said into the cancer-man's pre-paid, onetime cell. "Just you and me. No more Q and A. There's something you need to do. Get done, anyway."

"Just say —"

"No."

The neighborhood wasn't a place where a man like him could ask for help if he got lost. So I gave him real specific directions. And a time.

If being in a place full of nonwhites bothered him, you'd never know it.

If eating a meal that could be his last upset him, it didn't show on his face.

We were in my booth. In the back, against the wall that separates the main body of the joint from the kitchen. The bank of payphones was right behind where I sat, invisible but not always silent.

Max materialized next to me.

"This is —"

"Max the Silent," the AB man finished for me, his tone that of a man who was actually getting to *see* something he'd heard about for years but had never been sure existed. Like Bigfoot or Nessie.

"Yeah. And, behind you, coming this way, is the Prof."

He never turned around. His only reaction was to move to his left, making room.

"I need to speak with your boy," I told him.

He didn't bristle at the characterization, a man who didn't have the time for that kind of thing.

"Alone?"

"Yes."

"You willing to ink up a little?"

151

"So I can pass for one of your guys?"

"Yeah."

"Not for real. And I don't want to risk a temp."

"But I can tell him — ?"

"Anything you want. So long as he understands that he has to talk to me. It's not an option."

"You going to hurt him?"

I gave him a quizzical look.

"To make him talk," he explained.

"I thought you said he already *did* that."

"Yeah. And you're not buying?"

"Because I want to talk to him myself?"

"That's right."

"This isn't about the truth of what he said. It's about the truth of who he is."

"You've lost me."

"Burke's got powers," the Prof assured him. "He can get inside a man's mind as easy as me picking a lock."

Max tapped the man's forearm. Got his attention. Nodded. Nothing elaborate, but enough.

"So if he's lying — ?"

"It won't matter," I assured him. "Not to us doing the job, I mean. It'll just change *how* we do it."

"You believe those three — ?"

"Did it? Yeah."

"So what more do you need?"

"Why'd you come to me?"

"Silver said I could . . . Ah, all right, I get it."

"Can you make it happen?"

"I think so. It *is* okay, I tell him you're one of ours, right?"

"Right."

"And I can go along? Not come inside, wherever you do what . . . whatever you're going to do, but just come along with him?"

"He's scared bad, huh?"

"Those are three *big* dogs."

I gave him one of Wesley's smiles.

◆

Inside isn't the same for everyone. If you got a little county-jail slap, you've got different options: they mix the pre-trial detainees with the ones doing misdemeanor bits, so you can work the guys who haven't been tried yet for all kinds of nice stuff: phone relays, packages, maybe even get yourself introduced to their woman's girlfriend on visiting day.

But there's always people trying to work you, too. Pre-trial tanks draw more rats than Open House in a cheese factory, sniffing around for a little info they can sell to the

DA for a cut-loose. If the crime's headline-quality, and the proof isn't too tight, a jail-house snitch can buy himself a sweet life . . . provided he never comes back Inside.

When you're short-time jugged, the "homeboy" stuff won't do a thing for you unless you're one of those youngbloods who're still flying colors.

Anyway, if you've been down before, done *real* time, you stay far away from kids like that. Shank-happy fools act just like they do on the streets — stab someone over a bullshit diss, chest you to test you, act like they're actually *glad* to be there . . . more status for when they go back to the corner.

Like the Prof said years ago, "You spend too much time working on your cred, you spend a lot longer being dead."

If you're like me, you look for the older guys, guys who know how things really work.

There's rules: You never talk about your case. And you double-never ask about theirs. You find out if you know anyone in common, and you use the phones to start checking *him* out. You don't front; you don't profile; you don't sell tickets; you don't tell stories about how good you had it in the World.

You're always ready to do every single

minute by yourself, if that's how it has to be. You stay polite, quiet, respectful. But you don't step aside, you don't ass-kiss, and you never talk to a uniform. You don't play cards, you don't throw dice, you don't use dope — *no* kind of dope. You don't run a hustle, you don't open a book. You stay low and walk slow.

The penitentiary's a different life. There, you *have* to connect. You *can't* "do your own time," like every con says he wants to do.

Used to be a saying: "There's no Switzerland behind the walls." But that was wrapping a truth around a lie. Yeah, sure, Switzerland was "neutral" in World War II. But all that meant was that they didn't fight. And didn't give a fuck who won, like the poker parlor taking a piece of every pot.

So they stored art treasures the Nazis looted from the Jews, then did the same for those American commanders who handled the mopping-up operation after the Ultimate Aryan Warrior pulled the maximum punk-out.

Switzerland might not have *taken* a side, but they sure *played* them all — storing no-trace cash for power-men from Germany, Russia, America, Italy, Japan . . . and anyone else who made it worth their while. The way they had it set up, the only sure winner was them.

Forget that kind of game Inside. Everything's out in the open; no place to hide. So a jailhouse turnout takes a daddy because he thinks gang rape is his only other option . . . but he's safe only if his daddy can hold his own ground.

Some can't. And some of those who can, they rent out their property. Or sell it. Even if your daddy keeps you, and keeps you safe, you're still a punk, forever. And, Inside, no punk is ever really safe.

In all my time, I only ran across a few guys who were actually able to pull it off and stand alone. They didn't join, they didn't roll over, and they'd kill you if you tried to make them do either one. If you wanted to be left alone, one of the best reps to have was being a for-real psycho. You can threaten him for a few minutes, but you can't tell him what to do. Only the voices in his head can do that, and they're on the job twenty-four/seven.

No matter what liberals tell you, it never matters what *got* you there. There was this freak, Lenny, I forget his last name. A citizen, until he was caught. Some said he had been a pharmacist. Some said nurse; some said chemist. But everyone knew what

156

brought him Inside: the maggot poisoned his own three kids, for the insurance.

Lenny was Central Casting for "punk." Pale, fair-haired, chubby young white boy with rabbit eyes and lips so naturally red you'd think he used lipstick.

But nobody bothered him.

Turned out Lenny's fucking *hobby* was poisoning people. He loved to do it. And he knew a thousand ways to get it done.

One day, a guy named Uriah suddenly froze in the middle of chow, then started twitching like an epileptic on meth. When the guards got there, he was still doing his death-dance, but he was stiff before they rolled him onto the stretcher, already turning some color nobody'd ever seen on a human before.

Creeper got his name like you'd expect. And putting him behind bars didn't change his game. Nobody cared, because he wasn't a snitch — he just liked to watch. And he knew things.

A few days later, Creeper was telling his story. He'd been on the tier late the night before, and he passed by Lenny's cell. Lenny was jerking off, and not being quiet about it — moaning like he was getting a blow job from a porn star, with three others lined up waiting their turn. Lenny had a piece of paper wrapped around his cock. But when he was done, instead of flushing it, he crumpled it up and tossed it out into the corridor.

Creeper took the paper back to his cell — the same thing inside him that got him his name made him do it. When he opened the paper ball, it turned out to be an autopsy report. On the guy who had spasmed to death.

So, the next time Lenny started babbling about all the different ways you could make poison out of damn near *anything,* everyone knew two things: He wasn't lying. And he was the wrong guy to fuck with.

It turned out that this Uriah fool had given Lenny the usual "Shit on my dick or blood on my knife!" speech. Gave him twenty-four hours to make his decision — about as smart as telling a man you're going to break into his house as soon as it gets dark out.

After that, anytime you saw Lenny coming down the corridor with an aerosol can of shaving cream in his hand, you moved out of his way — fast.

Making other people afraid gives some freaks a bigger appetite for more of the same. After a while, Lenny put on a lot of weight . . . and started throwing it around.

Lenny knew chemicals, but he didn't know cons. He scared one of them so much that the guy hired Wesley.

◆

When I was Inside, they were just starting to have "programs." They always had the Bible classes, the AA meetings, stuff that the Parole Board was supposed to believe made you ready for the street. Provided that street was the Bowery.

The new stuff was different: art classes, literacy programs, GED-prep courses. And therapy, that was the trump card. Especially *group* therapy. Always run by some smug little weasel who was born a chump and then went and got a degree in it. Big thing was, you had to "confront" all the time. Not just yourself, you had to jump on anyone who wasn't "coming clean." See, the goal was to get you to "express your feelings." Criminals hadn't learned how to do that. Once they did, well, they could be citizens.

Inmates sucked that stuff up. Convicts wouldn't go near it. The Parole Board was appointed by the governor. Do the math.

The fancier stuff came along much later. Today, it's all the rage. Some "tough" guy beats his woman bad enough to be locked up, they decide it's all about too much testosterone. What a real man like that needs is some Anger Management. Get in touch with his sensitive side. Learn empathy. Learn to feel the pain of others.

Wesley was way ahead of his time — he could have been the poster boy for Anger Management. Nobody ever saw Wesley get mad. He'd step off for anyone, back down from any challenge. One guy — a crewed-up biker who must have ridden too long without a helmet — even slapped Wesley in the face once. Right on the yard.

Wesley took it. Just turned and walked away.

Action was heavy that night. Gambling action. I almost took the whole pool, betting ninety-six hours to the minute.

Fools went short, cons who'd been around awhile went long. Me, I figured two days to let the biker think he was the new bull on the block; another day to let him make some more enemies, so Wesley wouldn't be the only suspect; and one day to let dopes wonder if the stories they'd heard about Wesley weren't just jailhouse rumors, magnified over time.

But it wasn't until the fifth day they found the biker in the weight room, when they opened it for business. He was on his back on the bench-press slab, a length of wire stiffer than he was embedded in his carotid artery. How it got there, nobody knows.

"Nobody knows." That's how you answer any question about Wesley. "You get this much time to *do* it," he told me once, making a dry-click sound with his tongue, "but you might have to wait hours *to* do it. Even days, sometimes."

You know what they call an impatient sniper?

Dead.

◆

You can't kill time. It doesn't ever really die. Some of it keeps coming back, too. But you can make it pass.

If waiting was a martial art, I'd be a grand master.

The paper had a story about a coyote who'd been terrorizing Central Park, taking down dogs. "Beloved pets," the sob sister who wrote the column called them. Letting your dogs run off-leash in that place after dark — yeah, that's love.

The outraged city mounted a major effort, spent a ton of money, and finally bagged the coyote. They tranq'ed him out, put him in a cage — photo ops galore. More proof that one-bedroom walk-ups with no super and less service are worth a couple of grand a month just so you can live in the Big Apple.

The coyote died. Autopsy said it was from stress. Maybe it was too many flashbulbs in his face. Maybe it was the knowledge that he'd never run free again. Never find a mate. Never make another decision for himself.

All that time and energy, but nobody could find the gas money to drive him upstate, let him out in some forest, and leave him be, I guess. Always better to lock up the troublemakers.

I hate zoos. Lovingly supported by "nature-lovers," they're a crime against nature.

What's the point of saving a species from extinction if the only way they can live is behind bars? And if kids "need" the opportunity to see a rhino or a panda or whatever, why can't they just watch television?

Hell, why not have virtual zoos? Take the million miles of footage already stored, edit it down, and build long, dim corridors lined with giant, hyper-definition screens. Label each one, put a drop-down menu along the side, and let the kids get a better look at the animals doing what they *really* do than they could ever see in some zoo.

What's better, watching a polar bear cross a glacier, or pace around in tiny circles? What's more educational, a close-up of a tiger so tight you could count his whiskers, or smelling the foul rankness of his captivity?

Why pay extortion money to China to rent their goddamned pandas? Why pay big money for baby lions . . . especially when you know what had to have "happened" to their mothers for the "bring 'em back alive" heroes to harvest their crop? How do you put a great white shark in an aquarium and call it a "lesson" for children?

How many kids have the patience to watch a butterfly leave its cocoon? On tape, they can watch it whenever they want, just by pushing a button.

How the *fuck* do you call the "creation science" loons ignorant when you keep your own ancestors behind bars?

A hundred years ago, the New York Zoological Society — yeah, that's right, they own the Bronx Zoo now — actually kept an African Pygmy in a cage, right next to the orangutans and chimps. Sure, slavery was outlawed by then, but that only applied to humans. An "explorer" had captured the

163

Pygmy in the Congo, and turned him into an exhibit at the St. Louis World's Fair. When that show was over, the owner sold his property. It's the American way.

You know who finally busted him out? The forebears of the same "true believers" who are trying to stop schools from teaching evolution today. How can there be a "missing link" if the whole world went from Nothing to Now in seven days? That's downright ungodly. And America is a nation *under* God, isn't it?

Yeah, speak of the Devil.

After they got him loose, they gave the Pygmy a name — Ota Benga, I think it was. They handed him a Bible and taught him to use tools. He finally got to go home, the same way a lot of locked-down, no-hope kids do: he took his own life, is what it says in the history books.

By me, he took his life *back.*

I understand he used a firearm to do the job. Somebody must have taught him how to shoot. Too bad they never taught him who to aim at.

I looked at my watch. I'd been gone for . . . almost three hours.

Yeah, I know how to wait.

There's other ways. Michelle dragged me to this white-hot new club in the Village. Apparently, retro was in. The place reminded me of the club where I'd first seen Judy Henske — the goddess of torch-singing — live. I think she'd been on the card with Dave Van Ronk that night; I don't know where he is, but I do know that Judy can still bring it.

The club even had a Joan Baez type . . . a tall, dark-haired girl with an acoustic guitar and the transported look of a solo violinist. She only did one number, but she *drove* it:

A long time ago when we weren't at war
Even then we knew he was a political
    whore
His daddy tasted blood, so the son wanted
    more
And he's still killing today

She carried that torch all the way to . . .

And now the little weasel stands alone
A single step from his Magic Phone
You know he'll never call our soldiers
    home
Haliburton's still got its bills to pay

. . . and closed to a standing O.

"We have to stop this one!" she shouted, as she walked off the stage. "Our mothers and fathers showed us how!"

No, they didn't, I thought to myself. They showed us how to blow themselves up, or how to get their heads beat in by cops in Chicago, or to die at Kent State. Sure, some came in from the cold after a few years and told stories about how they had "renounced their white-skin privilege" while they'd been "underground." The ones who couldn't change their skin color, they were still in prison. Or "underground" . . . in a pine box.

But the dividing line was never as simple as color. Some of the whites had gone the distance, like Ray Luc Levasseur and Tom Manning. But it wasn't only the Vietnam War that drove their car: they'd been working-class guys who'd done enough thinking to realize that thinking wasn't going to get it done.

Levasseur is out now, after doing a ton, but Manning's going to die behind the Walls. Kathy Boudin's free after twenty, but all the others in on that fatal armored-car heist are serving for the duration. David Gilbert's never going home. Neither are all the BLA members they caught, even those who just helped out. Ask Marilyn Jean Buck.

The DA who prosecuted that "revolutionary" Brinks job later pleaded guilty to federal corruption charges. He'd been ratted out by his mistress, whose details of her sugar daddy's sexual preferences were enough to kill his reelection chances anyway. The DA got the "probation and community service" sentence they reserve for the non-violent offender, especially one who could tell a few stories of his own if pushed too far.

The Symbionese Liberation Army was firebombed and blasted out of existence, but a couple of survivors formed a new crew, with Bill and Emily Harris running the show. Whether Patty Hearst was their convert or their captive, only she knows. But it was the threat of her testimony that pulled guilty pleas decades later from everyone in on that bank job where a woman making a deposit was murdered because one of the "armed struggle" twits couldn't handle a shotgun.

And even *that* wouldn't have happened if someone hadn't informed on Kathy Soliah, who had been living aboveground as a community activist/housewife/mother for decades as Sarah Jane Olsen. They'll all be out in a few years.

All except Joe Remiro, the first SLA

soldier to be captured. He's got natural life. Rumors kept flying that the "underground" was going to bust him out. But the only "freedom fighter" they ever managed to spring was Timothy Leary.

Were the Panthers revolutionaries, or dope-dealers? The ones still behind bars aren't talking, and neither is Fred Hampton.

I knew where that whitewater rapid of thought was taking me, and I didn't want to be back in Biafra again. So I stepped outside, as if I wanted a smoke, pulled a cell phone, called a girl I know, and came up with another way to make the time go by.

◆

The guy selling supernotes — the counterfeit C-notes made in North Korea; supposed to be the best in the world — wanted way too much for the boxcar load he was supposedly trying to peddle.

The woman who wanted "a deep investigation . . . you know what I mean, right?" of the mother who was accusing her ex-husband — the wannabe client's current boyfriend — of sexually abusing their six-year-old daughter on "overnights" made a down payment and left. On the way back to her car, she had an accident. With any luck, she'll be out of the hospital in time for the trial.

The impeccably dressed Nigerian who wanted to make sure I understood the concept of "virgin cleansing" before proceeding further seemed greatly reassured when I recited the gospel for him: An HIV-positive male who has sex with a girl so young that her virginity is assured can transfer the disease to the child. Certain procedures must be observed. When the barrier is penetrated for the first time, only then can the disease itself be ejaculated out of the donor and into the recipient.

Of course, a physician's examination must precede the actual "transfer ceremony," he explained. After all, believe it or not, some unscrupulous individuals have been known to have a child's ruptured hymen surgically restored, so that the product could be used again. What an evil world this is!

I played the only cards I had, saying I had to meet his "principal" myself, to make sure he had the kind of money this was going to cost. The Nigerian smiled, opened his rhino-hide briefcase, and placed stack after stack of hard currency on the table between us.

I told him I would call when I had the package in my possession. Because I couldn't keep the little girl for long, his "principal" would have to come to wherever I was holding her to conduct his transfer ceremony.

I was told this was unacceptable; the Nigerian would continue to be the "bridge." When I was ready, he would bring the required amount and take the child with him.

The Prof watched him leave. Told us that the Nigerian's car had diplomatic plates. And that he was assisted into the backseat by a chauffeur who made no attempt to conceal the shoulder holster he wore.

A couple of nights later, while the Nigerian was on the phone getting the news he'd been waiting for, his chauffeur was enjoying a leisurely smoke outside the limo — he never saw whoever broke his neck. When the Nigerian came out, he was assisted into the backseat.

A couple of hours later, he finally acknowledged that he himself was the principal. Then we transferred a steel-jacketed lump of lead to his brain.

The papers called it a political assassination. They got it right — the same way a man who picks the winning number gets it right.

The way I see it, he got what he paid for.

I'd promised him he would never die from AIDS.

It was another week before the call came.

"He's yours," the AB man said. "Want to do it the same way?"

"No need for all that," I told him. "Drop by my place, pick up a couple of bottles. He takes the blue one. When you're sure he's ready, you take yours — the red one."

"So he doesn't see me —"

"Yeah."

"You must have given him a much heavier dose," the AB man said, watching the man on the cot across from us: still zonked, mouth open, trace of drool on his chin.

"Just gave you a much lighter jolt than you had last time."

"I get it. What do we do now?"

"Wait for him to come around. Then you tell him what I told you, the first time *you* woke up here. After that, you make sure he understands that talking to me isn't optional."

"I'll do that, brother."

171

I gave him a look.

"Just practicing," he said, straight-faced.

◆

The guy on the cot came around slyly, slitting his eyes so whoever was watching wouldn't know he was awake. The AB boss and I caught the angled overhead light bouncing off the whites of his eyes. We exchanged a look, but kept quiet.

What the guy on the cot saw was two men, each wearing a black hoodie draped to cover his hair and ears. The AB man's alligator eyes were enough of a memory-cue; mine were hidden behind wrap-around mirror sunglasses.

What we saw was a tallish runt with thinning dark hair, combed straight back from his forehead and moussed into what I guessed he thought was a style. His face was flabby, his chin was weak, and his eyes were little pools of greed and fear.

The AB man warned him about sitting up too quick, his voice soft and mechanical.

"Thanks," the guy on the cot said, moving very carefully. He wasn't the type to test his pain tolerance.

"This is the man," the AB man told him. "You already know how it's going to work.

You're going to tell him your story. Then he's going to ask you questions. You're going to answer the questions. What you're not going to do is *ask* questions."

Seeing us both smoking, the guy on the cot lit one of his own. "And then you'll decide if you're going to — ?"

The AB man stood up and walked off into the shadows, leaving me alone with . . . whatever he was.

◆

"Thorn — that's what your friends call you, right? — what I need you to do is start at the beginning."

He took a drag on his cigarette, gave me a look, as if he was making sure I measured up. Then he realized his mistake, and started talking: "It was somewhere between two-thirty and three in the morning when —"

"That's not the beginning," I told him. No threat, just a man making sure of the facts. "That's the night it happened. But these boys, they'd been to your place before, right?"

"Oh, yeah. Plenty of times."

"Because . . . ?"

"Because? Oh, you mean, them being just kids and me being . . . Yeah, I get it. It wasn't

173

like I *hung* with them or anything. I mean, they were high-school kids. Punks."

"And you were a dealer?"

"Just grass and pills."

"Pills?"

"Ludes, mostly. Once in a while, I had some speed — not coke, I mean amphetamines — and some downers, too. Like tranqs, you understand?"

"You had a steady connection?" I asked, acting as if I was reluctantly impressed at the operation he'd been running at such a young age.

"I had a lot of them," he said, back to being what he thought he was.

Sure. You had access to a doctor's office, a pharmacy, or a scrip pad. For weed, you just went down to The City, bought at street price from people who scared you, then doubled that when you sold it to kids who thought you were a real bad guy.

I kept those thoughts where they belonged, just nodded. That's how you do it if you really want to get it done. Never interrupt the flow, let them talk. No fish ever bit a hook with his mouth closed. But there has to be *some* bait, and letting the mark finish your sentences was always a good choice.

"So they'd been coming around for . . . ?" I asked.

"Maybe a few months, a little more. Carl was the only one with a license. Before that, they'd only show up when they were with older guys."

"So word was around?"

"Definitely. I mean, a little town like that, there wasn't really room for more than one dealer."

"So if *they* knew . . . ?"

"The cops knew, too? Fuck, yes, they did. Had to."

" 'Had to'? Meaning you never got shook down?"

"Not even once," he said, with the smugness of a vet explaining the ropes to a rookie. "See, even back then, I figured out how things work. It's not who's selling, it's who he's selling *to.* The cops knew I never handled hard stuff. It was what's called an 'unspoken agreement.' "

Showing your hand pretty early, huh? I thought. *Or are you testing? You that smart a sociopath, "Thorn"? Or are you trying to find out if I'm a stupid one?*

"Nobody ever got arrested for possession?" I asked him. "Ever?"

"You have to remember when this was. Just past Vietnam. Who *wasn't* smoking weed then? Besides, it isn't like I was an outsider."

"Because you had a house there?"

"I was *born* there. Same as those punks were."

"So your parents could — ?"

"It wasn't like that," he said, making a dismissive gesture with his left hand. "I was a *disappointment* to them. That house I had? It was really more like a cottage. And it wasn't them who bought it for me; it was my grandfather."

"You were tight with him?"

"I don't even remember him. Died when I was a little kid. Left me some money, but I couldn't get my hands on it until I was thirty or whatever. Unless I went to college. So the money was in trust, and my father got to 'manage' it for me. What he did was, he invested it in the cottage, see? That way, I had a nice place to live, and, instead of paying rent, I was *making* money."

"Your father knew you were dealing?"

"No," he said, barely suppressing a sigh at my slowness — he had my number now. "Real estate *appreciates.* Goes up in value. The idea was, I live in the cottage until I turn thirty, then I sell it for a lot more than they paid for it."

"I get it. So your parents, they just thought you had some kind of regular job?"

"They. Did. Not. Give. A. Fuck." Making

176

each word its own sentence: a sentence he was still serving.

"Okay. Did it work out like they planned?"

"You mean, sell the place when I turned thirty?" he said, chuckling. "No. No, it didn't."

"You were never arrested before the night the three kids came to you?"

"For what?"

"For anything," I said, indicating it wouldn't matter to me what he got dropped for; I was just getting all the facts. Doing my job.

"No. Unless you count some little juvie —"

"For anything. Ever," I repeated, icing my voice, letting him know I *was* going to do the job I'd been ordered to do.

"What difference could that — ?"

I had a choice then. I could have reminded him what his former paid protector had told him about not asking questions. That would get me an answer, but it would be a lie. When a guy comes into prison for the first time, the cons call him a "fish." Smart cons know there's all kinds of fish. Some you catch and throw back, some you eat, and some you don't want to be in the same part of the ocean with. A big fish doesn't necessarily mean a dangerous one, but even when they're easy to hook, they still have to be played.

This freak was as reactive as a rheostat, and you had to use a feathery touch on his dial. Frightening him would be easy work, but fear makes people untrustworthy . . . which is why torture isn't the way to get truth. *Only an amateur thinks being scared works the same way on everyone,* I thought, flashing back to what happened that time in prison, when Lenny had overplayed his fear-dealing hand.

"These kids trusted you," I said, making my voice into a blanket I could wrap around us both. "I mean, sure, they were scared out of their punk minds, but, if you think about it, what they trusted was your *rep,* see? Not just that you knew your way around, but that you'd never talk. When I was coming up, *everybody* did juvie. It was, like, some test you had to pass. Not just because those places are full of muds, and you have to stand up or they'll have you for supper. No, there's something else. Something that would count heavy with shaky kids.

"Nobody wants to be Inside," I rolled on, catching the knowing nod from him I'd been waiting for. Nibbling, but the hook wasn't in deep enough yet. "The juvie officers, they know that even kids with minor-league beefs probably run with *other* kids. Which means they know things *about* those kids. So — you get dropped, you almost always get the chance to slide, provided you got something to trade."

I felt him coming closer, now satisfied that I was coming to *him.* "The first time I went in, you know what it was for?" I confided, letting the bitterness in my voice come through, tightening the space between us. "Setting a fire in an empty house. Not to burn it down, just to keep warm. What total bullshit, right? But they took me in a little room, told me if I could tell *them* something I could go home."

"I get it now," he said, echoing my words from before — the hook finally set. "And you know what, I think you might even be right. In the town where I lived, going away was a *big* deal. It's supposed to be this huge secret — they can't put your name in the papers, nobody's even allowed inside Family Court — but word gets around."

"How long were you down?"

"The first time, it was only for a couple of months," he said, no longer worried about being judged, now that we had the same respect for each other. "I wouldn't have gone in at *all,* but my asshole 'father' thought it would teach me a lesson or something."

"Yeah?"

"Yeah. So I shot a lousy alley cat with my pellet gun. I'll bet half the kids in town did things like that. I mean, who doesn't?"

There it is! I thought. But I just nodded, this time to keep him going — I knew there was more.

"The second time was *really* lame," he said. "Attempted this; attempted that. All bullshit beefs. I didn't actually *do* anything. If I'd been in regular court, they would have thrown it all out."

"Attempted . . . ?"

"Just a couple of houses down from where we lived, there was this woman. Big, stacked blonde. I don't know if her husband was out of town a lot, or just got home late, but she was always getting ready for bed by herself. Put on a real show doing it. No *way* she didn't know she had an audience. She loved it."

"So they caught you in her yard and —"

"And dropped about a thousand different charges on me," he said in a stepchild's voice.

You had your pellet gun with you that time, too, didn't you? I thought. *Or some ninja crap you bought out of a catalogue. Or . . . whatever it took to show the cops that you had plans for that blonde. Who do you think* called *them, you freakish little maggot?*

"They offered you a deal?" was all I said aloud.

"No," he said, making that dismissive gesture again, telling me it wouldn't have mattered — a stand-up guy like him wouldn't have given anyone else up, even if someone else had been with him in the woman's yard that night. *As fucking if.* "I don't even think it counted."

"Counted?"

"As juvie time. They sent me to this place. It was all white this time. First thing I noticed. All we had to do was talk. All day, every day. Talk to them, talk to each other — you end up talking to *yourself* in that fucking nuthouse."

"How long that time?"

"Six months. Six months to the day. It wasn't a sentence, it was a fucking 'program.' By the time I got out, I was too old for the kiddie system anyway."

"And you never took another fall until —"

"Until when I met Claw, that's right."

Dumb fuck should have told me his Brand name, just in case, I thought.

"So you *did* have a rep," I stroked him. "People knew you went away. They didn't know what for, but they *did* know you came in by yourself, didn't give anyone up." Still feathering that rheostat — no point pretending he'd been a for-real AB, like I was supposed to be, but he *hadn't* ratted anyone out, and that *was* a credential.

In our world, "time will tell" has a different meaning. Six months in the County doesn't entitle you to call yourself a convict, even though that's more than enough time to get yourself seriously dead if you don't make the right moves.

"Yeah," he said, being all modest about it.

"Okay," I said, "let's go there."

◆

I wasn't surprised when he intuited that "there" was the night of the killing. He skipped back over thirty years, got right to it. No problem.

Maybe that's when I first realized that Thornton was an easy guy to underestimate. On my side of the border, that made him dangerous. Some are good with knives, some with guns. You get good enough at anything, you get a name for it, but that's not always a roadmap you can trust.

"A man's name don't always give away his game," the Prof had schooled me on the yard. "See Ruppo over there," he side-mouth whispered without turning his head, knowing I wouldn't turn mine — I'd already learned that trick in the "training schools" where I'd served my apprenticeship. "People call him 'Blade,' but they never peep his shade."

Ruppo's shade was big enough to provide plenty of it. That was the first time I'd seen Gigi. He was big enough to block the sun, and the sun was about the only thing he'd ever let get behind him, anyway.

Thornton was the same cut, only from a different fabric. He had a weak chin, coward's eyes, and a body that would probably reject steroids. His hard-guy talk was nice cover. He'd expect a man like me — a blooded-in Brand, vouched for by a former shot-caller — to see right through the pose, but be under orders not to slap him down.

What he wouldn't expect was that I could see his slimy mind. Not just the part he'd kept from the psychiatrists — the part he'd kept from the Brotherhood, too.

I could see him for what he was, but he could only see me for what I was supposed to be . . . what he *needed* me to be.

I remembered my lesson: "You do it right, they should never see you coming." Not the Prof's words. Wesley's.

"Where do you want me to start?" Thornton asked. "Claw already told you the story, so . . . ?"

"You told the kids — the three boys — that you'd take care of everything?"

"For a price," he reminded me. Making sure I wouldn't forget he wasn't some sucker who'd do favors for punks; he preyed on them, same as any real man would.

"Yeah. You went right out to this house where they'd left the body. . . ."

"It's called 'window of opportunity,' " he said, back to the superior tone a fool uses when he thinks he's teaching you something. "Late summer, it gets light early — there wasn't a lot of time for me to get everything done."

"Sure. The kids, they stayed in your place?"

"Fuck, no! I told them, move it! Get their punk asses back home, sneak back into their beds, make sure they were ready to alibi each other, if it ever came to that."

"They left before you did?"

"By a minute or so."

"What kind of car were you driving then?"

"A '71 Plymouth. The GTX. That car had *everything.*"

"Including a big trunk."

"You got it," he said, risking a wink. "Never know when that's going to come in handy."

"The rug?"

"I told you —"

"Me?" I said, toning my voice just enough to let his mind put me back in the role he'd cast me for.

"Oh. I see what you're saying. Truth is, I don't know where the rug came from. That was the punks' idea. I mean, they brought it with them when they snatched her. To roll her up in when they were done. It was still there. On the floor, I mean. Right next to her body."

"Were you gloved?"

"Huh?!" He paused too long before covering up with, "I mean, of course, man. Fuck, you think I'd walk into a murder scene so I could leave prints?"

"What'd you do with everything later?"

He was back in control by then. He wasn't being interrogated, he was a player, the one the boss had picked to brief a soldier for a mission. He visibly relaxed, knowing he was in about as much danger as a guy showing a map to the getaway driver . . . a map for a bank job he wasn't going to be involved in.

"Everything I had on me went into the furnace," he said. "I cleaned every inch of my car — I was always doing that anyway; I kept it *sharp*. But the trunk didn't just get cleaned, it got *bleached*. If the cops ever asked, I spilled a bottle in there when I was taking a load to the Laundromat."

"You didn't have a washing machine in your place?"

"Sure," he said, just the safe side of insulted. After all, he'd already told me that, besides being a master criminal back then, he'd been living semi-large, too. "But it was broke." He grinned around the words. "The repairman who came out gave me a bill anyway. Fucking robber charged me fifty bucks for a 'service call,' when it was nothing but a loose wire."

"Nice."

He lapped that up.

"So, okay, you've got her in the trunk, wrapped in the rug, and you're driving. By now it's, what, four in the morning?"

"Maybe," he said, rolling his eyes upward to show me he was trying to re-create as faithfully as he could. "Whatever, it was too damn close to daybreak for my taste. Which is why I took her to this place I know —"

"In the woods?"

"Not *deep* in the woods. Just enough for me to back the car in, so you couldn't spot it from the road. If I had driven all the way over to the place I wanted, the car could have bottomed out. Been scratched all along the sides, for sure."

"And made tracks."

"Right. I just put her over my shoulder and walked."

"Yeah?" I said, sounding just impressed enough to mute any trace of anxiety he might have left. "That must have been a bitch, carrying that much weight all that distance, especially in the dark."

"Ah, she didn't weigh much. And the rug was one of those thin ones, like for decoration? No padding or anything like that. Made it easier, actually — like having a cushion for my shoulder. The walk was maybe a half mile; I couldn't tell you exactly."

"How long did it take you?"

"To get there? Or to — ?"

"To get there."

"Ten minutes . . . maybe a little more."

"Okay."

"I knew the exact spot I needed," he said. "There wasn't time to be digging a fucking grave. I thought about the river — before I decided on the way I went, I mean — but the drive was too far, and there could be campers, or fishermen setting up early, or . . . a whole bunch of things. I had to think fast. I had to move fast. And that's what I did. When I got her to the spot, I just rolled her out of the rug onto a bed of dead pine needles, made like a mound on top of her with more of them, and then the log."

"Good thing you didn't have more time."

"What are you talking about? If I'd had more time, they'd never have found the little cunt."

"Exactly. Then it'd be a disappearance, not a homicide. *You'd* be the only one who knew where she was buried. You, not the three guys we have to touch. They could all pass polygraphs that they didn't know where she was. They've got money. They'd talk to lawyers. The lawyers would talk to forensic guys. Probably tell them, in the ground all those years, all anyone could ever prove is that it *was* her, not how she died. And that's if they had wanted to play soft."

"I'm not sure I —"

"They've got *money*," I reminded him. "There's guys, you put enough green on the table, they'll go dig up a body, take it somewhere else, and make it *really* gone. What kind of leverage would you have *then*? You'll go to the cops? Go the fuck ahead. What DA wants to try a murder case against three straight, clean, *rich* men with no body, no evidence, nothing but the word of an ex-con . . . especially an ex-con who'd caught a fraud beef? The only one who gets arrested in that scenario is the guy who tried to extort money from those good citizens. See what I'm saying?"

"Yeah," he said, slowly. "Because they found her body so quick, they *know* she was murdered."

"And raped, right?"

"Oh yeah. Fucked, stuck, and made to suck. For all I know, she could have choked to death on cum."

"Body pretty marked up?"

"I didn't look that close. And there was no light, anyway."

"I thought maybe you had a flashlight. You know, to make sure the log had her covered."

"Oh, that. Yeah. But I didn't use it for —"

"I got you," I told him, dialing down his rheostat with my voice as I listened to another voice in my head: Albert Collins, telling the truth on "Cold, Cold Feeling."

People like to say "the blues are the truth." Not where I come from. Down here, only behavior is.

I put Thornton back to sleep.

"Claw?" I said, a few hours later.

"It's a long story."

"I got time."

"So did I," he said. "Starting when I was a kid. Same as you, right?"

"Yeah."

"You know how they jump on you for anything in there? I don't mean just the color thing, anything they can fuck you around with — like if you're fat, or dumb. Well, the name I came in with was one I had on my school records: Claude. I took a lot behind that name. Where my parents came from, that was a man's name. But where I ended up, it was one of those faggy names . . . for a white man, anyway. You know, like 'Stanley' or 'Melvin.' A hard guy, he turns that into 'Stan' or 'Mel,' see? But what can you do with fucking 'Claude'?

"I was always a big guy, and good with my hands, too. But that name just . . . I don't know, it made some motherfuckers braver than they should have been. One day, I'm out in the yard, I find this rusty old pair of pliers. Now, I know that's a treasure, but I don't know what to do with it. Then, like a bomb going off in my brain, I *see* it.

"I put a piece of stone inside the lips of the pliers, and I squeezed it with all my strength. I kept squeezing until my hand froze. The cramps in my arm were so bad I almost cried behind it. But I knew I'd found

190

something that would change my whole life, if I had what it took to use it right.

"After that, I practiced all the time. Every chance I got. Sometimes for hours and hours at a time. One day, the stone *broke.* Right in my hand. After that, I found lots of other ways to work on my grip. I never stopped.

"I woke up one morning, and I knew it was here. My day. I couldn't wait to get out on the yard. Walked up to this giant nigger who was always ragging on me. He was fucking Mighty Joe Young with a brain, that guy. He could kill you with his mind. I hated him, but I admired him, too. You ever know anyone like that?"

"Inside *and* out," I said.

"Okay. So — I'm passing by and he says, 'What's up, Claude?' The way he said it, his whole crew got shit-eating grins on their faces. I didn't keep moving. I stopped, and stuck out my hand, like for him to shake. 'I'm good,' I tell him, 'but you got my name wrong.' You could see from his face he didn't know *what* the hell was happening, but he grabs my hand. And that's when I locked down and *squeezed.* I could feel him trying for power — the muscles in his arm were jumping like current was running through them. He kept right on grinning,

191

like it was nothing, but, that day, I was the pliers, and he was the stone. 'You said my name wrong,' I say, real relaxed. 'It's not Claude, it's Claw.'

"Christ, that was one *tough* nigger. I could feel the bones in his hand starting to go before he finally said, 'Thanks for putting me straight, man. Claw it is.'

"So I won that pot, but I knew I couldn't just take the money and walk away. I knew I had to *keep* what I won. And I did. Every day of my life since then, I worked this hand," he said, holding his right out for me to inspect. It was half again the size of his left. "By the time that wormy little fuck you just talked to met me, I could crush steel. And 'Claw'? That was my name. I earned it."

"Ever turn it into money?" I asked, frankly curious.

"One time, I went up against the arm-wrestling champ of a joint I was in. Guy had arms that made the iron-freaks look like toothpicks. Never lost a match. The odds were just insane. We're out on the yard, at the table, cons so thick around us it was like being inside the fucking Colosseum. We chalk up, lock hands, I clamp down, and he's paralyzed. His hand's broken, whole arm is dead. We had to rent space in a few dozen cells just to store all the smokes we won that day."

"That was beautiful," I congratulated him. "But no way the arm wrestler let it go, right?"

"No," he said, sadly. "He didn't."

"We need things we don't have yet," I said to Claw as he stubbed out his cigarette.

"Like what?"

"The girl was murdered. The dates are right. I got enough out of the punk to believe he could prove he was the one who dumped the body, but that doesn't get us where we need to be."

This time he didn't even waste the single syllable it would take to agree with me: a man driving on fumes doesn't floor the gas pedal.

"He came up with enough details that never made the papers so that only someone who actually had their hands in it would know. What I can't tell is if the cops finally put this in the deepfreeze. A few years ago, that would have been a sure bet. But as soon as something becomes fashionable, police procedure changes. Working cold cases, that's a hot ticket now. See what I'm saying? Instead of buried in some basement, rotting inside an evidence box, the file could be on some detective's desk right this minute."

"So?"

"So we're holding an ace — that your guy can prove he was involved — but it's not close to the full house we need to play this round."

"Why not?" Claw said. "All he has to do is —"

"What? Threaten to go to the Law, right?" He nodded.

"What's he go there *with?* A confession? That might put *him* down for life —"

I caught Claw's expression, said, "This is New York, not California. One, we've got the death penalty here, too; but it hasn't been used since I was a kid. And, two, there was a time when the Supreme Court threw out *all* death-penalty convictions. By the time some of the states were able to come up with new laws that would stand up, it was years later. A grace period, like. No-body's looking at the needle for this one."

"Grace period," Claw half-whispered, a tiny dot of rage buried in the iron of his voice.

"Yeah," I told him. "How come you think the Manson Family keeps going to those parole hearings?"

He shook it off — a fighter telling you if *that* was your best you're not going to be around at the end.

"You're right," I agreed. "Like we said, it wouldn't matter if those three guys were looking at six months in the County or a thousand years. It would still be worth the same to them to make it go away."

"What's missing then?"

"The *connection.* I spent hours with your guy. And here's the truth: He hasn't got one tiny piece of proof that points to *those* three as the ones he buried the body for. Nothing."

"But he tapped them for cash —"

"He *says.*"

"The bat they used."

"They'll say *he* was the one who used it. After he borrowed it from them, a few days before. Probably as imaginary as those Polaroids."

"That journal they kept. That should —"

"Prove they were obsessed with the girl? Maybe. *They'll* say they were writing a book, collaborating on a project, thinking they were creative geniuses. Free speech. I guarantee you, there's uglier stuff on the Internet every day. Kids write school essays about torturing a classmate to death, and if they so much as get an F on the paper, the ACLU's right on the job.

"And that's *if* it ever got into evidence. You don't exactly have a clean chain-of-custody going here — that journal's been in *your* guy's hands for thirty-some years. Maybe . . . *maybe* the lab guys could prove the approximate age of the thing, depending on the paper and ink they used. But it's too weak to stand up, never mind walk.

"And it gets even worse," I continued. "Even if you could dig up some old school papers they wrote, by that time, rich kids like those, they probably typed everything. Or paid someone else to do it. This whole 'handwriting analysis' thing is a whore's game: You bring your expert; I'll bring mine. Who's going to bring the best one? You think some little town is going to spend the year's law-enforcement budget trying to convict three of its most illustrious graduates, from three of its best families?"

"You said we needed a full house to play . . . and now we don't even have the ace we thought we had?"

"Yeah."

"So we're done?" Claw said. Like he must have said to the oncologist who gave him the news.

"No. We're down, not done."

"Down to what?"

"The tape. The one your guy made of them asking him to go bury the body."

"There is no tape. We already know —"

"That we're holding garbage? Sure. But they don't. Like a bluff in stud poker: we'll show them we've got *something* . . . but we have to make sure that's enough to scare them out of calling our hand."

◆

When I was a little kid, I never cried when they hurt me, not ever. Not because I was tough. Torture doesn't make you cry; it makes you scream. They loved that part.

Crying, that came later. When I finally understood that what they did to me was to show me what I really was. Property.

Only one thing ever made that crying stop.

When I got to prison — as inevitable for me as prep school for a Kennedy — I called myself a thief. The Prof straightened me on that, the way he taught me everything else: hard, cold, clean, and true. "You ain't no thief, chief. That's a man's game. An *experienced* man."

"I cracked plenty of —"

"You in here behind a gun, son."

I couldn't deny that. I'd lived in the basement of an abandoned building then. It was a foul little rat-hole, but it was mine. Someone wanted it for himself. Things happened.

"You lame to the game, Schoolboy," the Prof had said, giving me the name he's called me ever since. Among others. "A real thief, that's a *pro.* A kid who pops a punk he knows, that's an amateur."

"Not letting someone take what's mine, that makes me an amateur?" I said, hotly.

The Prof let out a long, sad sigh. "No, son. Letting him get to the hospital, *that's* what."

"I never thought he'd —"

"What?" the little man sneered. "Rat? Roll over? Give you up? Boy, there's *partners* who'd give you up; you think a fucking *enemy* wouldn't? You know pig Latin?"

"Huh?"

"Never mind. You ever hear a black dude — an *older* black dude — say the word 'ofay'?"

"Yeah."

"You know what it means?"

"White, right?"

"It means 'foe.' Get it?"

"The ones who say it, they hate whites?"

"No," he said, annoyed at my thickness. "Look, you want to play the role, you got to learn it slow. You doing time, you need to *take* your time, learn how to do it right. It's your call."

"I apologize."

He gave me a slow, appraising look. "Say why, Sly."

"Because you're giving me something, and I'm being disrespectful. I know everyone here respects you. I know you know things. I know you have . . . powers, or whatever they call it. I don't know why you picked me —"

"*Now* you cooking."

"I don't —"

"You white, right? So why should some old nigger be teaching you something if he wasn't running a scheme on the scene?"

I didn't say anything, ashamed that I'd been so trusting, but not regretting it.

"Southern blacks, they know the show. White man smiles at you, always got to be something he wants behind that. You know what Mr. Charlie says if a white tries to fuck with a black man that's worked for him all his life? He says, to the other white guy, 'Step off, that's *my* nigger.' They *all* put us last. Even the best of them, they always going with their own first. We know this right from our first taste of mother's milk.

"But, you think it through, you know it

199

can't be true. Got to be *some* white men who're righteous, for real. As down as old John Brown. You play it safe, stick only with your own kind, you miss some chances. That's my power, you see what I'm saying to you? I can *tell.* You . . . you can't tell nothing. So you got to decide with what you got."

"What have I got?"

"You got a gift, son. I can feel it in you. You learn to trust *that,* you trust me. You don't, walk on."

"How do I — ?"

"I'll teach you," the little man said. "But that means you mind me like I'm your father."

"I never had —"

"You think I can't *see* that, fool?"

"I . . . I know you can."

That was it, from that moment. It was the Prof who taught me the rules. "A *real* second-story man is a ghost, Schoolboy. He can unhook a pearl necklace from a woman sleeping on her silk sheets and never wake her up. I don't care if she's sleeping nude, and she's the finest piece of ass you ever seen. You *touch* her and you're over the line. Not a thief, not no more. You can never be one of us then, never.

"You can't be a thief unless you about the

200

money. Nothing else. So, like I'm saying, a real second-story man, he don't use weapons, he uses *tools*. No guns, ever — that's for another kind of work.

"Now, I'm not saying you can't be a stickup artist or a hijacker or even a gunslinger. 'Thief,' it's not about what you do; it's about what you *won't* do, okay?

"You want to be a pro slip-in man, you always move light and you always carry light. Don't fit in your pocket, you leave it. Only junkies steal TV sets. Any fool can count cash. You got to learn to tell a Timex from a Rolex, a diamond from glass, a piece of gold from a slab of brass."

"I thought you were here for —"

"What'd you do, boy? Ask one of the hacks? Tune into the jailhouse vine? Pull my records?"

"I just heard —"

"You heard I'm on this bit for dropping the hammer. But what I am, I'm a thief. I'm out there to steal, but sometimes some fucker will force you to deal."

"Dope?"

"Dope? You wasn't so damn childish, I'd be insulted behind that. Dope! They named it right, Schoolboy. Never went near it, and I wouldn't work with anyone who did. This bit I'm working on is for armed robbery.

When I say I'm a dealer, I mean I dealt it *out.* We were halfway out the door when the fool they paid to guard the place tried to earn his money."

"So if . . . ?"

"Look, now. Listen up. Hijacking ain't always smart, but it's not the same as dropping a dime, or taking your crime partners down with you. You want your rep to be carved in stone, you *always* go down alone. But if you got your ear to the ground, if you plugged in, if you *listen,* you keep picking up cards. When they got you — I mean, got you wrapped and trapped, jury ready to drop you, judge ready to top you — then it's time to deal."

"But if you can't give the cops anything —"

"You can't give them *yours,*" the little man said. "You can't even give them your own *kind.* But there's one kind I don't mind."

When he explained the kind of humans he was talking about, I knew he was my father. Every Child of the Secret wishes he had different parents. I was still a kid in my heart or I wouldn't have asked him, one day: "Prof? What's your real name?"

"What you think, boy?" the little man said as he drew himself up to his full height and pumped out his chest. "There ain't but one name the Man ever had for a nigger like me. I never went to class, and I never kissed ass. You can hang me from a tree, but I'm always going to be. I'm never gonna die, and that's no lie. You want my true name? I'm John Henry, fool."

◆

It was the Prof who taught me how to find a way in. "If you press, you stress, School-boy. Once you have the power, you have to lay in the cut until you see the gut. Stealing ain't about thrill; it's about chill. Let it come to you — then you'll know it's true."

I was trying to do that now. The clock was ticking for the cancer-man, not for me.

There's two places I can always go. For one, I get in the right position in front of a mirror I use — a round one with a red dot painted exactly in its center. I breathe the way I learned to do, until I fall into that dot. Sometimes, it's hours before I come back.

This morning, I was going the other route. I just relax — today, with a tall, frosted glass of pineapple juice and some roasted al-monds — and take in random information. I dial my subbrain to "scan," looking for answers to questions nobody has asked me yet. I don't know how it works, but I know it happens — one part of my brain takes in the info; another part is gnawing at it like a rat in a concrete cage.

I had WABC on for background music. Yeah, I know it's talk radio, but something about the Huff & Puff Show in the morning has the predictable tonal quality of a schizo arguing with the voice in his head. It's music, so long as you don't try to make sense out of the lyrics.

The newspaper was a comedy act. The feds had an ex–NYPD cop on trial, said he was actually working for the mob. Not just selling info, going all the way, right down to participating in hits. The ex-cop says it's all a pack of lies; he's never had anything to do with the mob. Then he puts up a couple of million bail, and hires John Gotti's old lawyer to represent him. Should have pleaded insanity.

One of the giant ISPs says that configuring its software so China can finger dissidents and send them to torture camps is just showing respect for another country's culture. Of course, *our* culture prevents them from IDing the kiddie-sex trollers who use their servers. After all, us Americans have the right to privacy.

If hypocrisy was a virus, the Internet

would crash tomorrow.

I killed the radio — the show had gone from its usual white noise to some other level. I hadn't realized there was anything lower than "dull" before. Time for a little TV.

Jurors were being interviewed. Must have been some kind of major case. They all agreed it was just disgusting that the killer hadn't shown the slightest trace of remorse. "He never shed a tear for her, not once," one blobby woman in a blue dress with a white Peter Pan collar said. Her own piggy eyes dutifully welled up as she reached for her personal *Oprah* moment.

I didn't know if the guy they were talking about was guilty or not, but I felt a wave of disgust for that jury, anyway. TV trials have turned jury service into a media opportunity, and the slugs know their lines by heart: If the poor bastard says he's innocent, they want to fry him because he's not "sorry." And if he blows any chance of appeal by admitting he did it, any tears that come out of his eyes are dismissed as phony.

It's all a show. Like those "Victim Impact Statements" in mandatory-sentence cases. It's really uplifting to watch people read their pre-typed scripts: "You're going to be in prison for life, but your mother can still visit *you*. The only place I can visit my son is in the cemetery." Yeah, okay, we *got* it already. We know dead people can't have babies, or go to college, or whatever dreams you had for them. Why tell the guy who made that happen? Think it's going to make *him* feel bad? Or did you just need "closure"?

The teleprompter-reader announced that Nigeria and China had just signed some sort of treaty, the centerpiece of which was cooperation between their governments. Nigeria announced it was irrevocably committed to a "one-China" policy, meaning, the day the Chinese decide to attack Taiwan, they could count on Nigerian oil to keep flowing to their war machine. Nice two-way street: if Biafra — or any other separatist movement — ever tries to rise again, and the Nigerian generals go back to their genocide program, China's going to veto any UN Security Council vote to intervene.

Dictatorships sticking together, forming mutual-support alliances. Doesn't anybody remember the last time that happened? Or maybe that info wasn't in the script the spray-haired "journalist" was reading from.

A man who survived Katrina by pulling his family out just in time was being interviewed. He told some girl "reporter" it was like he had been raped, but didn't understand why he felt that way. She made sympathetic noises, and cut to commercial.

I know why. Everyone knows that kids who've been sexually abused by strangers have a *much* higher recovery rate than when the perpetrator was inside their own family. It always comes down to what the victim expects for a response, and how close that expectation comes to the truth.

For Katrina victims, FEMA was the cop who tells a gang-raped woman that nothing would have happened if she hadn't worn that short a skirt and gone to that bar and let a stranger buy her a drink. . . .

Katrina didn't rape New Orleans. Everybody knows who the real rapist was. But do you think any of those organizations that live on government grants are going to say it out loud? You know who I mean: the same ones who run around gushing over how Congress is "protecting our kids." I mean, look at all they've done! Why, we even *register* sex offenders now, so any "father" who's fucking his own kid can go on the Internet and make sure his property's not exposed to danger from a stranger. The "missing children" thing went dry when the half-wits who run the show finally figured out that just about all of those "missing" kids were custodial interference cases, not abductions. So they just switched to "Amber Alerts" and slid themselves into the "Internet safety" business. Now the mother who pimps her kid can make sure some chat-room predator doesn't get to teach the kid how to make his *own* money.

I remember something a working girl told me, a long time ago. I'd done her a favor — her coat-hanger-loving pimp had never seen me coming — and she was trying to repay me in the only coin I wanted back then: survival skills. "You get a trick hot enough, he'll pay you the same for a hand job as the full ride," she'd told me.

She might have been talking about the people who vote in this country. She sure as hell *was* talking about the ones who don't.

◆

"I need some things," I said into the cloned-chip cell phone.

"What?"

"From him, not you."

"Can you say?" Meaning "say on the phone."

"Business records. His."

"From the joint he — ?"

"He might *have* them there, but I need to

go back much further than that. He started a lot of businesses, none of them worked out. *Those* records."

"His place isn't that far away from . . . from where you and me last ate. Under an hour, depending on the time of day."

"After dark," I told him.

◆

The "strip club" was a faceless slab of fatigue-cracked concrete, with the usual signs outside. Even the neon looked greasy.

"His office is in the back," Claw said. "No way in except through the front door. There's a bouncer, but he's about as much as you'd expect, a place like this."

"No."

"No what?"

"There's a fire exit out back."

"Yeah, but they're always locked from the inside. And an alarm goes off if you open them."

"Not tonight," I promised.

I backed the Plymouth into an open slot on the broken asphalt behind the club. He watched as I threw some switches, not asking what they were for.

The back of the building was completely tagged. Overriding all the graffiti was the symbol "MS-13" in huge white letters, edged in blue.

"What?" Claw said, watching me stare at the sign.

I stepped back into the deeper darkness next to my Plymouth, nodded an "okay" when he took out a smoke, knowing he'd cup it. When he had it going, I explained why we were waiting.

"In this city, the only way you get a piece of anything is to take it. If you're reaching from the bottom — new kids on the block, no politicians in your pocket, no cops on your pad, no unions, no nothing — your only way in is with product or power. The Colombians brought both. They had their own pipeline, and they were truly vicious bastards, too. The Russians had the gas scam locked down tight: no-tax gas in this town is gold, if you can guarantee enough stations regular deliveries. Then the Albanians decided they wanted to play, too. They didn't have any sources, so they had to go psycho. It all got settled one night in the Bronx. The tanker was right there, pumping, when they had their meet. Everyone had guns, but the Albanians brought hand grenades. The Russians told them, you toss those things near the tanks, we all get blown to pieces, where's the profit in that? The

Albanian boss told the Russians every man he had with him came there to die. The Russian boss didn't read it for a bluff."

"You think it was?"

"No."

"So what's with that MS-13 thing?"

"Mara Salvatrucha. Started on your coast, all guys from El Salvador. Got together for the reasons anyone crews up. Same reasons you did. At first. Then they started pulling from all over Central America: Guatemala, Honduras, like that.

"You grow up with death squads owning the night, people 'disappearing' all the time, the threat of dying doesn't have any impact on you after a while. Some of them were street kids who got across the border; some of them were the same soldiers who used to hunt them. They're not into 'organized' crime . . . at least, not yet. Dope is the same as robbery or a shakedown to them — a thing you do for money. But they never hire out — they get money *by* violence, not *for* it, see?"

"They ink up?"

"*Big*-time. Some of them, right on the face. In Honduras, an MS-13 tattoo buys you serious time. Just for the tattoo, I mean. So it's a commitment. In for life, whether it's on the bricks or behind bars. They're big on messages. Heads on stakes. The kind of thing the newspaper clowns call 'senseless violence.' But it makes perfect sense to them. Works, too.

"See, they've got no rules, no boundaries. Never had a treaty with anyone. They can't be infiltrated — undercovers can slip into the Mafia if they're good earners, but MS-13 wants to see you make a body, up close. Got to be with a blade, and it's got to be slow. They don't even *pretend* to be legit businessmen. Forget the tax boys, forget the wiretaps, forget the forensic accountants to catch them laundering money.

"Their life expectancy is death, see? They're proud of being crazy. And anyone who's *not* crazy is scared of them. Scared to death."

Claw tuned right in. Prison is a pyramid. Actually, a row of pyramids. In some joints, especially down south, you have convict bosses running the dorms or the blocks. But even the biggest bulldog isn't going to scare an elephant, and if the *real* boss — the warden — decides he wants to change the regime, that's all it ever takes.

Not so many years ago, it was right out on Front Street. They had cons guarding cons. *Armed* cons, ready to shoot if you made a break from the fields. No problem making sure *those* boys walked the line: one slip and they're back in the fields themselves. With a life span until sundown.

Today, they just use bus therapy — move the problem to another prison, a prison that's already *got* a boss. Where Claw had done his time, they do it different. Known gang members are deep-freezed, dropped down into the Shoe — that's how you say Special Housing Unit, SHU. The only way out is to "debrief." The ones who do it for real, give up all they know about their gang — codes, leadership hierarchy, signs, stashes — they get released into "protected housing." Putting them back into Population would make them the prize in a shank lottery.

The stand-ups sometimes make it out of the Shoe on their own, especially if they've got real lawyers on the job. Men like them would never take a voluntary PC, and they go right back to the block, certain their rep will hold.

But their crew can never be sure. And some of them might decide not to take the chance . . . especially if the man who was running things while the boss was away got to like his new job.

"You think they're shaking down our guy's

place?" he asked.

"They marked the territory."

"Just because other gang kids didn't overtag them doesn't mean —"

"I don't care what it means. They could be bleeding the place dry, it's nothing to us."

"So why are we watching?"

"They're not talkers," I told him. "If they're inside right this minute, they're either collecting or they're using their machetes. There's some parties you don't crash."

Fifteen minutes was enough. We stepped through the shimmed-open fire door in the back. Claw pointed to his right. I followed him down an unpainted plywood-walled corridor, pulling my watch cap down into a ski mask. Music — or something like it — boomed from the front of the building. We passed an unmarked door. I was guessing bathroom, but I didn't like the idea of a door opening behind me, so I switched stances — still following, but with my back against the wall.

The last door had the kind of sign you buy in a hardware store; peel off the back-

ing tape and stick wherever you want: PRI-
VATE.

I pulled my short-barreled .357, pointed
my left hand at the door twice, once at Claw.

He opened the door, stepped inside.

The girl who came out was moving quick,
keeping her head down — like she'd probably just *been* doing — making sure whoever was outside could see she hadn't seen
them. All I could make out was that she was
short and real skinny, long black hair in
pigtails, carrying some kind of blue robe in
one hand, shoes in the other.

I went through the open door.

Thornton was behind an office-surplus
desk, in a red vinyl chair, looking like what
he was. Claw was to my left, positioned so
he could watch the corridor.

"No! I —"

Thornton cut himself off as he saw the
pistol go back inside my jacket. "Just talk,"
I said. "Like we did before."

"Oh! You're —"

"Yeah. You don't need to see my face, do
you?"

"No. Of course not. I mean, all I want —"

"We know what you want. I'm not here to
go over all that again. I'm here for something that could help make it happen."

"What could I have that I haven't already

given you?"

"You told the big man" — if he noticed that I didn't call the other man "Claw," like he did, it didn't register on his face — "that, before you went down, you tapped them a few times, right?"

"Not for —"

"Yes or no."

"Yes."

"Two things first. One, how'd you make contact? Two, how'd they make the delivery?"

"I'd just call their office —"

"They don't work together, right?"

"Right. I just meant, whichever one I was going to —"

"I get it."

"I'd just call, say I was an old friend from back in the day. Tell whoever answered that I realized Mr. Whoever wouldn't be able to come to the phone, but I'd appreciate it if I could leave a number, and Mr. Whoever's assistant could just leave a message on my machine, telling me when it might be convenient to call."

"The machine wasn't where you lived."

"I'm a lot of things," he said, superiority slipping back into his voice now that he wasn't scared, "but none of them are stupid."

"Okay . . ."

"I'd always get a call back. There'd be a number for me to call and a time. I'd call — from a phone I was never going near again — and there'd be some man at the other end. Not the one I called, but I wasn't expecting that. This man — I know they had to be different men, all the times I did this, but, I swear, they all sounded like the same voice — he'd say he understood I was calling to negotiate a small venture-capital project, and, depending on the reasonableness of the request, it could probably be arranged.

"And I'd *make* it reasonable. We'd have a nice talk. I'd give him my 'business plan,' we'd talk about stuff like 'anticipated rate of return,' crap like that. Anyone listening, it would sound like it was all plausible. I mean, sure, maybe my 'new concept' was a little shaky — good cover when the 'investment' went sour — but enough for them. . . . I figured it was all being recorded."

"But they never paid by check, so what diff— ?"

"Who said 'never'?" he said, giving me a triumphantly sleazy smile.

"You did."

"Every time but once," he said. His teeth

217

looked gray in the pus-colored overhead light. "Naturally, I never did a hand-to-hand. I wasn't going to meet with anyone *those* guys sent. FedEx to one of those mailbox-rental joints; I used a different routing every time. They *get* it; they *send* it . . . right back out. By the time whoever they were using ran the trace, I'm gone. With the cash. But, one time, Reedy actually sent a check. Didn't have his name on it or anything, just some 'company' he probably got opened and closed in a day. I guess he figured I'd have to cash it somewhere, and the canceled check would tell him . . . I don't know, something."

"How big a check?"

"Twenty-five K."

"You remember the name of the company he was — ?"

"I got better than that," the weasel said, smirking like he was casually turning a winning hand faceup.

◆

Only tourists think of Manhattan as an island. Most of the people who live here travel underground to get anywhere — some subway stops have longer distances between them, that's all.

Now, Staten Island, *that's* an island. But it doesn't get tourists.

Neither does the part of the Bronx where the Mole lives. Everything's the opposite of Manhattan — the subway goes there all right, but it rolls outdoors, on elevated tracks. It's the Mole who lives underground.

I knew if Michelle ever found out I'd made the ride without asking her to come along, she'd go ICBM on me. I also knew the Mole wouldn't talk. Thing is, he wouldn't lie, either, not to his woman. But I needed him for what I had to have, so I risked it.

I celled him from Bruckner Boulevard, heard him pick up. I knew he wouldn't speak until he heard a voice, so I asked, "Okay to come by now?"

"Yes."

I thumbed the cell into lifelessness and concentrated on negotiating my way through Hunts Point until I got to the junk-yard. Passed by burned-out buildings, so far gone that the gang graffiti had faded — turf not worth claiming. Abandoned cars. Abandoned people. Hungry dogs. Needy junkies. Blood-bank winos. And, not far away, the humans who turned all of that into cash.

The city has a seat at that table, too. I passed by Spofford, the "community-based" juvenile detention center. After one look around the "community," you could decode *that* message pretty quick.

The fence looked even rustier than ever, but the flesh-ripping concertina wire woven through and over it was the same smoke color. I knew the Mole had me on visual somewhere, so I just waited for the first gate of the sally port to open, drove inside, locked up behind myself, opened the second gate, docked the Plymouth, and started walking.

The pack popped up suddenly, like meerkats checking for predators. Except that these dogs *were* the predators. The most dangerous kind — they were still evolving, learning how to be better at what they do. After so many years running wild, feeding off whatever the nearby Meat Market dumped — and anything else that couldn't outrun them — it was as if they'd become a breed of their own. They ranged in color and markings, but most were kind of a smog shade, with only two body types: barrel or blade.

"Simba!" I called out, quickly.

As the old beast moved toward me, the pack parted like the Red Sea. Simba was many years past being able to hold his position if any of the young bulls wanted to try him. None ever did. Anyone who says dogs don't understand respect hasn't seen a permanent pack.

Simba wasn't moving fast, but he played it off like he was taking his time, sizing me up. I didn't move toward him. I understand respect, too.

"Simba-witz!" I greeted him.

He nudged against my leg. I scratched him behind what was left of one ear, knowing his eyes were too filmy to actually see me, trusting his other senses to tell him who I was.

We walked all the way to the clearing outside the Mole's bunker together. Two good pals, taking in the sun, bragging about old times. I never once looked behind me — the rest of the pack would go piranha on anyone stupid enough to try entering without a passport.

The Mole was outside, sitting on a bucket seat wrenched out of one of the hundreds of junkers that littered his lot. Simba ambled over to him, lay down at his feet. The Mole thumped the monster on the top of his triangular head a couple of times. Simba made a sound in his throat.

"Downstairs?" the Mole said. Meaning: did I need him to do some work, or had I come to talk?

"Here's good," I told him, taking a seat on a milk crate with some kind of spongy-looking pad on its top.

I let a couple of minutes slide past. Neither the Mole nor Simba was ever anxious, and they didn't like it when others were.

"I have a check — a photocopy of a check — that was written a few years ago. The company that wrote it was a fraud, but the check was good. I need to trace the check so I can connect it with a certain man."

"Canceled check?"

"No. The guy who cashed it made a copy before he did. It's all I have."

"Bank records?"

"This'll be a long, twisty trail, Mole. Shells inside shells. The company was probably formed just for this one check. No PI could track this. Even if you could get a subpoena — which is impossible here — it would dead-end way before the connection was made. You'd need government-level access to . . . a whole bunch of different sources."

"Just the check?"

"There's also some . . . files, maybe. Or evidence boxes, maybe in deep storage. Inside a police station."

"City?"

"Suburbs. *Rich* suburbs."

"It *would* take the government."

222

"Yeah. But not necessarily —"

I shut up. The Mole knew what I was asking for. The Israelis have had a spy network running in the U.S. for decades, and whatever units they have on that job are as good at what they do as the ones they sent to Entebbe. I had met Mossad men in this same junkyard. The Mole had done plenty of work for them, but it was never for money.

"Would this be about my — ?"

"No," I said, some part of my mind hearing Claw tell me that he trusted me because he knew I wouldn't lie to my own. I know how to push the Mole's button: You say "Nazis" to the dumpy little man and those faded-denim eyes behind his Coke-bottle lenses catch fire. Then his mind — a mind that would make the most powerful AI program on the planet drop to its knees and worship — would start to laser-burn through any obstacle in the way.

But the Mole was my brother. And the Prof had taught me right.

"What, then?"

"Justice and vengeance."

"Those are the same."

"I guess so. And money, Mole. That's there, too."

He shook his head.

"Justice for a little girl, Mole. Raped,

tortured, and murdered. And the rich guys who did it walked away. Walked away laughing. More than thirty years ago. Can this be right?"

Mole wasn't just my brother, he was Michelle's man. And Terry's father. That was another reason I wanted to make sure I came to him alone: I wasn't going to play those last cards, or even show them, with either one around. And I don't think the Mole's woman or his son knew about his special friends, either.

"And I did something for your . . . friends, too. Remember?" I reminded him.

"Yes," he confirmed. "So do they. Are you saying — ?"

"Uh-uh, Mole. I got nothing to trade this time. If I knew something I thought they didn't, I would have brought it to you soon as I found out."

He nodded.

Simba made a sound I hadn't heard before.

"The Bible says —"

"The *what?*"

"The Bible," the Mole answered, looking at Simba as if for backup.

"I thought only Christians —"

"The Old Testament, not those novels they wrote later."

"But you're a . . . a man of science, Mole."

"I am a Jew."

"Yeah. But that's not a religion, it's a . . . tribe, right?"

"To the Nazis, we are a race, not a tribe. A different breed of human."

"Not just to them."

"I know."

"But the *Bible,* Mole? You believe that stuff? Like Eden was a location you could find on a map?"

"Not that," he said, in a "you can't be *that* stupid" tone.

"What, then? Jesus was a Jew, right? Didn't he tell people not to marry because the end was coming?"

"Revelations is not the word of God."

"How the fuck *could* it be?" I said, angry without knowing why I was. "What, the son of *God* called it wrong? Bet on the wrong Four Horsemen?"

On the Mole, sarcasm was about as effective as Mexican law enforcement. "A book can contain truth without *being* truth," he said, calmly. "The Torah is the Law. The Law came from the Old Testament. The Law is the code of conduct for our people — how we are to act on earth."

"So you don't buy the Seven Days thing?" I asked.

"Evolution is a theory —"

"So is Christianity. And Islam. And any other explanation. Just because you can't prove something doesn't mean it isn't true, right?"

"Yes," he admitted. He should have; he's the one who taught it to me.

"So life's nothing but a goddamn horse race, and we're all two-dollar bettors? 'My soul, on Allah, to win.' Or on Jesus. Or Buddha. Or a pile of rocks. There's your 'proof,' Mole. How can there be more than one God?"

"Or, how can God allow six million of us to — ?"

"Right. It's a long list, brother."

"Yes. That is why it is called 'faith.' Not because it cannot be proven; but because it is the only way to reconcile that which refutes it."

I looked at Simba for a long minute.

"You don't buy any of it," I said, finally.

"This is truth," the Mole said. "Objective, proven truth. Our people have been persecuted since the beginning of our time on this earth. We have learned there is only one way, and that way is not inside the temple or the Torah."

"Self-defense."

The Mole made a sound in his throat that

only someone real close to him would recognize as a sort-of laugh.

"Mole, I came in here naked. I got nothing to trade. That . . . service I did for your friends, it's no secret that there was something in it for me and mine. You were *there,* for chrissakes. This thing I'm in now, I'm bound to do it."

"Because of the little girl?"

"Yeah."

"What you want, there is risk?"

"Got to be. Even if the paper trace I need doesn't hit any trip wires, getting into a police station and removing —"

"*Real* risk," the Mole said. Meaning: was there going to be any anti-personnel work anywhere along the road? There's work you can do without leaving a trace, but some you can't do without leaving a body.

"Not for them," I promised.

◆

The subway runs to Brooklyn, too. The building was one of those old factories being converted into luxo-lofts. A work-in-progress, its value growing faster than the construction. The front was coated in some high-tech glaze that wouldn't protect spray-painted messages against a water hose. But some tagger must have figured one day's worth was good enough for what he wanted to say:

what came first: computers or icons?

I stepped inside, between two industrial-looking pillars. By the time I got to the man sitting behind a table covered with what looked like architectural plans, I'd been photographed, scanned, screened, and recorded.

The man behind the desk looked up. The two men moving in from different corners were wearing tool belts and hard hats. I knew what tools they were good with, and I knew those hats would turn a bullet.

"My name is Pearl," I said to the man behind the desk.

He watched me the way a mother-to-be watches her first sonogram.

"I'm here to see Mr. Gentile."

The man behind the desk pointed to a staircase that looked like it might be worth a fortune on the *Antiques Roadshow.* It was so deliberately discordant in that place that I knew it had to mean something . . . but not to me.

I started climbing. Footsteps behind me, making no effort at masking their sound. As

I moved, the occasional microdot flash told me the whole staircase was photo-celled.

At the first landing, I kept climbing. Saw nothing but beams and girders until I reached the top floor.

I crossed to what looked like one of those steering-wheel doors they use on bank vaults. There was a faint hiss as it swung open.

I stepped into a windowless area I immediately realized had been constructed within the core of the building, invisible from outside. I'd been in dirtier operating rooms.

"Yes?" A woman's voice, about as soft and sweet as liquid titanium.

I turned in her direction. She was medium-height, with long black hair worn in an elaborate French twist. The white lab coat wrapped her body like a sheath. Her prominent nose gave her a hawkish look that her dark eyes didn't diminish even a little bit.

"Leolam Lo Odd," I answered.

"Come," she said, turning her back on me as she stepped through a door to my left.

I followed her, not too closely. And not because it was a treat to watch her walk. Just as well, because she suddenly spun on one heel and turned to face me, moving in very close.

"The password you gave, do you know what it means?"

" 'Forever no more.' "

"In English?"

"Never again."

"You learned this where?"

"From my brother."

"Your brother? No. Your half brother, maybe?"

"You're a geneticist?"

She stepped back a fraction, trying to gauge whether I was deliberately insulting her. But all she said was, "Your face has been altered."

"It wasn't cosmetic surgery."

"I see." She stepped very close. Even her perfume was hard. She put her hand to my face the way a blind person does, feeling for truth. "You are Rom, yes?"

"I don't know."

"How can you not — ?"

"I had no mother."

"Every man has a mother."

"Whoever gave birth to me left me in the charity ward of the hospital."

"Yes," she said, undeterred. "But on your birth certificate it says . . . ?"

"Baby Boy Burke," I told her. "For 'mother,' the hospital used whatever name she gave them, made up on the spot. For 'father,' they just put in 'U-N-K.' You understand?"

She nodded, lowered her eyes for a second, then said, "You have a Gypsy face. But a Gypsy woman would not leave a child. Children are treasure to them. As they are to us."

"And they were right behind you on the line for the camps."

She nodded again, but kept her eyes on mine. "So, when you say 'brother,' you don't mean blood."

"I *do* mean blood," I said, explaining as much as I was going to. "I just don't mean DNA."

She nodded again. Said, "Come."

◆

Another room. I expected the row of computer screens, the anaconda cables, machinery I didn't recognize . . . but I wasn't ready for the occupants.

Kids, they were. Not one of them looked as old as twenty-five. A full-spectrum array, from army-surplus jackets to pineapple-colored spiked hair to unlaced combat boots to what looked like a white tuxedo jacket with red velvet lapels.

Someone had hand-painted a rust-colored sign across the top of a side wall . . .

LUCK is only perceived when results
exceed information
No luck means no BAD luck
Service is not faith, it is WORK

. . . or maybe it was done in dried blood — at least a couple of the girls looked Goth enough to have gone that way.

"Chill the testiculating!" one of those snapped at a young man with a shaved skull and a hole in one earlobe big enough to put a thumb through. "You're so 404, it's a sadness."

"Fuck you *and* your co-signer," the kid fired back.

The woman in the lab coat looked the entire room into silence. "Daniel," was all she said.

A kid with a fifties flattop with matching motorcycle jacket and engineer boots came over to where we were standing. Maybe he didn't know the wire-frame glasses spoiled the look. More likely, it was *his* look.

"This is the man you were told about," she said.

The kid looked at me. His eyes reminded me of a chrome champagne flute. An empty one.

"Come," the woman said again, this time including the two of us.

The air in the next room had a chemical undercurrent. The walls looked like those at Attica, built out of acoustical tile. The carpet didn't try to hide that it was nothing but a pad over a grid of wires.

In the precise center of the room was a round table and three chairs.

The woman in the lab coat made a gesture. I followed Daniel's example and took one of the chairs. She took the last one.

I'd sat down with stone killers plenty of times in my life and still been the most dangerous man in the room. Because I wasn't alone. My family may not have known where I was, but the people in the room, they all knew who I was with.

Some of them may have known the Prof. They all knew about Max. Some maybe just knew his rep; some may have seen him work. But they all knew there was more where that came from. My family. And what they'd do if I didn't come back.

But that was never my trump. There's plenty who think they could handle the Prof if they caught him without his scattergun. There's gunmen in this town who think they could take Max down if only they could keep distance between them long enough — shooters think like that. But there isn't anyone in our world who didn't fear Wesley. Even today, my ghost brother was always riding my shoulder, like a cape of invisible vipers. That's because the whisper-stream is always flowing, and there's currents in there too dark and deep to see. The Prof said it best:

"You saw the show, but you can't never really *know*. And if you can't be sure, you never knock on his door. Never. Don't matter what you pack, you can't chance that Mystery Train coming down your track."

This "international assassin" thing is for thriller-writers who think the CIA is an "intelligence service." Guy gets a phone call, hops on a plane, flies to a country he's never been to in his life, learns the language on the way over, pops his target, and disappears into the shadows. Then he flies back home, puts on some Mozart, fixes himself — hey, he's a "loner," right? — a glass of something special from his wine cellar, and contemplates the meaning of life.

Wesley? He was the truth.

But the people in the room with me weren't from my world. They were specialists — the kind who don't care about going wide because they live only for going deep.

Whoever had ordered them to give me whatever they were going to hand over, *they'd* know Wesley. But even if they believed he was still around, that wouldn't make them blink. After all, they were in the same business, just working for different wages. In the parallel universe they occupied, if you weren't the other man's target, and he wasn't yours, it was the same as a truce.

The woman made a hand gesture, then rapid-fired in something I guessed was Hebrew.

The kid turned to me, watching my hands.

"What?" I said. "You don't think I'd bring a — ?"

"We know you're not armed," he said. "What I'm telling you is, no notes, understand?"

I nodded.

"There were eleven, *eleven,*" he said, emphasizing the word in a tone meant to convey reluctant admiration, "separate shells. Like one of those Matryoshka dolls, one inside the other. Some of them existed for less than twenty-four hours; some of them are still alive. But even those are empty — just minor money on their books, sitting offshore and stagnant."

I set my mind to Intake, sat with my hands folded in front of me like a kid at school.

Which, to them, I was.

"The check you're interested in, it was drawn on an American bank."

I held his eyes, expressionlessly.

"Only it was one of those S&Ls that went belly-up during the early eighties. That should have made the records disappear — Reagan was in charge then, and there were a bunch of senators who were pals of the principals. Only it turned into a big enough scandal for a federal audit, because too many people lost their life savings, the media started screaming, and the politicians did what a raccoon does when his leg is caught in one of those steel traps. They chose survival.

"Of course, those records are sealed. Very interesting cases, some of them. In one, the defendant was a personal friend of Senator John McCain. Didn't seem to help him much. Or hurt McCain, either, in fact. The judge was someone named Ito."

I said nothing.

"The corporation you're interested in — DrepTechDepth Drilling — was opened with a cash deposit of thirty-five thousand dollars. A checkbook was issued by the bank. Only two checks were ever actually written, numbers 2077 and 2078, which means the checks were just pulled out at random.

"The person who opened the account was one Lester T. Ambrose, a licensed private investigator in Nevada. Check number 2078 was made out to him.

"Ambrose is well known to the local authorities. Suspected — never arrested — of a variety of offenses, from forging documents to wiretapping. Some divorce lawyers use him rather frequently."

I sat there, waiting.

"Two days before the account was opened, the passenger manifest for TWA flight 609 from JFK to Las Vegas shows a Mr. James LeBrock in first class, seat 3B. On that same day, Mr. Ambrose rented a car, a 1997 Cadillac SLS, from Hertz. Both men stayed at the Aladdin that night. Each checked out the next day. You know the Aladdin, right? It's the hotel that was demolished in 1998, so the owners could build a brand-new one on the same spot."

I made a noise that could mean anything.

"Mr. Ambrose did not rent the car under his own name. However, the credit card he used traces to a separate identity he had established and had in place for several years. Mr. LeBrock also booked his flight — and his hotel stay — to a credit card. A company credit card. And, although its bank account has long been closed, the company itself still exists. It's a closely held corporation whose stated purpose is real estate investment. The owner of all its shares is one Carlton John Reedy. Date of birth matches the one you gave us; Social Security number squares with his tax returns, home address is —"

"Son of a bitch," I said.

The kid took it as the statement of admiration I meant it as. The woman in the white lab coat turned to me, said, "That is our part, do you understand?"

I did. It wasn't the first time a beautiful woman had told me not to come back. Never again.

◆

"Isn't that enough?" Claw asked.

"We bet the Daily Double, Ace," the Prof answered for me. "So far, we only bagged the first race."

The AB man gave him a look. Clarence's hand flew to his chest — he wasn't checking for a heartbeat.

"Easy, son," the Prof reassured the young gunman at his side. "My man digs our plan; he just wants the time to rhyme."

Claw gave the Prof another look. No

mistaking this one: respect.

"Remember what I told you before?" I told the cancer-man. "This is five-card stud, okay? Table stakes. And we only get to sit in for one hand. So we've got to come in holding so heavy that we don't get called behind what we're *already* showing, make it so they don't *want* to make us show them our hole card."

Claw nodded his acceptance. He was a man used to waiting. Used to counting, too. And his chances were down to one.

◆

"I went your way," the Prof said, as soon as the AB man left. "But I don't get the play."

"What are you saying?" I answered, signing to Max at the same time.

"We think we already got enough in the tank to make major bank, Schoolboy? You thinking, let nature take its course, then —"

"You know I can't do that, Prof. I gave my word."

"To Silver."

"Yeah. To Silver."

"Okay, so you *not* just waiting on that Double-H motherfucker to check out for us to score. But you *still* holding back, Jack. That other stuff you asked the Mole's people to get . . ."

"Yeah?"

"It could take — fuck, I don't know — *months* to set up a job like that. What could the cop shop have on a murder that old that's going to tie our three pigeons into it? They were never even suspects, right? Never questioned. So no statements. No searches. No . . . nothing."

"What're we doing this for?" I said. Not flipping the script, just enlarging the type.

"This scene ain't about nothing but green."

"Yeah. One with three targets."

"You want to be sure before you go for the cure," the man who raised me said. It wasn't a question.

"Nobody ever paid," I admitted. "Now some people want to *get* paid for that."

"That little girl, she really put you back, didn't she, son?"

I looked down at the table for an answer. Our last job had turned over rocks I hadn't even known existed. And shown me things I'd never imagined underneath.

A child I'd been paid to rescue from a pimp a long time ago turned out never to have been his victim at all. Even at her age, she had been playing the pimp, not the other way around. And I'd returned her to the place where she'd learned those tricks. Yeah, I'd gotten paid for doing it. But what I was really looking for back then was pay-*back.* To me, the freaks are a tribe. Anytime I take one from Them, that's one for Us.

Beryl had been the little girl's name. Twenty years later, a man hired me to find her again. Not her father this time: a sucker she had fleeced and released. He wanted me to find a woman he knew as Peta Bellingham, but as soon as I saw her picture I knew who she really was. What her real name had been, anyway.

A few minutes after he'd hired me, the ripped-off sucker was taken out by a hunter-killer team. One so smooth and professional it was clear that they weren't paid just for a hit — this one was all about sending a message.

I figured Beryl was next. So I found her, even though there was no one left to pay me. Figured I could . . . I don't know . . . rescue her one more time. And this time for real.

But what I finally found was a predatory sociopath so twisted I wanted to stop her viperous heart.

I didn't do that. Instead, I fixed it for her to collect reparations in the only coin she wanted: vengeance. Then I bought a baby from her and gave it to a real woman.

Before Beryl came back into my life, I had dismissed my mother as a teenage whore who carried me until she went into labor, then hung around the hospital just long enough to pop me out and get back to work.

Me, I was a trick baby. Whoever had planted the seed that became me had wanted to fuck an underage girl, probably paid extra for it. Couldn't be any other way — no pimp would ever let a moneymaker be out of circulation for that long . . . especially if his stable held only one horse.

But the pain of what Beryl shoved in my face opened my eyes to a possibility I'd blocked with such perfection that only one "truth" had ever touched my core. Was my mother the whore I'd always assumed she was? Or could she have been a hero, like Belle's sister had been, giving up her own life to spare her child's? What if my bio-father was *her* father? What if she gave her baby the only chance he ever *could* have, and went on the run before the freak could start using her again?

Had I gotten that vasectomy when I was just a young man because, somewhere inside me, I knew?

Bad blood. That bad blood Belle always said was in her — her big sister, the woman who'd traded her life for Belle's, had also been her mother.

When I'd been tracking Beryl, I'd gotten help from the woman I've always loved. Wolfe. But she'd given me my chance — twice — and I'd fucked it up.

Another woman who told me, "Don't come back." The one that hurt the most.

Wolfe had only helped me find Beryl because I swore to her that I was back to being the man she first met — hunting the humans who prey on kids.

Over the years, I'd slipped away from that. Too many times, I'd found kids who didn't *want* to be "saved." One was working in a low-rent whorehouse. I told her I thought runaways took off to find a better place. She said she had.

You ever wonder why so many working girls call their pimp "Daddy"?

I didn't bring that girl back, but the man who'd hired me still paid for it . . . just not the way he figured on doing. I never did a legit piece of work in my life. Yes, if one of Them walked across my path, they wouldn't get to *keep* walking, but that wasn't what I was about anymore. It just seemed to . . . happen, sometimes.

The Prof knew. I didn't owe Melissa Turnbridge a thing. But I owed whoever did . . .

what they did . . . to her. Yeah, I was going to get paid. Everyone was going to get paid.

But only my crew and Claw were guaranteed to be paid in cash. The others? That's what I needed those old police files to decide.

◆

I was just coming back from visiting a guy tall enough to dunk on Wilt and skinny enough to do it through the eye of a needle. That is, if his legs worked. He needed one of those two-handed walkers to get around, but his hands were as good as any surgeon's.

I pulled into the chain-link cage behind the two-pump gas station that never seemed to have any fuel to sell. The Plymouth was now a resplendent shade of Mopar's infamous Plum Crazy, instead of its usual urban camouflage, a mottled pattern of dull black and gray primer.

That's what the guy I had visited wanted to show me. He had a way to apply a full-body decal to any car. Looked exactly like paint, even up close. It took him a while to put one on — the less chrome to remove the better, and my Roadrunner was a perfect candidate — but only a few minutes to peel it right off. Especially if you had help.

"Think of it as a getaway driver's condom," he said, smiling with teeth so perfect they had to be replacements.

My plan was to test it for a couple of days, including running it through a car wash. If it worked, it was worth every dime the man was asking.

The new color didn't faze the three pit bulls ambling out of their own two-story condo. I don't know if dogs can see color, but I know they never rely on it. If they hadn't recognized me in whatever way dogs do, even the plastic tub of pulled-pork BBQ I brought with me wouldn't have distracted them from their job.

As usual, the old male got the first deep snarf of the goods. His humongous head plunged viciously, shook once, and then turned the concrete into a dinner plate. The two females went right for the booty, but one of them, an orca-spotted beauty I'd been courting for a long time, gave me a look over her shoulder first. I made a "come here" gesture with one hand. She immediately trotted around me, deftly snatching the solid cube of steak I held out behind my back, without breaking stride.

After I slammed the three-pound padlock closed, I walked back to the flophouse.

Darkness was down, and I wrapped it around me the way a rich man's mistress does her mink. It was mine, and I'd paid what it cost to make it so.

"The kid's upstairs, boss," Gateman greeted me.

"Alone?"

"Yeah," he said reluctantly. To Gateman, both Terry and Clarence were kids, but he only called Terry by that title, because Clarence was a fellow gunman. The naked unhappiness in his voice was because Terry had come without his mother — Gateman's unrequited adoration of Michelle had never been expressed once he found out she was the Mole's woman. Never expressed to her, that is.

"Bad?" I asked. Meaning: was Terry on the run? If he'd been down here and got caught in a bad spot, this is where he'd come. Getting past Gateman would be a hard job for a couple of pros, impossible for amateurs.

"Nah," Gateman dismissed my worries. "He had a message for you, said he had to deliver it in person."

Something happened to the Mole! flashed in my mind, but I let it go just as quick. That was the case, Terry would have been with Michelle, for sure.

246

"Why didn't he wait down here with you, Gate?"

"Oh, he did, boss. Got here *hours* ago. We sent out for sandwiches and everything. But I had a little business to do, and I didn't think you'd want . . ."

"You'd make a good father, Gateman."

"Probably would have made a good sprinter, too," the man in the wheelchair said.

I tapped fists with him, acknowledging his recital of the truth we all learn: you play what you're dealt.

Then I hit the stairs.

◆

"Hey, son," I greeted Terry as he looked up from his laptop.

"Burke."

"Gateman said you had a —"

"Dad needs to see you."

"So why not just — ?"

"Now, okay?"

"Do I need — ?"

"Nothing." Meaning: No weapons. And come alone.

"Nice ride," I told the kid. I'm not a rice-burner man, but I could feel the Scion tC we were riding in had been major-league reworked, even if the boost gauge on the A-pillar hadn't tipped me off.

"I had a big fight with Mom about it," he said, not quite smiling.

"The only thing Michelle knows about cars is how good the leather on the seats is."

"Not that. She wanted to buy it for me, and I wanted to pay for it myself."

"She should have been proud of you."

"She *was*. But she said . . . Well, you know how she gets."

"Amen."

"I told her she and Dad were already paying for college, and —"

"She reminded you that you're on a full scholarship, and you're not too big to forget you were raised to respect your —"

"Exactly." He sighed. "She got kind of upset, Burke. I asked Dad. You know what he said, right?"

I shrugged.

The kid burst into laughter. "Yeah. That *is* what he said. I mean, he's not exactly *afraid* of Mom or anything, but . . ."

"I know."

The kid handled the car expertly. I wondered who'd taught him, maybe feeling a little hurt that he hadn't asked me. I knew it hadn't been the Mole; he drives like Ray Charles on Valium.

"Burke?"

"What?"

"You know Mom. You maybe know her better than anyone."

"Sure. She's my kid sister."

"Yes," he said, quiet and serious. "Why did she get so worked up about the car? If it's none of my business, okay. But don't tell me you don't know, okay?"

If I still smoked — I only do it now when I have to play a role — that would have been one of those times when I'd have reached for one. I took in a long, shallow breath. Let it out.

"You're pulling away, T."

"From *Mom?!* Are you — ?"

"No. Not from your mother. Or your father. From The Life, understand?"

He turned and gave me a quick look.

"Terry, you know where we all live," I said, treading softly. "None of us are citizens. None of us are ever going to be. It's not that we picked our own paths; it's that those paths crossed. Each one was our way out, and we can't go back. The Mole and Michelle, you know they don't want that for you."

"But I'd never —"

"Yeah, you will," I told him, straight to the heart, the way he deserved, from the uncle who loved him. "You have to. We don't *want* another generation coming up with us. We live underground; we want you to live in the light. Whatever we teach you, it's for 'just in case,' okay? Not to earn a living."

"They always said . . . something like that."

"Not 'always,' son. When they thought you were old enough to understand." *Understand that the freaks who sold you are our blood-enemies; you're one of us now. And we never give up our own.* But I didn't say that out loud, just: "It's not so much about what they *want* from you; it's about what they *expect* from you, see?"

"No," he said. But he wasn't telling the truth. Or just refusing to face it.

"You don't change the world from underground, Terry. You don't cure cancer, or isolate the enzyme in mosquitoes that kills the malaria inside them, or figure out how to locate trauma paths in brain-wave patterns or —"

"People are already working on all that."

"Cut it, kid. You know what I mean. Exactly what I mean. Can you even *imagine* what your father could have discovered if . . . if things had been different for him, earlier?"

"And if Mom —"

"Yeah."

"You, too, Burke."

"Me? Look, I was talking about —"

"You know what Dad once told me about you? He said you know more about people than any man he ever met. And that, if you'd been a cop, no freak on earth would ever be safe."

"Okay," I said quickly, trying for a nerve block.

"But if Mom *wants* me to go —"

"She knows you *have* to go, Terry. She knows it's right. It's hard for her to . . . deal with sometimes, that's all."

"Me, too," he said, setting his jaw.

As far as he knew, I never saw the teardrop track his cheek.

◆

Terry slipped the metallic-ruby coupe inside the junkyard without a trace of drama. Walked through the dog pack like it was a fur-and-fangs turnstile, just like his father

251

always does.

We walked the rest of the way. Found Simba sitting next to the Mole's empty chair.

"I'll wait here," Terry said.

I entered the Mole's underground bunker, moved through the dark with the confidence of a blind man in his own house, turned the corner — and there he was.

"Sit," he said, as he turned from a table covered with tiny bottles and glass tubing.

I took the special chair Michelle had bought him for Father's Day a few years ago. None of us ever celebrate our birthdays. We don't even acknowledge them. Except for the kids: Terry's, sure. Flower's, not an option. Max might let it slide; Immaculata might understand; even Flower would let it go. But Mama would . . . well, none of us were brave enough to find out.

The Mole dragged over the four-legged wooden stool he sat on whenever Michelle wasn't around.

"My people, they want something."

"They've got it," I said, knowing there was no other answer.

"This was not expected," he said, almost apologetically. "But those I know, they have the younger ones coming. To those, I am not so much a . . ."

"I get it."

"There is a traitor. An old man now. My people cannot touch him."

I can't speak Hebrew, but I can translate Mole. Some fools think the Rosenbergs were Communists. Or did whatever they tried to do for money. I guess you're not supposed to spy on your allies. I asked the Mole about that once. "Ally?" he said. "You mean, like Saudi Arabia?" So, when he said "traitor," I knew he meant a man who had sold one of Israel's citizen-spies to the *federales.*

"He is a wealthy man," the Mole said.

Meaning: he could afford security. Nothing the Mossad murder-magicians couldn't penetrate, but they couldn't be connected. Or even suspected. This was a job for thugs, not spooks. Maybe a burglary gone bad . . . ?

"He sold his daughter," the Mole said, controlling his voice with effort. "If she is convicted, she will be sentenced to life in prison."

I looked a question over at him.

The Mole's faded-denim eyes glistened behind his thick lenses. Something . . . something I couldn't read.

"If he's gone in the Grand Jury already, they can still use his testimony if he's 'unavailable' at the time of trial," I told him.

The Mole nodded. Meaning: We know. And it's not a problem.

"You know I can't involve my own —"

"There is a budget," my demented genius brother said, softly.

"They expect me to just go out and —"

"Do you remember — a long time ago? — you were looking for something you needed very badly? I took you to a house. We met a man. The agreement was that he would talk with you. Talk *freely.* But you could not hurt him."

I said nothing.

"You *wanted* to hurt him. This was known. You gave your word this would not happen. But the . . . people who made him . . . available, they insisted I come with you."

"I remember," I finally said.

"You did nothing to him. But something *happened* to him. Later."

"Scumbag like that, just a matter of time."

"He was a very valuable asset. Some of my people, they have not forgotten."

"Why are you telling me this?"

"Because what they want from you this time — and this I swear — is the opposite of what they required from you that last time."

"I see."

"No. No, you don't, Burke. I am saying to you — what they want, it is something *you* want, too."

"For real?"

"For everything," the Mole said, holding out his hand. "Yes?"

"Yes," I answered, closing my hand over his.

He turned, grasped the handle of a metal file box, held it out to me.

I took it, and turned to leave.

"Sei gesund," my brother said.

◆

"Fifty K?" Gigi said. "That's —"

"The front money," I finished for him. "Half."

"For that kind of cash, you're looking to buy —"

"You may not have to do anything. Depends on what this guy's got in place around him. Could be you just sit there and watch. Could be you have to take someone off the count."

"Same pay either way?"

"Either way. What I'm buying is what you can't get anymore."

"Good help?" the Godzilla said, chuckling.

"Time-tested," I told him, speaking in the

language only men like us understand — by then, Gigi knew the whole story of my new face.

"I'm no good with guns anyway," Claw said.

I hadn't used any of the Mole's "budget" to buy him in. Whether he believed me when I told him that I was trading the job we were going to do for the second half of what we needed to move on our targets, I don't know. But he believed me when I told him that, if I didn't get this one done, I couldn't do the one he needed.

Or wouldn't. From where he was sitting, same thing.

It took me three days and nights just to work through the stuff the Mole's people supplied. I'd never seen surveillance work like it. They had draftsman's-quality blueprints of everything, right down to the wiring of the apnea monitor; terrain maps; wiretap tapes; camera work — telephoto to macro. Plus, CAD/CAM 3-Ds; the combination to the floor-mounted safe; and even a list of weapons the bodyguards carried.

There were two of those, and they never left the place. Slept in shifts sometimes, but they were both always on the job when it got deep-dark.

"You get the shooter," I told Claw. "The karate guy's yours," I said to Gigi.

"I already got the car," the humongoid assured me. "Motherfucker's put together like a jigsaw puzzle. We can leave it anywhere and walk. But we can't get stopped."

I nodded. We each had our own reasons, but none of us were going back Inside. If some trooper lit us up on our way back from this job, court was in session.

◆

"Cocksucker!" Gigi cursed. Again. "You didn't tell me this was gonna be no fucking cross-country trip, man."

"There's no dogs, inside or out," I said, softly, into the soft night. "The old man's afraid of them. No fence, either. What do you want to do, drive up to the front door?"

Claw never said a word. He wasn't even breathing hard.

The house was mostly dark. A few lights on, all on the first story. The key I'd been given opened the back door. The security codes I punched in clicked.

Then we started working.

The bodyguards were in one of those "great rooms," their eyes magneted to the gangbang porn playing on a wall-sized plasma screen. Claw had his spike deep in the shooter's neck before the glazed-over slug could even touch leather, but the karate guy caught the peripheral flash and was out of his chair like a rocket, launching a kidney-killing side kick at Claw's back. Gigi plucked him out of the air like a gorilla snatching a butterfly on the wing.

I went up the carpeted stairs, rubber-soled and plastic-gloved. A faint glow spilled from the room I wanted. I slipped inside. The old man saw me. I wasn't wearing a mask. He had to know what that meant, but he didn't move.

I knew what he was, right in that moment. The kind of human that would make lice jump off his skin and vultures refuse to eat his flesh.

I crossed to him. The room's shadow shifted, darkness inside gloom. Before I could whirl, a heavy forearm wrapped around my neck like constrictor cable. Something slammed into the back of my thigh. I slid down, not resisting, trying to get my chin tucked while I still had time.

The choke artist came down with me, still locked on. Darkness was closing.

I thumbed my sleeve knife open and stabbed his cabled forearm deep, raking the serrated edge through muscle tissue. He made an ugly noise as his grip loosened. I slipped out, stepped back, sucked in a deep, ragged breath. The choke artist, a powerfully built black man, staggered to his feet, left arm limp at his side. I circled, buying time, hoping the knife would make him hold off long enough for me to get more air into my lungs.

But he knew, and he stepped right to me, firing a Shotokan right hand off his front foot. His balance was off enough for me to slip the punch, toss the knife to my left hand, and hook him to the liver with it. He made a sound I recognized as he went down.

Quick! rang in my head as I spun toward the old man. He still hadn't moved. Hadn't reached for a phone or a panic button. Just kept staring at a portfolio-sized display case, standing open on a shelf. Inside were dozens of tiny compartments, mirror-backed.

"I warned that filthy little cunt," he said, rheumy eyes blazing with righteous conviction.

His last words.

I heard a crack-snap noise behind me. Spun again, weaponless. But it was just Gigi, making sure the bodyguard the Mole's friends hadn't known about wasn't going to bleed out.

◆

We ransacked the place like amateurs on angel dust. Grabbed all the loose cash, cleaned out the medicine cabinet, chopped off the shooter's ring finger, and left it there — some TV-trained cop would spend a lot of time checking pawnshops for a ring that had never existed.

But the prize was the display case: constructed of what looked like Hawaiian koa wood, it folded into the size of an artist's portfolio. The intricate fastening clamps were gold. I saw the OCR-font printout from one of the pages the Mole had given me as clearly as if it was projected on the wall:

Among certain individuals, it is well known that Target possesses these items. They were created a minimum of two hundred years ago, each of handcrafted ivory. One of a kind, every one. Unduplicatable. Literally priceless, but could never be sold openly. The security Target employs is to protect his treasure, not his person.

I couldn't stop myself from looking before I closed the case. Each tiny figurine was really two: an adult male and a girl child. I wished the craftsman whose magic hands had created such intricate, complex scenes on such a small scale was still alive. So I could take my own trophy.

While I was doing the hophead-burglar thing — opening the chest of drawers starting at the top, then turning each one upside down — Claw was razor-slitting a bunch of cushions, the way you do when you're looking for a hidden stash and don't have much time. He made sure to take the shooter's piece — looked like a Sig P210, way too expensive for junkies to pass up, even with the serial number showing — and empty everyone's wallets. He even snatched the karate guy's G-Shock watch and platinum neck chain.

Gigi just wrecked everything, including a

261

Sub-Zero that it should have taken two men even to move, much less turn over.

We went out the way we came in. Standing outside, Gigi kicked in the back door, then smashed the wall next to the security box with a brass-knuckled fist. Claw immediately reached in and cut the wires.

Then we split for real, leaving enough clues to keep crime-scene techs busy for months. Every meth-head within fifty miles was in deep trouble.

Back at the car, we all stripped, tossing everything we'd been wearing into a thick canvas bag. I tied it at the top, wrapping the wire around one of the Mole's little boxes and put it in the trunk. Anyone who tried to open that bag before it got to the crematorium would destroy a lot more than evidence.

We'd gone in double-sheathed; all our prints were in the system. But we'd also splattered some random DNA — carried in baggies, emptied by hands covered in surgeon's gloves — in a few spots.

For cops, the only thing worse than no clues is too many.

Gigi dropped Claw at a subway on the West Side. Dropped me on a corner in Chinatown.

"It's mine from here," he said. "This" — meaning the car — "is a big fucking paperweight in a couple of hours."

We'd already divided up the cash — equal shares. Everything else went into another bag for the Disposal Three-Step: cremation; sledgehammer; then the river. The "collection" was going to stay inside the paperweight. I trusted Gigi to handle that part. He was a stand-up con, and he wouldn't back-deal a partner. Plus, even if he looked, he'd know he'd have to reach *way* out to sell something like that. But trust only goes so far — I'd spent the return trip sitting in the backseat, carefully using a pair of needle-nose pliers to crush each of the figurines into ivory dust.

I didn't need to get word to the Mole; it was all over the papers. TV, radio, Internet. Every media outlet had a different version of what happened. Every "expert" had a different guess as to why: cults, criminals, or crazos. The cops were "still evaluating the evidence." Too bad the maniacs — "probably flying on speed," one genius solemnly intoned — had busted up all the computers. I mean, that's the first thing you check, right?

◆

"Call for you," Mama said.

I got up from my booth, picked up the phone, said, "What?"

"It's Bishop, man."

"Sorry. You must have the wrong number."

"Hey! You haven't even heard my —"

I hung up on him. Bishop was a menace. Not to society, to any thief who went near one of his ideas. He was a lifelong failure — the kind of guy you usually have to pass through a metal-detector to visit. The hapless fool never falls hard — small-time all the way; no violence, ever — but with Bishop, falling is such a guarantee that the Prof calls him "Gravity."

I'd met him on Rikers a long time ago. I was being held for trial — a trial that never happened, when a pimp who'd taken a bullet developed a medical complication: loss of memory. Bishop, he was doing ninety days because . . . well, because of what he was. A softhearted judge had let him off with "probation and restitution" on his last job. He paid the restitution immediately . . . with a rubber check. Bishop was the kind of master planner who could always figure out how to come out on the bottom.

"He's supposed to be so smart," I said to the Prof once. "I mean, he's got, like, a Ph.D. or something, right?"

"Why you think they call a diploma a 'sheepskin,' son?"

"I don't get it."

"A *real* teacher, he wants the ones he teaches to be better than he is. Smarter, sharper, slicker. Wants them to *rise,* okay? But all they teach those poor kids in college is rinse-and-repeat, see? That's 'cause those teachers, they're the kind of punks who stay up by keeping folks down. And they've got lifetime gigs doing it."

"So college, it's a waste of time?"

"It don't *have* to be. It's like the Good Book," he said, switching from Professor to Prophet. "You got to read the book itself, not the book *reviews,* see? A teacher's like a fighter — got to bring some to get some. When they can't bring it, they just sing it. And most of those kids going to school, all they ever learn is to just sing along. Memorize the words, so they can spit them back out. How's that gonna make you smarter?"

"So a guy like Bishop . . . ?"

"Oh, he's smart for real. But the mother-fucker's radioactive, son. Dealing with him, it's like swimming in the swamp. You might pull it off once, but you try it too many times, something in there's going to pull you down. You see that man coming, you cross the street, hear?"

I never went to college, but I never forget what I've been taught. Any of it.

I don't forget the people who taught me, either. Any of them.

◆

I walked through the shadows, sadness-shrouded by how at home I felt there. And how I could heat this whole city in the middle of winter with the flames from all the bridges I've burned.

My car was where it was supposed to be. So were the pits. This time, I was carrying top-quality tribute: a massive T-bone. The male and one of the females each took a bite and played tug until a slab came loose for each. My orca girl took a fat cube of filet mignon from behind my back.

I drove my purple Plymouth to the bad-lands, stripped off its condom inside the chain-link as Simba came over to keep me company. I couldn't just slog through the pack the way the Mole or Terry did — I needed the old warrior to walk point.

The Mole had us on visual all the way. He was waiting outside. We both followed him down — me to his Father's Day chair, Simba to the gorgeous sable coat Michelle had abandoned after deciding that wearing fur was a badge of low character. It was Simba's curl-up spot now.

"*Nu?*"

"You know it's done," I said.

"Not that. Was I right?" Meaning, was killing that piece of filth something I would have wanted to do, even if I didn't have to?

"Or?"

"Or what?"

"Or are you checking to see if your own people lied to you?"

"I already know."

"How?"

"I can feel it coming off you. So can Simba."

The beast made a throaty sound. I took it for recognition of his name; the Mole took it for agreement.

"He was —"

"I know," he cut me off.

"So his daughter —"

"Yes," the Mole said. "There is what you wanted."

I followed his stubby finger to the corner where it was pointed. Six more metal file cases, with carrying handles. Duplicates of the one he had given me originally.

"The deal was for just this one —"

"Yes, yes," he said. "Those boxes are not another . . . job. They are what you wanted."

I met his eyes. Saw the truth.

"You had the stuff all the time," I said. Not an accusation, saying aloud what I just realized.

"I was trusted," he said. Three words — a thousand meanings.

◆

If the pits noticed that my Plymouth had been restored to its night-blending color scheme, I couldn't see it on their faces. I had stopped by the flophouse first. No way I was going to tie up both hands trying to carry all those file boxes through the route I had to take. Or make six trips, either.

By the time I got back, Max was sitting with Gateman. He took two boxes in each hand. I followed him up the stairs.

We sat down at the poker table. Max

spread his arms in an "Is that all of it?" gesture.

"That's what they say," I told him.

◆

It took the Prof and Clarence almost two hours to show up. By then, Max and I had figured out that every single piece of paper in the file boxes was a copy, even the color photos. I was guessing Xerox didn't make whatever the Mole's people had used for the job.

"Motherfucker!" the Prof burst out, when he saw the mountain. "What'd those fools do, rob a paper factory?"

"It's all on the case," I said. "I don't know how much work they really put in, don't know how much of this is just cops playing CYA, but it's all on Melissa Turnbridge, Prof."

"So you're saying, if we're not gonna cheat, we gotta check every fucking sheet?"

I didn't even answer him. The reason so few crimes actually get solved — if you don't count informants, or fools who don't clean up after themselves — is because of prejudice. Not black-white kind of prejudice — that's what pins crimes on the wrong man, sure, but that's not what muddies the water if you're really looking for answers. I mean the kind of prejudice that makes the investigator start with a bent mind.

Psychologists call that "cognitive distortion." You view the world through a prism, refracting the images to fit your needs. That's how freaks resolve their "internal dissonance." They know sodomizing a baby is nothing but pain and terror for the victim. But not having a conscience doesn't mean you don't know right from wrong; it just means you don't let stuff like that get in the way of your fun. Or, more likely, the pain *is* the fun.

The "treatment community" believes this means the thought process of child-molesters is distorted. Baby-rapers don't see a victim being used; they see a child being "loved." And all children want love, don't they? Isn't love *good* for them?

For decades, they've been building sex-offender treatment on the foundation of this quicksand: *If we can just alter the poor man's cognitive distortions, we can change his behavior.* The treatment twits aren't wrong about cognitive distortion — they just don't understand that *they're* the ones who have it.

The whole concept was probably a deliberate plant, suggested to a therapist who believed some freak had achieved "insight." The therapist repeats it, like a trained parrot, only he calls it a "discovery." Eventually, "repeat-and-believe" becomes the formula, and, before long, there's a whole new industry springing up.

The pipeline opens, and the money flows. Politicians pass the "right" laws, judges do the "right" thing, and the right people get "treatment."

It's the perfect scam, because people *want* it to be true.

I just read this test some researchers conducted. Ah, it was a beaut. The researchers didn't care about sex-offender treatment; their field was statistical measurement, and they wanted to know what sort of factors might affect results. So they asked this whole group of imprisoned baby-rapers who had been placed in a "treatment unit" a series of questions. The first job was to measure the percentage who reported "cognitive distortions" concerning sex with children. Amazingly, virtually all of them did.

Then what the researchers did was to tell the "subjects" that they were all going to be given the same set of questionnaires again, only this time they would be polygraphed to see how many had been truthful. And

271

the *only* thing that would be disclosed to the Parole Board was whether they lied or told the truth.

Get it? Maybe you don't, but the freaks sure did.

They passed the polygraph at an astounding rate. Nearly every one of them was absolutely truthful. That time, only a couple of them — probably the ones with the lowest IQs — still reported cognitive distortions. Baby-rapers only lie when there's something in it for them.

Actually, the whole "polygraph" thing had been a fraud. The researchers were interested in validity-reliability methods, not sex offenders. The real test was to see if people changed their answers when they had something to gain by telling the truth.

And it sure told the truth about the whole "cognitive distortion" game.

Sex-offender treatment is like performing an exorcism on an atheist.

Making assumptions is the same as volunteering to be stupid. When I investigate, I'm never invested. I'm looking for whatever the truth is, because that's the only combination that will open the safe I need to crack.

"Put in the time you can," I told them. "We won't ever finish this in one shot. Everybody just come and go when you need to, okay?"

Max stood up. Sat down again. Made gestures of a man rowing the arms of his chair.

"You're right," I said. "No reason Gateman can't help with this. Even Terry, if we can slip around —"

"You bring her boy into this mess, his momma'll set fire to your chest, Schoolboy. And put it out with an ice pick."

"He's just at the research end, Prof. No way he goes past that, okay?"

"I could send him documents," Clarence said. "Over the —"

"No," I cut that off. "Nothing leaves this building except by way of the smokestack."

The way the Mole's ancestors had. The thought ripped into my mind like a supercharged chainsaw, shredding the resentment I'd been nursing. His shadowy friends had made me take some life-or-death risks, sure. But they played for the same stakes, every day. Where would I draw the line if I thought someone was trying to exterminate my whole family? When it comes to fighting off genocide, there's no rules.

"What are we looking for, boss?"

"I can't say, Gate. Something that's not right."

"Whole motherfucking thing's not right," he said, his eyes as cold as the custom 9mm semi-auto that he carried the same way an artist would carry a paintbrush. "You're thinking — what? — the blue boys got paid?"

"That plan won't scan," the Prof cast his veto. "Sure, a badge ain't nothing but a license to steal, but something like this, there's too many to pay to make them *all* stay away."

Max made the sign of a man writing something in a notepad, looked up, cocked his head as if listening, wrote some more.

"Sure," I agreed. "Reporters had to be all over this one, too."

"Yes, mahn," Clarence confirmed, looking up from his computer screen. "The coverage was all very critical; the police took a lot of heat for this."

"Don't forget the reward," Terry added.

I nodded in his direction. "A hundred grand the girl's parents put up. Thirty years ago, that was enough to shake every tree in the forest."

Max rubbed his first two fingers and thumb together, then shook his head disdainfully.

"The dragon pulls the wagon," the Prof said, pointing his finger at Max as if acknowledging a major contribution to a big score. "The Max-man's clue is true. Any of their fathers had even *tried* a bribe, their kid would've ended up taking a ride."

"You're saying the cops really went after it?" Gateman said, skeptically.

"I think they did. Come on, bro: would the locals ever call in the Feebs if they weren't desperate? It's the same as admitting they don't have what it takes."

"FBI made the scene?"

"Yes, Father," Clarence answered. "Many of the later news accounts refer to them, some by name."

"So what're we looking for?" Gateman asked, again.

"See this?" I said, pointing to the transcript of my conversation with Thornton. Everyone had a copy. "It should match. Well, not match, but not be . . ." I paused, trying to put words to the pattern-recognition software that keeps people like us alive. And makes us the best hunters on the planet. "Look, you're rolling down the street," I told them, signing for Max as I spoke. "Something's just . . . wrong, okay? Some . . . disturbance in the visuals. Nothing major. Wrong posture on the guy near the lamppost. Wrong jacket for this time of the year. A flash of color you've seen somewhere before, earlier that same day, in another part of town. This isn't like when a hawk's in the sky and all the animals go quiet and still. Citizens won't ever see it. But we will."

"Like when a guy hits the yard walking robot?"

The Prof was talking about how a man who expects to be facing a blade will wrap himself with layers of newspaper under his jacket. Maybe not thick enough to turn a shank, but enough to stop it from getting all the way in.

"*Just* like that," I confirmed. "Something that draws your eye, tells you something's off. Yeah?"

The Prof nodded. Max and Gateman, too. Clarence was a lot younger, but he'd come up as a gunman, and he got it, too. For Terry, it was a theorem, not an experience. Still, he had his father's mind and his mother's soul — I knew he'd find his way to the same place. I didn't want to tap any trigger-point in his past, but I couldn't pretend it was anything other than

276

what it was.

Even though we all wanted him to walk a different path, we knew he might someday need what we could teach him.

◆

I took the subway to a three-bedroom, two-bath rent-controlled apartment on the Upper West Side. It was occupied by an elderly lady with half a dozen diseases ravaging her wasted body. She didn't have long, and she knew it.

Death didn't scare her, but she wasn't the type to hoard her pain pills, either. She knew, the second she checked out, the rent would rocket from $595 to maybe four grand, minimum. And that's if the owner didn't "improve" the unit, upping it even more.

The building's owner would end up as swine-swollen as a CEO treating his "boys" to a night in an upscale strip club to celebrate the company's latest creative-accounting triumph. Nothing like glancing over a glass of sucker-priced champagne to convince yourself it's your raging testosterone that's attracting such a cooing herd of for-sale flesh to your table.

But this pig had a problem — the old

lady's nephew. He occupied two of the bedrooms. And because she'd adopted him when he was nine, he'd inherit the right to keep occupying the place . . . at the rent-control price.

The nephew was around thirty years old. What his parents had done to him had bent his neurons and snapped his synapses. He had an incomprehensible mind, a one-occupant world of torture, degradation, and horror.

He never left the apartment.

He never had guests.

His brain didn't register the past. He thought he'd been born when puberty struck, and the warp opened.

But his aunt's mind was still as clear as Bush's agenda.

And she never forgot.

So when she gasped out, "Theodore, this man is very special to me. You must do whatever he asks," between hits of oxygen, all the damaged boy said was "Yes, Auntie."

While he was waiting for me in his rooms, I again swore to the old lady that my lawyer — a bull elephant named Davidson — had the battle plan against the landlord all mapped out, and was looking forward to it. Her nephew was always going to have his home.

"I'll be watching," the old lady said.
I believed her.

"I hate what they do to animals," the nephew said. A demon-eyed wraith, he had a voice that was pure Asperger's, utterly devoid of emotion. "Do you?"

"Yes," I said, knowing there's always a toll.

"What do you hate?"

"Zoos."

"All zoos?"

I told him about my idea for virtual zoos. He nodded, bored. Not because the idea was so simple, but because his idea of protecting animals was to eliminate humans. He held his misshapen head in his hands for a minute, then looked up at me.

"You know those games where you can buy points from other players?"

"I don't think so."

"Online," he said, as if that explained everything. His fractured-iris eyes searched mine, instantly registered my level of knowledge, readjusted. "Some of the games have thousands of players, all over the world. If you're good, if you have skills, you can acquire different things. Like weapons, for example. Or maps to where they might be.

You can *sell* these — to other players, I mean. For actual cash. So if you spend money, you increase your chances of winning."

"I get it."

"I'm designing a game. Right here," he said, pointing to a computer housed inside a transparent casing full of vibrantly colored wires. "In *my* game, the prize — if you can get it — is that you can destroy it all."

"The game?"

"Yes. People spend an *incalculable* number of hours playing. It's kind of like The Sims, but what *you* do impacts the other players. If you can get enough points, you get to take the whole game down. It could take years to do it, but all those people, all they invested, it would be gone. Not just the money, *everything*."

"But if the players knew something like that could happen, why would they — ?"

He gave me a look of profound pity.

◆

"You want a poison pill," the nephew finally said, a couple of hours later. He had been listening to me, asking questions, listening some more. He was never impatient, never annoyed. I meant less than a cockroach to him, but when his auntie told him to do something, the one pipeline to humanity still inside him opened. He'd kill a planet to hear her say, "Thank you, Theodore. You're such a good boy."

"What's a — ?" I asked.

"Never mind. See this?" He held up a thin, rectangular piece of metal. "It's disguised to look like a memory stick. Plugs into any USB port. All you have to do is insert it *before* you boot up the machine, and it recodes everything inside."

"What good would that do?"

"You know what the Enigma Machine was?"

"Yeah. It was —"

"This is a thousand times more sophisticated. A team of top cryptographers couldn't hope to crack it. Even a mainframe would fry its circuits trying."

"But you could read it?"

"Yes," he said, the way a polite person talks to a retardate.

"Could you make one that restores, too? So I could plug that one in, turn the whole hard drive into gibberish, then plug in the other and make it good again. Like the antidote for the poison?"

"Yes." He sighed, as patient as Einstein explaining long division.

"Why did you design it in the first place?" I asked him. I'd long since gotten what I'd come for, but I didn't want to disengage too abruptly. When you find yourself too close to a land mine, you back away very, very slowly.

"To hurt things," he said, as if that was the only sensible answer to any question.

Satan must have been burning up in frustration that the nephew never left the apartment. If that mutated-by-terror maniac ever played his games with real people, he'd make Ted Bundy look like the Dalai Lama.

"Was Theodore helpful?"

"Yes, ma'am. Very helpful."

"It's not his fault," the old lady said.

"I know."

"Will you come back? And visit, some-time?"

"Of course," I lied.

"You are a good man," she lied right back.

◆

I thought about her nephew on the way back to the subway. I guess there had always

282

been creatures like him, but technology seems to have changed the game. It's cool to be cruel now. Some human puke who thinks he's "cutting edge" makes a video of puppies being doused with gasoline and incinerated. Putting that video on the Internet for all to admire is about what you'd expect from a maggot like that. But when people actually pay to *download* it, I wish I could get them all together and show them what "cutting edge" means to some of us.

On the side of a building, someone had sprayed DAM in huge yellow letters. To make sure the droll cleverness of the multimedia artiste was fully appreciated, *Mothers Against Dyslexia* was written out beneath it.

◆

"I don't think we can wait," I told the Prof late that night. We were in my Plymouth, parked at the end of a prostie stroll just a few blocks east of the Hudson. The real-estate agents call the area "Clinton." Who's going to want to pay seven figures for a bare loft in a neighborhood called "Hell's Kitchen"? That's why there's no Lower East Side anymore. And why's there's a "TriBeCa," and a "SoHo."

But the name game isn't just for the real-estate pushers. The Bureau of Child Welfare calls itself the Administration for Children's Services now. Of course, it still pays its workers a ton less for dealing with humans who treat their children like garbage than the "sanitation engineers" who empty the cans people leave at the curb.

In this city, the agencies copy the criminals: when there's too much heat, they just switch to an alias.

Dannemora used to be the state's worst place to do time, a max joint so far north you could walk to Canada. That icebox was so synonymous with extreme isolation that we called it "Little Siberia." It's still there, still doing what it always does. Only now they call it "Clinton," just like the neighborhood. But this one's never going to be gentrified.

"You the one behind the wheel," the little man said, mildly.

"Yeah. I know. I wanted to . . ."

"Right. You looking for truth, but all we *really* need is proof. This scheme is for the green, Schoolboy."

"That check?"

"You got two packages from the Mole. That first one leaves us holding the gun. The other . . ."

"You're saying, what difference?"

"Dead is dead. Ashes to ashes, dust to dust. Whatever that little girl was, she wasn't one of us."

"I can't just scam my way past all the barriers that a guy like that —"

"There's three of them."

"But we only have that one check, Prof. Besides, if it happened like that Thornton scumbag says it did, how's the one guy *not* going to reach out for the others? I don't care how rich he is, why should he pay the whole thing himself?"

"You mean the money?"

"What else?"

The little man didn't say anything. To him, I was a pane of glass, and he always carried a bottle of Windex.

◆

The girl who poked her round, sweaty face into the side window of my Plymouth might have been sixteen under that amateur paint job. Maybe.

"You look like a man who wants a date," she sex-whispered.

"Get your ass around this side," the Prof snarled, speaking across my chest, jerking his thumb as a summons.

I watched her as she passed by the windshield. Cheap white halter top over cheaper red satin hot pants, baby fat jiggling. About as sexy as watching a drunk vomit on a curb.

"Hey!" she blurted out when she saw the Prof. "How old are you, anyway?"

"Old enough to be your father," the little man shot back. "Young enough to be your daddy, too . . . if I was enough of a two-bit simp to be running some R. Kelly bait like you."

"Hey! I'm —"

"I know what you are," the Prof said, letting another organ-stop into his voice, shifting into a reach-out. "You some little child who ran away, got pulled by a punk who talked a lot of junk, and now you think you gonna be a star."

"You've got it —"

"My song ain't wrong," he dismissed her. "They all the same, child. They charm you; then they harm you."

"Tway-Z isn't —"

"He isn't *nothing*. And that's what you are to him, child. You nothing but a piece of toilet paper to that slimy little snake."

"I make —" she started to say, defensively.

"What you *make* ain't the same as what you *take*, you dumbass little bitch. What you *keep* is what counts. Please don't tell me how some faggot motherfucker is 'taking care' of you, either. You see this?" he said, holding up a thick wad of bills, fanning it so she could see nothing but hundreds. "You want some?"

She licked her lips, on home ground now. "Sure, Daddy."

"I'll give you two yards for an hour."

"I usually get —"

"You 'usually' get a twenty to suck some stranger's cock, maybe a little extra if you take it without a rubber," the Prof cut off her lie before she could finish it. "You hear me? Some *stranger.* Could be a psycho with a straight razor in his pocket, could be a freak with AIDS who wants to take a whole bunch of little whores with him when he goes. Could be *anybody,* ready to do *anything;* what do you know? You ain't no 'escort,' bitch. You ain't got no security, no protection, no nothing. Remember that word: *nothing.* That's your *real* name."

Her face twisted. The Prof grabbed her wrist. "You want money? I'll give you the two bills for an hour of your time, and you don't have to give up nothing."

"What do you mean?" Scared for real now.

"There's a place. In the Village. We drive you there. You talk to the lady inside. One hour. Then you do whatever you want."

"I don't . . ." She looked over her shoulder,

breathing hard.

"You think your 'man' is out there, watching your back?" the Prof sneered. "You think, we wanted to snatch you, you wouldn't already be snatched? You got a panic button? Nah, you don't even know what one is. Your 'man' ain't a man at all. Look, bitch, I'm not trying to pull you; I'm trying to pull your coat, get it?"

◆

It took longer than it usually does, but she finally climbed in the backseat, holding the Prof's two hundred in both hands, like a cross to ward off vampires.

We dropped her off. If the program could talk her into staying, Tway-Z was going to be one girl short . . . which should empty his stable. If not, we could find her again.

And then she would lead us to what I'm always looking for.

◆

Michelle was dressing me for my frontal assault on Reedy when her cell phone trilled.

"That's —"

"I know, honey," I said, shrugging off her apologetic face.

She stepped out of the room to take the call. When she came back, I read her heightened color like it was Caller ID.

"You have to — ?"

"Not until . . . later. And I can get Terry to come and pick me up, baby. Don't fuss."

In all the years since they first connected, this was the first time the Mole had ever called that Michelle hadn't asked — hell, *demanded* — that I get her out to his place, personally and pronto.

I let it go. She tossed a fifteen-hundred-dollar suit into the corner like it was a dust rag, yammering, "Classic doesn't mean ancient, you idiot."

I wasn't enough of an idiot to say anything.

"And we can't have tomorrow's look, either," she rolled on. "You're supposed to be . . . ?"

"A problem-solver."

"Yes. But not a thug. And not a con man, either. What we want to show is *expertise,* understand?"

I didn't say anything. What would be the point?

"Not just expertise, *successful* expertise. You're not some criminal who stumbled across a piece of information in a bar. You're a professional. A spider, at the center of a web. When the web trembles, you know you've got something, so you go and take a look. Most of the time, it's garbage. But when it's gold, you know the spot price. The going rate.

"So what we're after is dignified, baby. Not mortician-dignified, okay? Calm, self-assured, confident."

"You can *dress* to be that?"

"Oh, you can dress to be anything," my little sister said, dismissing any argument with an airy wave of her hand. "But the best that does is get you in the door. After that . . ."

I took a deep breath.

"And nobody's better at it than you, baby," she said, fiercely. "Nobody."

◆

My wheels dressed the part, too. The graphite Mercedes E500 sedan was a generic in the parking lot of the bronze glass building, which only a discreet brass plaque identified as the home of QuisitionDevelOp Enterprises, LLC.

The security guard at the green-veined black marble desk had the resentfully dull eyes of a retired cop who hadn't quite gotten used to the idea that his authority had been handed in with his badge. His eyes took me in, figured me for someone it wouldn't be a safe idea to get all TV-show with. I might have a mug-shot face, but Michelle was right — the outfit spoke louder. To this fool, anyway.

"Sir?"

"I'm here to see Mr. Reedy."

"And you are — ?"

"My name is Thornton," I said, smiling. "And, no, Mr. Reedy is not expecting me. I'm an old friend. I was in the area, and thought I'd take a shot at inviting him to lunch."

"I'm not sure he's even in the building, sir. I'm sure you understand —"

"That Mr. Reedy uses a private entrance? Or that there's a helipad on the roof?" I cut him off, smiling again.

"You got that right." He chuckled. "Well, let me call up and see."

I stepped back, deliberately showing respect for the delicacy of his position. He was on the phone for way longer than he should have taken.

"Yeah," he said, gesturing for me to approach. "Just like I figured. Mr. Reedy's not in. In fact, he's not even in the country at the moment. If you want to leave your card, though, I'll make sure they —"

I was already handing him a card. Delicately engraved on off-white vellum, it identified me as:

Donald R. C. Thornton

Nothing else was on the card except a 212 number in the lower left-hand corner, and "By Appointment Only" in the lower right.

◆

I knew they had me on video from the time I walked in the door, but didn't expect the black Dodge Magnum wagon to be in my rearview mirror so quick.

I drove like I had no idea I was being followed. Motored sedately down to Bronxville, where I used the Mole's code-grabber to remote-open the door to a three-car attached garage standing a covered archway's distance from a fieldstone home whose owner was at work. His wife and kids were visiting her mother in Pepper Pike, Ohio — he was going to join them that weekend.

I went out the open back window of the garage, drab green mechanic's coveralls over my suit. The stage actor's cheek-altering clay, black mustache, and red-rose "tattoo" decal on my right hand were all sitting in my pocket.

Michelle would turn my hair back to its natural steel gray from the jet black they'd have on their videotape, and cut it, too. I'd be three inches shorter without the lifts. And a good long soak would remove the acetate from the pads of my fingers and thumbs.

I was through a short patch of woods — half an acre was a big piece of property in that neighborhood — and into the Honda EV while the two guys in the Magnum were still waiting for instructions.

The electric car didn't make a sound as I moved off. That's me: green is what I live for.

I don't know how the guy who owned the house was going to explain the stolen Mercedes in his garage to the men who would be coming to call, but I knew he could pass a polygraph that it was all a mystery to him.

◆

I left the Honda in an underground garage just over the border, keys in the ignition. I exited via the freight elevator to the loading dock. The Roadrunner — now a bilious yellow with Mopar-heresy red bumblebee stripes around its rear end — was waiting.

The Honda was probably gone before I was; that place is always full of thieves. Max had been waiting within striking distance, but it took Clarence a couple of minutes to come down from the roof.

I dropped them both off at the flophouse first, not wanting to introduce the dogs to strangers. The pits enjoyed the random assortment of deli sandwiches I tossed out. As I was converting the Roadrunner back to its original camouflage, the orca-blotched female sat next to me . . . pretty close.

She'd already had her special bribe, so I didn't think this was about food. The battle-scarred male watched as I knelt and cooed to the girl, but he didn't move.

The distance between us shrank as she approached, bouncing in the way pits do when they're making up their minds. When she got close enough to nail me, I risked a gentle pat on her wedge of a skull. She sat, as if in response to a command. I scratched her behind the right ear.

"You're a beautiful girl," I said, softly.

She gave me a look, then trotted away to join the others.

"Fucking amateur probably got the mark's guard up," the Prof said when I'd run down the past few hours. "Tapping that baby-killer like he was a fucking maple tree."

"I do not understand," Clarence said, his face alive — not from puzzlement, but with the joy of learning something from his father.

"Blackmail is a one-stop shop," the little man told him. "Hit and run, son. One jack, and you never go back. Even if the well ain't dry, you *still* fly, understand?"

"So because this . . . person kept going back to him, over and over again . . . ?"

"Could just be corporate," I said. "Who's got the kind of serious money our guy's holding without putting some protection in place? Figure he hears the name — the one I used with the security guy in front — and he grabs me on video, live feed. Doesn't recognize me, but he knows I'm not Thornton, so he figures he better find out who that weasel may have sold him to. Good luck with that."

"Sure," the Prof said, sourly. "But it didn't get us in the door."

"He's got the card I left. When the trace goes dead, how's he *not* going to call? A man like him, information is plutonium. Worth a fortune in the right hands, blow you off the planet in the wrong ones."

Max held up three fingers. Pulled the middle one back toward his palm.

"Yeah," I agreed. "There's still two left, but Reedy's the only guy we can actually connect to Thornton. Besides, he's probably already gotten word to the others."

"And if he don't call . . . ?"

"I don't have a Plan B, Prof. But that doesn't mean we can't —"

One of the cloned cell phones I keep in individual charging cradles made a sound I recognized. I walked into another room, pulled it loose and opened the channel. Said, "Uh," which is all anyone was going to get until I knew who I was talking to.

"You get more Paleo every day." Michelle, her voice even waspier than her waist.

"Huh?"

"Well, it *must* have not come off, or I *know* you would have requested my presence by now."

"Yeah," I admitted.

"I'm sorry, baby. But there's more than one —"

"Yeah," I said, again. I know my little sister loves me, but some things you just don't need to hear more than once.

There's parts of Chicago I've always loved, ever since the first time I went there. Just a kid, picking up a package for some guys in Brooklyn. Had to go to this fleabag hotel in Uptown — they called it "Hillbilly Harlem" then — and wait for a man with a blue-and-yellow flight bag. They said he'd be there between ten and noon, but couldn't be sure what day he'd show. The nights were mine.

I was so young and dumb then. Hell, I'd once taped a plastic bottle to the front end of a revolver and thought I had a silencer. Now, when I have to work quiet, I use one of Clarence's custom-built semi-autos, the magazine packed with hand-loaded poison tips, the casings cast to luminesce in the dark, so I can pick up my brass without a flashlight.

I didn't know Chicago, but I didn't want to be inside that dirty little room at night, so I roamed.

The blues bars of Chicago in the sixties were merciless. Anyone who thinks Darwin got it wrong should have been there, down in the crucible. If you wanted to try, you looked for a nod from the leader, climbed up on the tiny little stage, plugged in, and took your shot.

If you could bring it, they'd let you know. If you couldn't, you had to go.

"Good enough" was never good enough in those joints. Either you killed the crowd, or the crowd killed you. For every Buddy Guy, the West Side produced a thousand who didn't make the cut.

"Magic Sam" wasn't a stage name; it was a title, earned in the ring. I don't mean some two-bit "belt," handed out like a rigged-bid contract by one of those licensed-to-steal "sanctioning bodies" who rule boxing today. No, Magic Sam won his title in matches where the crowd picks the winners.

His signature song was "Sweet Home Chicago." A Robert Johnson original, transplanted but still rooted in Delta soil. Like Sam himself. But "I Found a New Love" was always my favorite.

I loved the city's architecture, too. Supposedly, the whole town is built of stone because no wood construction was allowed after the Great Fire. But the first time I saw the Robert Taylor Homes on the South Side, I saw the future of America. *Miles* of housing project, sixteen stories high, overlooking the Dan Ryan Expressway, the outside walkways covered in chicken wire so the inmates could look out from their cages on the world passing them by. It

298

became its own world. Gangland. Just like the planners planned.

The Robert Taylor Homes are gone now. The inmates have been relocated . . . to where they were intended to spend their adult lives since birth.

This time, I could have driven — it's only about a twelve-hour trip, with all kinds of disinterested motels between Ohio and Indiana.

But this was a hit-and-run. I'd sent a message and given it a few days to work its way through to the guy I asked to do something for me. I knew better than to think he'd talk on any phone. All I needed was five minutes with him, alone. Plus, I owed Claw some speed after he did the job inside the rich old freak's house on just my word.

O'Hare is famous for a lot of things, but on-time landings isn't one of them. I walked through the terminal's glowing tunnels on my way to the CTA line. That was another reason I hadn't driven: where I was going, I wouldn't need a car. Paper is a fingerprint — you can't go through life without touching anything, but you avoid it whenever you get the chance.

As I approached the airport exit, a young woman came toward me, towing one of those wheeled suitcases behind her. As we

passed each other, she smiled. Not flirting
— an anxiety reaction to any man who
looked like me. A momentary "please don't
hurt me" flash in her too-wide eyes.

I knew some humans who would get
aroused by that look. Just as the Prof knew
the truth about why I'd come all this way
just to draw to a gut-shot straight.

◆

The receptionist took the name we agreed I
was always going to use, said, "Someone
will be out to get you in a minute, sir."

The "someone" was wearing a skirt tighter
than spray paint and four-inch strappy
stilettos instead of business pumps. She
walked ahead of me, letting me know that
the man I was there to see was getting his
money's worth. And that he hadn't learned
anything from the last time he did.

I'd had to clean up that mess for him —
that was the favor he owed me.

"I could only get something off the radar
on one of them," was his greeting. He didn't
get up from behind his free-form desk, or
offer to shake hands. Didn't even invite me
to have a seat.

I watched his eyes.

He looked away from mine.

"Reggie Bender is leveraged."

I made a "So?" gesture.

"Yeah," he said. "Doesn't mean anything, all by itself. But he's got some very heavy plays going in nonprecious metals. And he borrowed against his own holdings to go that deep. If copper jumps, he's in megabucks. If it goes the other way, he could have to sell off some big pieces. Moneymaking pieces."

I spread my arms, palms turned to the ceiling.

"Who knows?" he answered my unspoken question. "Maybe got word of something. Maybe he's gone all Hunt brothers — remember what those loons tried to do with silver? — and wants to corner the market so he can set the price. He doesn't need the money, and the risk *looks* stupid, but . . ."

I made a fist, extended the little finger and the thumb, held it to my ear.

"I don't have a direct line for him," the man behind the desk said. "But I can certainly get him *on* the line; he'd return my call. You want me to tell him he should speak to . . . whoever?"

I shook my head "no."

"Would a home address help?"

I gave him the same answer.

"He doesn't have the kind of . . . interests

301

I do," the man who owed me offered.

I made my wrist limp, asking the obvious question.

"No. I don't mean that. It's just that he's a straight arrow. Wife, four kids. Church. Doesn't get out much. Or around. Far as I could find out, anyway . . . without making anyone curious. Sorry. I wish I could have been more help."

I made a "no big deal" gesture, walked out, took the elevator down forty-eight floors, walked to the El, and caught the three o'clock to LaGuardia.

◆

Nothing makes people more outraged than being wrong. A few years back, I was in a bar, waiting for a man who said he had a job for me. Michelle was there, too — not only is she the perfect cover, the job was the kind of thing she'd be in on if we took it.

We were there early. Too early, as it turned out. Michelle was looking past my shoulder when she saw someone coming, signaled me it wasn't our man but someone *she* knew.

The woman was big-city pretty, about as fresh-faced as a Kabuki dancer, indigo cocktail dress, black-pearl necklace, perfect manicure, no rings. She slipped into Michelle's side of the booth, hip-checking her way into the spot facing me.

"Who is *this*, girl?"

"My brother," Michelle said, sweetly. "My big brother."

"Oh!" Meaning: she'd heard the stories. But she made a little gesture to summon the waiter, ordered a gimlet — "Absolut Mandarin, please" — and settled in.

I looked at my watch, telling Michelle we had a half hour, tops.

The girl — "If Michelle's not going to introduce me, I guess I'll have to do it myself. I'm Tommi" — was asking Michelle about people she hadn't seen in a while. I tuned out. Until I heard Tommi say, "I voted for Nader. I mean, really, there was no difference between Gore and Bush, anyway."

"I hope you remember that the *next* time you need an abortion, bitch!"

Michelle was still giving off steam long after Tommi jumped up and split like the place was about to be raided.

"I'm sorry, baby," Michelle said. "It's just that —"

I held one finger to my lips, nodded my head up and down to tell her I understood.

And I did. None of us can vote. We're not

citizens. But we can't figure out how citizens can't be bothered to. Or, worse, throw their vote away so they can say something they think is precious-special in their blogs.

Like the Prof always says: Nothing you can do about being born stupid, but *volunteering* for that job means you need a proctologist, pronto.

Sure, politicians are whores. But even in a whorehouse, you'd want to pick your own, right?

And certain whores, you pay them enough, they'll do anything. Even the right thing. I still remember Michelle bursting into Mama's holding a copy of the newspaper in her hand. She was always beautiful — that day, she was incandescent, glowing with joy.

"Look!" she yelled, too excited to say anything more.

We all gathered around, staring at the story she was pointing to. And felt it pulsate through us all . . . together. A law had just been passed that closed the "incest loophole" forever. Used to be, in New York, you fuck a neighbor's baby, you were going *under* the jail. But if you fucked your *own* baby, you'd probably never see the inside of a criminal court. Maybe, if the case was *real* serious, they *might* bring you down to Family Court, that secret room where the predator gets "therapy" and the victim gets fucked. Again. By everyone.

Say some maggot sneaks into a ten-year-old girl's bedroom one night and tells her to suck his cock or something terrible will happen. That's Rape One, a Class B felony, with a twenty-five-year top. But if the maggot is smart enough to grow his own victim, and does the exact same thing to his ten-year-old daughter, then the DA could charge him with "incest." And *that* was a Class E felony . . . meaning, even if he was convicted, they could still just put him on probation.

Happened all the time. Very clear message: Children are property. You can't mess with your neighbor's property — that's holy — but you can do whatever you feel like doing with your own.

And now that beast was dead.

"How the hell did *this* happen?" I asked Michelle, still shaking inside because New York finally, after all those years, had called incest what it's *always* been — rape.

"I know," she said, as gleeful as a little girl with a new doll. "There's this PAC — you know, political-action committee, like the NRA or the AARP or whatever — and all it cares about is protecting kids. It's called the

National Association to Protect Children, okay? Anyway, they put this huge package together . . . the whole works. I saw the boss of the New York chapter on TV — *gorgeous* Asian girl — and you could just tell, she was in this to the death. I don't know how they got it done, but who cares?"

"Amen!" from the Prof.

I looked over at Max. He put both hands over his heart.

Mama came over. Read the story in silence. Then she stood up, walked to her register. When she came back, there was a wad of cash on the table.

"Yes!" Michelle said. And instead of crying about how this came too late for any of us, my steel-hearted little sister said, "Ante up! I saw their site on the Web: <protect .org>. It shows how to join. We can't do that. But that machine runs on money, and I've got the deposit slip right here."

She pulled a FedEx box out of her giant purse, already addressed. You're not supposed to send cash that way, but our kind don't play by your rules.

I couldn't wait much longer, but I couldn't come up with a way in. A guy with "office help" like Reedy had wouldn't answer his own door at home. Or even open his own mail.

Going backdoor didn't appeal to me, which was why I rejected the Chicago guy's offer to set it up so that one of the others would take my call. Too many ways that could go wrong. Reedy was the only one I had anything on to tie him into the killing, not counting Thornton's nonexistent tape.

"A straight arrow" is what the Chicago guy had called Bender. Said he was leveraged heavy, too. I get him to take my call, first thing he does is run to Reedy.

I replayed my debriefing of Thornton in my head. All it did was remind me of questions I hadn't asked. The plans those three punks had for that little girl, was that some sort of collective enterprise, or one leader and two followers? Was this a *folie à trois* crime, or the kind one of them would have done on his own?

If Reedy was the power man in a triad, using Bender as a messenger was all wrong. Prison taught me that. There's killers who'll draw the line at torture . . . but no torturer will ever draw the line at murder. If the whole plan had been Reedy's, Bender's family was going to be cashing life-insurance policies.

307

And if Bender was cash-poor, he wasn't any good to me, anyway.

The other one — Henricks — was in Europe somewhere. Not relocated; on business. I only knew that because *The Wall Street Journal* had a little squib about him meeting with some big players in the Netherlands — neutral territory? — about putting together a consortium to run a natural-gas pipeline from the Russian icelands all the way down to a Y pipe. One channel to go to countries where they paid in euros, the other to one that paid in anything you wanted, from warplanes to harvested organs.

Reedy.

I thought of something Wesley told me once. "It's easier to take a man's life than his money. He don't always carry his money around with him, but you can put the crosshairs on him wherever he goes."

◆

I was walking down lower Fifth, between the New School and the Arch, when I heard a cell phone go off. Knew it wasn't mine — that one is always set to "vibrate" when I'm working.

I saw a homeless guy, sitting on an old army blanket, his back to a building, holding a sign, THE VA THREW ME OUT!, hand-lettered on a piece of cardboard, a dented coffee can in front of him for contributions. He furtively looked both ways, reached inside his olive-drab jacket with a name stenciled on a piece of tape over his heart, and pulled out a fold-flat cell.

"I'm at *work,* bitch!" I heard him growl as I passed by.

"Feel anything, Gate?"

"Just that it's wrong, boss."

"Wrong, like in . . . off?"

"When is a fucking skinner *not* 'off,' man?" Gateman half snarled. "I haven't looked at the whole thing, just what the kid brought down for me, but . . . I don't get what you're saying."

"I don't know if I'm saying anything," I admitted. "Just feeling it."

"This all came out of some evidence locker?"

"Yeah."

"Cops," Gateman said. Saying it all. There could be pieces missing. Pieces we'd never see.

"I think they went for it, Gate."

"I kinda think they did, too, boss."

"Yeah?" I said, frankly curious. "How come?"

"Nobody ever got jugged, right? Girl like that, crime like that, *town* like that, that's heavy pressure. If they weren't really looking to do the right thing, how hard could it be to come up with a George Whitmore?"

I slapped Gateman's held-out palm; hard, signifying complete agreement. The "Career Girl Murders" had shocked New York back in 1963. Daughters of the rich and famous, found raped and murdered in their own apartment. A headline story, so big that it pushed the surrender of a gutter thug who had helped kill two cops in a bar for the fun of it down to the second lead. That murder had been in Jersey, but the punk had given himself up in New York, where he and his partner had run to, looking for a place to disappear. His partner had made the other choice: they put enough bullets into him to stock a lead mine.

Months went by before some cop got a mentally impaired black man named George Whitmore to confess to the Career Girl Murders. Big press conference. Medals and promotions. But it only took a few more months for some investigative reporters to figure out Whitmore couldn't have done it. We're not talking about CSI stuff here —

Whitmore was in another state at the exact time the sex murders were taking place. The only "evidence" was his confession, which was about as believable as a used-car salesman deep into a nasty loan shark over his gambling debts telling you the odometer was accurate.

But just in time — before the papers started calling for deep investigations into "police practices" — they caught the "right" guy, a dope-fiend burglar named Robles.

Well, they didn't actually "catch" him. What happened was that a three-time felony loser got popped for a homicide of another street-level dealer. This was when they still had the electric chair in Sing Sing, and this guy knew he was a prime candidate. He told the law that Robles had confessed to *him,* and he wanted to trade. Told a great story, about bloody clothes and a knife he had disposed of. Did such a great job of it that nobody could ever find them. So the cops wired him *and* his apartment, and waited for Robles to admit everything.

When they got tired of waiting, they arrested Robles. A few months later, New York abolished the death penalty. By then, it was such common knowledge that Whitmore had been framed, people finally realized an innocent man could be executed. The abolition vote wasn't even close.

Robles was convicted. Nobody down here thinks he did it, either. But, more than forty years later, he's still up in Attica.

Supposedly, he finally "admitted the whole thing." None of us bought that one, either. Oh, we believe he said it, but we know who he said it *to* — the Parole Board. By then, Robles had been jugged for at least twenty years, and he'd learned the convict's Three "R"s for dealing with the Parole Board: Remorse. Repent. Release. If you don't say the first word, nobody even listens to the rest.

Where I come from, the cops always get their man. Whether it's *the* man isn't always top priority.

Anyone who thinks there's only one law in this city is a tourist. Whitmore had been convicted of other crimes — all on "confessions" — so the man who became district attorney of Brooklyn, Eugene Gold himself, personally petitioned the court for the poor bastard's immediate release. I still remember reading how Gold said the evidence "renders the case so weak that any possibility of conviction is totally negated."

Years later, Eugene Gold — yeah, the same one — gets charged with aggravated rape of a child, a ten-year-old girl. Happened in Nashville, when he was attending a convention. The victim was a prosecutor's daughter. Gold pleaded guilty to "fondling," and the court gave him "probation and treatment." He was on the next plane to Israel.

I remember that one because I showed the paper to the Mole. Got a blank stare for my efforts.

Yeah. Citizens read the news. But we know the truth.

◆

"Dad wants to see you," Terry greeted me as I walked into my place.

"So why didn't he just — ?"

"Just you," the kid said, not happy about it.

"What's with the mope, dope?" the Prof asked him, not looking real happy himself.

"I can't say anything to Mom."

"There are things I could never tell my mother, mahn," Clarence put in, trying to smooth things.

"Did your *father* ever tell you that?" Terry shot back.

"You know I didn't have no —"

"But I do," Terry said fiercely. "A mother *and* a father. Never once did my dad tell me not to say anything about . . . anything. Ever."

Max touched his heart, made the sign for "child." Pointed at the daughter who was not there, put his finger to his lips. Nodded forcefully. Meaning: Sometimes, it's better to keep things from your mother. And he'd asked his beloved Flower to do that himself.

None of this was doing Terry any good.

My turn. "What happens if Michelle finds out I'm going to meet the Mole, kid?"

"She'd have to . . . Ah, I'm just stupid!"

"The day *you* stupid is the day I join the Klan," the Prof scoffed. "Listen to Burke, boy. He knows the road."

"A man's entitled to his privacy," I said, in a just-the-facts voice. "So is a woman. You give up that in one of two ways. Voluntarily — that's why you're in my house; because *I* gave you the address — or when they take it from you. Those of us who had it taken, we know how precious it is. The Mole not wanting Michelle to know something, that does *not* mean he's keeping secrets from her, understand?"

"I . . . guess so," said the young man, still scared. Even the word "secret" made him tremble in places he wished he didn't have. But he knew his secrets weren't secrets to me, so he listened. And trusted.

"Can you even *imagine* the Mole getting some on the side?"

This time, the kid finally laughed. "Mom would —"

"And dig his fool ass up and do it all over again," the Prof confirmed.

"This isn't them, Terry," I told him. "It's something between me and the Mole. Something we've had working for a while."

"About this?" the kid said, waving his hand to indicate the big room, papered with the photocopies of the police file on the rape-murder of a little girl that happened way before Terry had been born.

"Yes," I said, lying now. The Mole had already turned over everything. I'd done my part, and his people had done theirs. So I, for real, didn't know what he wanted. But making sure Michelle didn't get involved meant it was something that could end ugly.

"But Mom already knows about —"

"Your mother doesn't know it all," I said, very quietly. "A man has the right to protect his wife. That's his *job,* okay?"

"And a good son respects his father," Clarence added.

Not a single person in that room thought he was talking about bloodlines.

"I'll drive you," Terry said.

Figuring the Mole wouldn't have gone through Terry if he hadn't wanted the kid involved somehow, I went along for the ride. I knew something was hard-core the minute the kid pointed at a beige Toyota Camry sedan, a car about as noticeable in this city as pigeons on the sidewalk.

It was getting dark when we approached the junkyard. This time, Terry just drove on in instead of walking, so I knew the anonymous Toyota wasn't going to be my ride back.

The Mole was waiting for us. Simba, too.

We took our seats. The Mole turned slightly to face his son. "Burke has taught you pattern recognition?" Social preamble was a foreign language to him, but that didn't throw Terry at all; he knew his father.

"Well, I know about it. Clarence and I —"

"Not pattern-recognition *software*," the Mole cut him off. "Not for catching criminals, for decoding. Application of logic."

"I —"

"Did Bush believe Iraq had weapons of mass destruction?"

"How could anyone know what he *believed*?" Terry shot back, showing his credentials.

"I know," the Mole said, showing his. "And you should, too." No contest.

"But how could I — ?"

"If Iraq did have weapons of mass destruction, what would they have done, the moment they were invaded?" he asked.

"Fired them off," Terry said, no hesitation. "That's what happened the last time. Those SCUD missiles."

"Yes. And where were they aimed?"

"At Israel."

"Did Israel retaliate?"

"I . . . I don't think so."

"No," the Mole said, his voice shifting subtly. "And why not?"

"Because . . . because they had a deal with us? And, anyway, the war was over so quick that —"

"Because those missiles were counterfeits," his father interrupted. The Mole hated speculation, but he loved crushing it with the pile-driver of logic. "The consequence of tyranny is that such a country never develops its own thinkers. When great minds are discovered, instead of being nurtured, they are eliminated. That butcher bought his weapons from Russian outlaws, but none of his own people had the skill to check their viability. So he *hired* people to do that, the way a man who can't get a woman to love him buys sex. And smart whores always tell customers whatever they want to hear. So the experts he hired told Saddam they were in good working order. It wasn't just for the money; they knew what would happen to them if they responded any other way. Do you understand?"

Terry nodded. Said, "If those missiles had actually worked, if a lot of people died, then Israel would have —"

"Correct," the Mole said. "Now imagine if, instead of mere explosives, Israel had been hit with chemical and biological weapons. The key word is not 'destruction,' it is *'mass'* — do you understand that, too?"

"Like what happened when Hitler . . . ?"

"Leolam Lo Odd," I said.

The Mole nodded, gravely. "If Israel were hit with such weapons, Iraq would have disappeared."

"Nuclear?" the kid said, just short of shocked. "That could start a —"

"Holocaust?" the Mole spat bitterly. "Is that the word you search for? Listen to me, my son. For a Jew, better the whole planet vanish than we go back to the camps. Nobody doubts our commitment to this. Otherwise, Israel would not still exist."

"So, if Bush thought Iraq actually *had* the weapons, he never would have invaded!"

the kid said, angry himself now. "He would have been the man who kicked off a nuclear war. Instead of a hero, he'd be a . . ."

"Pattern recognition," the Mole said.

"Is it . . . teachable?" the kid asked, back to the cold-logic place in his mind that always comforted him.

"You can teach almost anyone to play chess," his father answered. "How many become grand masters?"

"So it's a . . . gift?"

"At its highest levels, yes. One can learn all that can be taught, but the top of the mountain is only for those who have the gift."

"You have the — ?"

"Me?" the Mole said, quietly. "No. I can apply logic and reason. But I don't *sense* things; I have to work them through. Your uncle, *he* is the gifted one. So you learn from both of us, yes?"

"That's what I've been doing," Terry assured him. "But if it takes —"

"Oh, you have the gift, my son," the Mole assured him. "It probably comes from your mother."

The kid stayed outdoors with Simba as I followed the Mole downstairs. When we were seated, the underground man faced me squarely, as if we were going to fight, not talk.

"You think my devotion is blind, yes?"

"To Michelle? Don't be —"

"Stop!"

I spread my hands in a "What the . . . ?" gesture.

"You think I would do anything for my people," the Mole said, an edge to his voice I'd never heard before. "And you are not wrong."

"That's not news."

"But I never had to make a choice," he said. "You are my brother. Just as Terry is my son. And Michelle is my wife. Yes?"

"How else could it be?" I said. When the Children of the Secret form a family, blood-lines never count. And that's not just for us: if Malcolm X could say he hated every drop of white blood in him, couldn't this Felton guy Claw had told me about hate every drop of black blood in himself, too?"

"Everybody trades. Even allies. They bargain, they make deals."

"Not between us. Not in our family."

"Yes," he said, sadly. "I know. And I am ashamed."

"Mole, I don't get this. *Any* of this. You think I'm mad because you held back the files until your people saw I got the job done?"

"I looked at the files," he said, refusing to take his eyes off mine. "You are . . . back. When we first —"

"Yeah. I know."

"Yes. *You* know. But me, the man who taught you *'Leolam Lo Odd,'* maybe I never taught you the meaning."

" 'Never again.' "

"A slogan. It actually means we are never to *forget.* That does not mean just building memorials or writing history books. It is literal. I know why you wanted those files."

"I never said —"

"I know my own brother," the Mole said. "I know the man who brought me my son. I know why. And I have been guilty of forgetting all that."

"Look, Mole, I never —"

"An apology is words, not behavior," he cut me off. "And only behavior can be the truth." He reached behind him without taking his eyes off me, pulled something off his workbench, and handed it to me.

"What the hell is this?" I asked him, holding a dull-gray box, maybe five times the size of a cell phone, with twin antennas in the closed position.

"It is many things," the Mole answered. "It is a satellite phone, with an embedded harmonizer and a GPS-diverter."

"Huh?"

"When you speak into this phone, your voice will be digitally reprocessed — broken apart and reassembled. It will not be *your* voice, but it will be a human voice. Even if recorded, voiceprinted, subjected to stress analysis, it will be as unique as a snowflake, and just as untraceable.

"The diverter will retriangulate any trace attempt. The caller's number will not be blocked, so the person being called will recognize it on their Caller ID and know it is authentic. But their equipment — *any* equipment they have — will tell them the call is coming from . . . well, from random places. You cannot set the diverter yourself, so their trace will show the call as coming from anywhere at all — from next door to the other side of the world."

"What do I need this for?"

"Open it up," the Mole commanded.

I did. It looked like a big fat phone: keypad, viewing screen, the usual.

"I still don't see . . ."

"The buttons are pre-set," the Mole said. "That is one reason it is so heavy. If you press '88,' you have approximately two-point-five seconds before a charge ignites. Like Semtex, but much more potent. That is one reason it is so heavy, the shaped charge inside. Anything within a fifty-yard radius is unlikely to survive. As they get closer, and the space they occupy is more enclosed, the possibility of survival drops to below measurable."

"So it's a bomb. Why all the — ?"

"You can press remotely, if you are connected at the time," he went on, as if I hadn't spoken. "Understand?"

"If anyone I'm on the line with presses that '88,' I vaporize. Why set it up that — ? Never mind," I said, interrupting myself as I began to understand what the Mole had built.

"If you press '11,' " he continued, in the same patient voice you use when you're making *sure,* "the screen becomes a receptor — a real-time receptor — and the person dialing *into* it can send whatever image they wish."

"Mole . . ."

"There are other button combinations, too," he rolled on, inexorably. "For proof, you will use '22' and then '23.' "

"Proof? Of what?"

"I will explain, be patient," he said. "If you press '33,' it will ring the personal cell phone of one Carlton John Reedy. He is the only person to carry that phone, and only a few *highly* trusted individuals have the number. This does *not* include his wife, his children, his mistress, or his friends. If that number rings, he *will* answer it."

"Son of a bitch!" I shook my head at the power of what my brother had just handed me. "I knew you could build a bang-machine this small, Mole. But that number —"

He held up his hand, meaning "Enough!" as clearly as if he had shouted it.

◆

"Your father is a real man," I said to Terry on the drive back in the kid's tC.

"You think I need you to tell me that?" the kid snapped at me. The Mole was right — he had his mother in him, all right.

"No," I said. "I just felt the need to say it out loud, and you were the only one here."

"I'm sorry, Burke. I know you weren't —"

"And I never would, T."

I levered my bucket seat so it was almost reclining, closed my eyes.

After a few minutes, Terry turned on the radio. Must have had a satellite hookup, because doo-wop flowed from the speakers.

Some things never die. Dion always was a bluesman, even back in the day. I hear he's doing the traditional stuff now. Not walking a new road, going back to where he'd never known he'd started from.

But this was some weird station the kid had tuned to. The play list was all covers: the Cadillacs' version of "Gloria" going back-to-back with the one by the Passions, the Willows and the Diamonds both with "Church Bells May Ring," then "Will You Love Me Tomorrow" by the Shirelles, followed with a version by what sounded like Kathy Young and the Innocents. I recognized "There's No Other Like My Baby" by the Crystals, but the next version rang through like Rosie and the Originals. I thought they'd only done one record — I flashed on me and Flood, slow-dancing to Rosie's "Angel Baby," just after she dueled a freak to the death. His.

"Love You So" always hit me. A teenage girl sent me the lyrics when I was locked down as a kid. Only she sent them as a poem. It wasn't until later that I realized those weren't her words. Or her feelings. That was the Ron Holden version. But the cover by Little Isidore and the Inquistors didn't touch me at all.

When "A Thousand Miles Away" came on, I came out of my altered state. Something about . . . then it hit me. Shep and the Limelights. Or the Heartbeats, whatever they were calling themselves back then. They'd earned their way in the same way Magic Sam had: you didn't get to do one of Alan Freed's live shows unless you could deliver the mail, and the crowd at the Apollo was downright savage if you showed weak.

"Shep" was James Sheppard. His textured lead vocals are a model for doo-wop revivalists to this day. But *his* day was over real quick. They found his body on the Van Wyck Expressway in Queens one January morning in 1970. He'd been beaten with ugly precision, then stripped. Maybe it was the blows, maybe he froze to death. Another murder, never solved. I wondered if anyone was looking for the killers.

◆

"Who's sponsoring this flimflam, Western Union?" I heard the Prof sneer as Terry and I walked in.

I guessed they were all taking a break, sprawled around the TV, watching a boxing match. At least the Prof was limiting his running commentary to his disgust with fighters who telegraph their punches, and not still trying to talk Max into entering one of those "ultimate fighting" leagues. I'd heard him pitch that proposition a dozen times. Every time, Max would show him how deaf he could *really* get.

"You got money on this one?" I asked, finding myself a seat.

"Money? I don't bet on pig races, School-boy. Only mystery in this fight is which one of those out-of-shape slobs gasses out first. This is so pathetic, motherfuckers be changing channels even if it was pay-per-view."

"I got something . . ." I started to say, just as one of the fighters collapsed to the canvas from a slow-motion left hook to his flabby side-pillow. His opponent staggered to a neutral corner, sucking in huge gulps of air through his mouth.

The Prof waved a disgusted hand at the screen, hit the "mute" without waiting for the count.

"We got a shot?" he said, turning to me.

"Yeah. Just an idea I'm working on," I told him, signing to Max by tapping my temple.

"Let it cook till you can set the hook," the Prof answered. Meaning: whatever I had, I didn't need to say it in front of Terry.

I nodded agreement. "I need to go over those files again."

"If we just knew what you were looking for, mahn . . ."

"I can't know that," I explained. Again. "But when I see it, I'll know."

"It has to be there for you to see it," Terry tossed in. His father's son.

"Dog hears a whistle you can't," the Prof said. "What's that mean, there wasn't no whistle at all?"

"Okay," the kid said, throwing up his hands.

◆

"The soup is the best you ever made," I said to Mama.

She shrugged, but the faint pink that suffused her cheeks was the truth-teller.

The Prof raised his mug — a white one, with BARNARD in bright-red letters — in agreement.

"This could never be duplicated," Clarence echoed.

Max tapped his heart twice, either in appreciation of the soup or of the fact that, from the moment his daughter Flower had chosen to attend Barnard, Mama switched from her traditional small bowls to the mugs that displayed her granddaughter's achievement.

The mugs were for family only, same as the soup. Hell, it *should* be — we'd all been kicking in a piece of every score "for baby's college" since Flower had been born. I figure the kid had enough cash in there to attend grad school on Mars, and come home on holidays, too.

I ran down what the Mole had given me. They all listened in silence until I was done.

"So it ain't just Terry that's out," the Prof said. "Our girl can't play, no way."

"Right."

"So we're down to four."

"Claw could play a role," I suggested. I'd never told any of them about how he already had.

"Those boys are all dogs," the Prof dismissed the idea. "And the only trick I want any of them to do is play dead."

"I'm not saying take him in with us, Prof. But when you've got a man with nothing to lose . . ."

"We ain't gonna get but this one shot. That's *if* the man even picks up the line."

"He will," I said, maybe with a little more confidence than I felt. "But he's a wild card. We need them to come up with a *lot* of cash. And, from what I heard in Chicago, Bender may be illiquid."

"Stuck in a paper rut," the Prof translated for Clarence, as I signed the situation out for Max.

"Not only that, but Henricks may be out of reach, at least for a while."

"So you think this one guy is going to come up with enough to cover all their tabs?"

"I don't know. Don't care. I know he *can*. And we all know that he's still good for the murder. He was sixteen when they did it, remember?"

"When you gonna call?" the little man said, giving in.

"Soon as you buy into us bringing Claw in. The best I'm going to get out of a call is a meet. And it won't be in any back alley, or waterfront warehouse. We need a man who can work close."

"Who's better than Max?" the Prof demanded.

"Who's going to stick out more in the kind of place we want Thornton to trust?" I shot back.

"All white is all right," he said, giving in.

The phone was picked up on the third ring.

"Where are you calling from?" a voice demanded. A boss, expecting a subordinate.

"That doesn't matter," I said, through the harmonizer. "I'm not who you expected."

He made a sound I couldn't translate.

"But you know me," I went on. "I called at your office a little while back. Left my business card."

"If this is some kind of —"

"You know what this is 'some kind of,' Reedy. This is a call from a professional problem-solver."

"And that's you?" he said, coolly, fully recovered, back in control.

"That's me. Not the name on the business card I left. That, that was the message."

"Message?" Playing for time now.

"You've got this . . . condition. You've had it for over thirty years. Every time you think you've gotten rid of it, it shows up out of nowhere. You pay the doctor bills and it goes away. But that's just remission — there's never been a permanent antidote. Like, say, a tapeworm. Either you get the whole thing cut out, or there's always the chance it could go back to feeding on you."

"I don't have a clue —"

Word games. He heard the "tape" in "tapeworm" clear enough. And wasn't going to put himself on another one.

"Thing is, I do. But that's not what matters. What matters is that I've got the antidote. The *permanent* antidote. And it comes with the kind of guarantee you can take to the bank."

"And I'd have to *rob* a bank to buy this 'antidote,' I suppose?" Just enough sarcasm in there to distance himself from anything resembling self-incrimination. You get as rich as he was, dealing with extortionists comes with the territory.

"There's a cost for the service, naturally. But, obviously, that cost should be split three ways."

"You don't know what you're talking about."

"We've got him," I said. "Understand? *Got* him. We don't want to keep tapping a vein like he's been doing. We want a quick in-and-out. Yeah, a big one. But, like I said, a permanent one, too."

"Even if something were to happen to . . ." Still vague enough to stay on his side of the line, but he wanted whatever information I was willing to give up.

"I said a guarantee, and I meant it."

"Spell it out."

"Over a cell phone?"

"Leave a number; I'll call you back."

"You have the number."

"On that card?"

"No. The one on your screen now."

I hit the "end" button in the middle of whatever he was about to say.

"Need a meet," I told the cancer-man.

"Just say —"

"Northeast corner, Houston and Thompson. Two hours enough to get there?"

"Half that."

"Done. One hour. Hail the cab with the Off Duty light on."

"He's not going to do it," Claw said. He was sitting next to me in the Plymouth's passenger seat. Max was behind him. Clarence lounged against the front fender, showing the world a long black coat topped by a Zorro hat; his right hand rested inside his coat. The Prof was leaning against the trunk, facing out, his sawed-off against his chest, dangling from a rawhide loop, only half concealed by the white cattleman's duster that came to his ankles. In this part of Red Hook, we didn't want anyone mistaking us for DEA. Or a scouting party for a new player.

"Sure, he will," I assured him. "Once we explain the scam, he'll love it."

"Didn't you learn anything Inside?"

"Just because he's . . . what he is . . . doesn't make him stupid. But anyone who plays him for that sure the fuck is."

"Now you want to rank me, too?"

"I've treated you like a man from the beginning, pal. You want to do your elder-statesman number on someone, go find some skinheads. No, wait: didn't your boy Pierce — his wife was Latina, but I guess the leader gets to make his own rules, right? — didn't he say they were all a bunch of morons and animals?"

"All I'm saying —"

"You're not here because I want your advice," I told him, not raising my voice. "You're not my partner. You came with a proposition. I bought in because you came with references. But you're a role-player, got it? This is a job, not a consensus-building exercise. And where there's a job, there's a boss. That's me. Not you, me. You're out of your league here. I don't have a green shamrock on my hand, but I already *spent* a lot of green on this. It's my money on the blanket, so I get to throw the dice."

"It's your money, yeah," he said, "but it's my life."

"Your life? What's that to me? My word to my brother, that's what means something. And if that's not enough for you, just walk your own road. Starting right now."

"You know I can't just —"

"You can't do *anything* with me and my crew. You proved yourself with a man I trust. You proved yourself with me, that last thing we did. I know your clock is ticking, okay? But think about it: whatever Silver told you about me, there's one thing I *know* he said."

"Yeah?"

"Yeah. He told you I can get things done."

The AB man nodded, not arguing.

"You're not going to be the one to talk Thornton into the play. That's my job. But you've got to make sure he carries it through."

"But what if he — ?"

"He'll fucking *love* it," I promised. "But I need to talk with him first."

"I can get —"

"Not yet. I'm not ready. But soon, understand?"

"I got it," he said, holding my eyes. "I got it, boss."

"You own this?" I asked the green-eyed beige man behind the wheel of a dark-turquoise Maserati Quattroporte.

"All of it," the man said, moving his index finger in a 180-degree arc. I was looking at acres of razed land. The only building left standing was a one-story lump of cinder-block that had probably been the staging area for the operation that had done all the wrecking work on the rest of the assembly plant that once had covered all that empty ground.

Another one of those "Enterprise Zone" projects with enough minority names on the paper to score the government contract. You know, the ones that were going to revitalize the community with jobs, vocational training, affordable housing. . . .

Sections of chain-link were still standing, Y-shaped at the top to hold the coiled razor wire. Looked like what was left of a demolished prison.

The driver was a slim, elegantly dressed man, with a complexion models would kill for. Only his marcelled hair gave a clue to his age.

"Electricity still hooked up in there?" I asked him.

"It's *nice* in there, man. Got A/C, heat, carpeting, big bathrooms. Even dish TV. Better than plenty of places folks could ever hope to live in."

"Or die in."

He tapped the custom wood wheel with pianist fingers. A heavy emerald ring caught the fading light. "This, this squares us? For real, I'm off the list?"

I nodded, said, "You got security on this parcel?"

"Twenty-four/seven."

"Patrol, or live-in?"

"Nothing *to* patrol. But this neighborhood, junkies will tear up pavement just for the copper."

"Dogs?"

"To keep off some junkies? No way. Dogs, you either got to keep them behind a fence, or you need a man who can handle them. Just a waste of money."

"How much notice would you need?"

"About ten minutes, man. I touch the right button, that place empties like it was on fire. And nobody comes back until I touch another button."

"Show me."

"Now?"

"Right this minute."

"All I got is your word that —"

"You'll get more than that," I told him. "We do this thing now, you get the name of the person who paid to —"

"Wait," he said, holding up his hand. A white French cuff shot out from his sleeve, displaying his initials, monogrammed in green thread. "If I was on . . . the list, how come I'm still . . . ? I mean, nobody's even *tried*. And word is, your . . . well, that he's gone, man. I mean, it was on TV and all."

Wesley had been gone a long time. But nobody knew. Not for-sure, bet-your-life knew. And that's just what you'd be doing. Even the whisper-stream current that said Wesley's ticket had been canceled said that he'd done the job himself. Nobody else could have.

My ghost brother. And I still had Wesley's book. Not just the jobs he'd done — every detail, from who paid to how much to what he'd used to make it happen — but also the contracts he still hadn't executed before he'd left.

The green-theme man behind the wheel had been one of those. Wesley had gotten his usual half up front. Maybe whoever had paid so much for his finale was still waiting for it to happen.

He wouldn't be waiting much longer. I said his name.

338

"Quinones?! He thinks, I'm gone, he could actually *run* things? Man is insane! We let him play *el cacique* for so long, he forgets it's just a role."

I shrugged.

"Hold up. If Quinones paid for me to be taken off, why didn't it happen? Everyone knows —"

I cut him off with a silent chop of my hand. I knew what he was going to say: the one crime Wesley would never be charged with was *attempted* murder.

"It wasn't supposed to happen until after the *next* round of elections," I said, with a "Get the point, fool?" raise of my eyebrows as I spoke.

"Cock*sucker!* That fits. That *gusano* always did love his dominos."

I said nothing.

"So he's *not* gone?"

"Ask Quinones."

"I'm *gonna* ask him."

I wasn't worried about Quinones telling the truth. I knew he'd deny everything. The man sitting next to me had another trademark besides the color green: anyone he wanted answers from got wired to a battery first. Quinones had a quadruple bypass last year, while he was "fact-finding" in Puerto Rico on the taxpayers' dime. The first jolt would be more than enough.

"It's perfect," I told the Prof. "Got everything we need."

"Almost," the little man said. "But we can bring that."

I didn't say anything.

"You calling in a lot of markers for this one, Schoolboy."

"These are bad people, Prof. All wolves, no tickets."

"Yeah, yeah. I got it. But I ain't lame enough to think all this is about a money game, son."

"You love me?"

"What kind of stupid — ?"

"Just say it. I want to see if you're still the best liar on the planet."

"Michelle . . ."

"You won't?"

"I love you, honey. You're my baby sister."

"Then why aren't I in on this?"

"I never said —"

"*I* said. I said I was in on it. And you, you've been slipping around ever since."

"It's just not time yet."

"That's not it," she said. "That would never be it. So it can only be one of two things: either you got my husband involved, or my son. I know I can't do anything about *him*" — she half smiled, making it clear she meant the Mole — "but you know the rules."

"Terry's a grown man, honey."

She slapped me so fast I almost didn't see her hand move. When she was on the street, a tiny little tranny with nothing but herself for protection, she'd made a scorpion look slow with that same move. Only, this time, her hand hadn't had a straight razor in it.

"Oh!" was all she said. Then she started to cry.

◆

It was a long time before she let me hold her, wrapping my arm around her like when we were kids, sleeping wherever we could find shelter. "He's *not* in on the hard end, honeygirl. I swear it."

"I . . . I know you wouldn't do that, baby," she said, as soft as a feather. "I know he's . . . helped before. With his mind. But ever since he and Clarence —"

"He's the one teaching Clarence," I said,

341

quickly. Truth, when it came to computers. But the lessons had gone two-way. I warned the kid that if he ever let Michelle see how he could handle a pistol, I'd fucking kill him myself. "This is still about the pattern recognition —"

"Yes, yes," she said, beyond bored.

"His piece is just about over."

"Just about?"

"It's jumping off soon. One way or the other. I set the hook, deep. If the mark calls, he'll want a meet. And he's odds-on to make that call — I already showed him I can find him, and that I've got access to what he wants."

"This meet . . . Terry wouldn't be there?"

"He won't even *know* about it, honey."

"Well," she said, flashing a witch's smile as her long red fingernail tapped against the vein on the underside of my wrist, "I know one way to make sure of that."

"You!?"

"Me," I assured her.

"After all this time, huh? You must want a nice quick fuck. What's the matter, don't have time to troll?"

"Yes or no?"

"How do you know I'm not with some-one?"

"How do you know *I'm* not?"

"Yeah." She chuckled.

There's more than one way to kill time.

Luella probably noticed the thick bulge in the side pocket of my jacket. Probably thought she knew what it was. Sure as hell didn't care.

"Ever going to call me again?" she said, when we finished.

"Sure."

"That's what you said the last time."

"And I *did* call, didn't I?"

"You're such a bastard." Her pout was as real as a Zimbabwe election. "You couldn't even bring me flowers?"

"The shops were all closed," I said, pressing some folded bills between her two silicone mountains. "I was hoping you might be willing to shop for some tomorrow."

◆

"You're sure you got this?"

"Cold," Claw assured me, giving the cinderblock building one more walk-through. "You know anything about Nietzsche?"

343

"You're not going to babble some of that 'whatever doesn't kill you' crap, are you? I know a lot more about your boy than you think. You know where Aryan Paradise was supposed to be? Not in Viking country, in Paraguay. That freak's sister opened a colony there. Naturally, it failed. See, if you want *true* racial purity, you've got to breed true."

"So?" he said, more interested than he wanted to admit.

"So what that means is, you have to breed *back,* get it? Sons fuck their mothers, brothers fuck their sisters. Sound good to you?"

"Look, all I'm trying to tell you —"

"The colony — I think the degenerate whore called it Nueva Germania, get it? — had deep roots. You think it's an accident that Mengele lived in Paraguay? You think he was the only one?"

"What are you now? A Jew, too?"

"My brother is."

"Silver? Get the fuck —"

"I've got a big family."

Claw took a last drag on his cigarette, ground it out on his palm. That didn't impress me — I've seen it before, too many times — but pocketing the butt did. I didn't bother explaining that there wasn't going to *be* any DNA around when we finished.

"Look, man, I don't care if you're a nigger-kike-spic-gook super-mutt. I played it straight, down the line, and I came with references. What else do you want?"

"I already told you. Just spare me the Nazi shit, understand?"

"*You're* the one who's not understanding," he said, dragging deep on his just-lit cigarette. "You said, before, that I thought Thornton was stupid. I know he's not. I know him better than you ever could. Once he sees this" — he reached into his gym bag and pulled out what looked like a miniature version of the Jaws of Life they use to extract car-wreck victims — "he'll be fine. You know why? Because he knows that what doesn't kill you might make you stronger . . . or it might make you wish it *had* killed you."

"What the hell is that thing?"

"It's called an Alligator Lopper. Walk into any hardware store, they'll sell you one. Regular old Black & Decker tool. Perfect for cutting off tree limbs with one hand. Go through bone like it was cardboard."

"So what's so special about — ?"

"It's not the tool, it's the knowledge," he said. "And Thornton knows."

"I'm still not seeing —"

"He knows I'll use it. I'll spell it out for him, exactly how it's going to work. One chop, he faints. Won't even feel the blow-torch I'll use to cauterize the area. When he comes around, he'll still be a freak in his mind, but he won't be able to do anything about it."

"How do you know?"

"I told you. I know *him.*"

"I know he talked to you. You hear something you haven't told me about?"

"It doesn't have anything to do with this job."

Not to you, maybe, I thought. *Or maybe you just told me something about yourself.*

The Mole's special phone rang. Digital readout showed a pictograph of a sweeping searchlight.

"Go," I said.

"You said not over the phone." Reedy. His security people must have told him that a trace would be easier at a time when cellular traffic would be light. Or maybe he just figured I was a man who worked nights.

"Just you and me."

"Of course," he counter-punched with a lie of his own.

"I pick the place. It'll be in downtown Manhattan. This Wednesday."

346

"Just —"

"*You* just be downtown, anywhere below Canal, by noon Wednesday. I'll call then, give you forty-five minutes to get to the spot. I don't want surprises."

"And I'm not walking into some —"

"It'll be outdoors, public place. We'll be two businessmen, doing business. When you see what I've got, we'll only need one more meeting and then we're done."

"You can *prove* — ?"

"If you walk away from the meeting anything but one hundred percent satisfied, you'll never hear from me again."

"I only have your word for that."

"And I'm betting, betting a *lot,* that once you see the property I want to interest you in, you'll buy. You don't want to even *look* at it, that's your choice."

"So if I don't come to this meeting . . . ?"

"Then we're done," I repeated. And hit "end."

◆

"I don't see why we have to keep doing this."

"I'm going to explain that to you," I told Thornton. "I'm going to explain it to you with respect. This is a complex operation,

347

and I need you *with* us on it."

"I already said —"

"Just listen, please," I said.

"I'll be right outside," the AB man assured him. And stepped away, closing the door behind him.

"I thought you worked for Claw," Thornton confronted me, his eyes honed sharp by fear. "How do you get to give him orders?"

"It's not orders," I said, gently, "it's professionalism. Claw's the boss, the shot-caller, Inside or in the World. But let's say he told one of the crew to crack a safe, okay? He wouldn't tell the man *how* to do it. And if the man needed some special tools to do the job, well, the boss would get them for him. This is no different."

"You're no safecracker."

"That's right," I agreed, amicably. "I'm an extortionist. A blackmailer. Whatever you want to call it. All Claw knows about that line of work is 'Pay up or get stuck,' am I right?"

Thornton nodded. When you've been Inside, you know "stuck" means one of two things, and it had been the AB that stood between them both for him. After he paid.

"I told the boss that I can't do my job without another private talk with you first. This is all about finesse, and that's my specialty."

"How much finesse could this take? Either they pay up or I —"

"You want half a million, cash."

"So? That's pocket change to —"

"You think we're all working for *you?*" I asked, almost in a whisper. "Everybody's got to get paid here. If you weren't in so tight with the boss, we could make more just bringing those three guys your head."

"What?!?"

"Think about it," I said, very calmly. "You've got nothing but your word about what happened. You don't have any tape, no photographs, nothing."

It was just a little tic-movement at the right corner of his mouth. But I had been watching his face like it was a cardiogram.

"They'll have left DNA," he said. "If they exhumed the corpse, I'll bet they'd find —"

"On a *skeleton?* After thirty-plus years? You've been watching too much TV. Truth is, we're down to a bluff and a threat. If we had a tape to play for them, that'd make it another game. But with only your word, how much do you think they'd pay us to make sure you never opened your mouth?"

"Claw wouldn't —"

"Now you're getting it. Here's the cold truth, Thorn. If we could vote on this, all of

349

us would rather just offer them your head in a box than go through this fucking dancing around. But the boss said that was off the table. This isn't a democracy. We're Aryan warriors, and there's a chain of command. So we can't touch you. Ever."

I let my eyes shine with the absolute obedience of a Nazi dog . . . a dog who wanted to rip out a throat, but obeyed his master's command to "stay." After all, isn't that what "Master Race" means?

"But you're not sending me in there without putting some more cards in my hand," I went on, nice and well mannered. Always ready to be reasonable. As flexible as piano wire.

"I *still* don't —"

"You remember what your lawyer told you when he first took your case?"

"He told me a lot of things, the miserable piece of —"

"He told you that you had to tell *him* the truth. You didn't have to tell anyone else. Not your wife, not your mother, not the law, even though he was going to advise you to cooperate. Right?"

"He said that, yeah."

"And he told you why?"

"Because, if he got surprised anywhere along the way, I'd be the one who fell through the trapdoor, not him."

"That's it. I don't want to be surprised, Thorn," I said, giving him my "I know. And I *understand*" look. "But, the way I see it, there's no reason for the boss to know."

"Know what?"

"What you're going to tell me. And show me."

"I already told you everything. And I don't have anything to —"

"Let's start with the pictures," I said, my tone free from judgment, as impersonal as typhoid.

"What's this?"

"It's an Internet Tablet, stupid."

"Michelle . . ."

"Think of it as a cell phone with an Internet connection. Wi-fi. Just the thing a businessman like you would be scanning while waiting for a client to show up."

"Why can't I just read a newspaper?"

"Why can't I be a blonde? Oh, wait! I *am* a blonde," she said, tossing her golden mane.

"Jesus H. Christ."

"Oh, just stop! This is a more challenging task for me than usual. No way you are going to out-dress *this* one. And we don't want you to, either. What we're looking for is a no-look look."

"I love you, honey. But you just might be the world's biggest pain in the —"

"*Will* you be quiet? I can overink that tattoo on your hand again" — meaning the hollow blue heart between the last two knuckles of my right hand; my tribute to Pansy, not the temps I sometimes use when I'm working — "but your face will have to go as is. That stage makeup will fool a camera, but it won't stand up to an up-close-and-personal. We're going to have to go jet-black with the hair. And I can extend those eyebrows, too."

"Fine," I said, surrendering, as we both knew I would.

"Charcoal," she finally pronounced. "It's making a comeback, anyway. White shirt, red suspenders —"

"What?"

"Red suspenders. It's the kind of detail people remember. Kind of passé, but you aren't trying to look Wall Street. And a plain blue tie — I'll find the right shade."

"The restaurant is locked?"

"Locked? It's tighter than that, big brother. You didn't know Mama held the paper on it?"

"No," I said. Not surprised, though. Mama hated anything that wasn't working, and money was no exception. She even owned a nice co-op in a building she'd never visit. Cash-purchased it from the girl I'd given the baby I'd taken from Beryl — the most righteous rescue of my life.

Loyal, the baby's new mother, her *real* mother, got the purchase offer for her co-op through Davidson. I don't know who owns it on paper, but I know the current renters are paying through the nose — they wouldn't want the lease on the ID they'd bought from me to get canceled.

"And Max had those crazy boys visit, too."

"Crazy boys" was Michelle-speak for the Blood Shadows, still the most feared of all the Chinatown gangs. Their allegiance to Max was something they could never explain, but so precious to them that their own boss never so much as questioned them about it.

"You know it could get stupid. This guy, I don't even have a guess how he'll play it . . . if he shows at all."

"You think?"

"Enough," I told her, holding up both hands.

The restaurant was one of those "fusion" joints, this one French-Asian. Light food, heavy presentation, short wine list, major attitude. The outdoor patio was small, exclusive, and sidewalk-blocking illegal.

Just four tables out there. I was at the far left corner, alone, consulting my Internet Tablet, waiting for whoever was going to join me. Michelle and Clarence were at the other end, their chairs pulled close enough so they could whisper to each other. Clarence was in subdued peacock mode: metallic threads from his burnt-orange silk jacket sparkling in random patterns whenever he shifted his weight. He looked drab next to Michelle, who was wrapped in a silver-foil sheath, with matching hat and veil.

A passing couple stared at them. The girl tugged the guy with her to a stop just as they came to where I was sitting. He was a man of the world — a veteran of the harsh reality of crime movies — so he broke it down for her. Just a high-class pimp trying to sweet-talk a racehorse whore into switching stables, he explained, swollen with his own coolness.

Maybe he could work the scene into whatever "noir" screenplay he was writing that week.

A gay couple took up the inside table closest to me. Looked like they were celebrating a wedding anniversary. Lots of hand-holding, an occasional kiss.

The table inside Michelle and Clarence was empty, a big RESERVED sign making it clear that there was no point even asking the red-jacketed young Chinese who stood in the open doorway without moving, hands behind his back.

A couple of guys with gym muscles under their nice suits tried anyway. It didn't take long.

I picked up the Mole's phone, hit "33."

"I'm here." Reedy's voice.

I gave him the location — the restaurant's and mine — and killed the call.

I stood up and rotated my head on my neck, two circles in each direction. Just working out the kinks.

The homeless man sprawled against the wall on the other side of the street, wrapped in several layers of blanket despite the weather, may have seen me.

My Internet Tablet was tuned to the wire services. Cambodia's ruler — a former

Khmer Rouge "soldier" who calls himself the Prime Minister now — announced he was banning certain cell phones, because they had the capacity to send video images. His beloved country had to be protected against pornography. After all, what if some innocent child saw such images?

Images. Liberia was once ruled by a dictator who called himself Samuel Doe. He was overthrown by another of his kind, Charles Taylor. Only Taylor's ambitions overreached his borders, and he ended up financing the mass murders in Sierra Leone, an endless slaughter that gave "blood diamonds" the name they carry to this day. Taylor's in The Hague now, awaiting trial for genocide. Nigeria gave him up. They've got oil over there, but they've got to keep up a nice front with the UN, because they might need to crush a rebel movement themselves at any time. Not like the Saudis, who don't have to worry about such things — they let Idi Amin live in one of their castles until he died. Didn't hurt their image a bit.

Images, yeah. Samuel Doe was tortured to death on orders of one of Taylor's freakish followers, with every shriek of agony carefully captured on videotape by a Palestinian "journalist" they invited to watch the fun. Running a dictatorship and reinforcing it with the occasional pogrom is one thing, but Doe's regime had recognized Israel, and supporting the Zionist Oppressor is a crime against all humanity. That tape is "still commercially available," in the words of *The Economist.*

A couple had just been arrested. For the kidnap, torture, rape, and murder of a young girl, all captured on video. By the killers. Another one of those snuff films the blasé bloggers will call an "urban legend," I guess. After all, this was just a home movie, not "produced for commercial purposes," so it doesn't count. And the video, I guess if it shows up on the Internet for free it *still* doesn't count, right?

Image. It's everything.

A couple in Milwaukee — both wealthy physicians — were found guilty of forcing a woman they imported from the Philippines to work sixteen-hour days for less than prisoners are paid to make license plates. She was their slave for nineteen years, but it wasn't prime-time material. After all, she hadn't been a "sex slave." Didn't photograph well, either. Lousy images.

A "team" of humans who paid a fortune so they could add climbing Mount Everest to their "life accomplishment" list came across another climber on their way up.

Looked like he was already too far gone, they said, so they trekked on past, leaving him for dead. They didn't owe the guy anything. They might have saved him, but there wasn't any law against looking the other way. Ask David Cash. But don't try asking a little girl named Sherrice Iverson.

The murderers who run Burma decided Suu Kyi, the woman who won the election the generals had voided with bullets, needed to stay under "house arrest." She won a Nobel Peace Prize more than fifteen years ago, so their decision was sure to spark some heavy discussions in the UN.

Yeah, what a scary thought. There's already four million slaughtered in the Congo, and blue helmets on the ground are about as effective as Tom Cruise working a suicide hotline.

Joseph Kony was a witch doctor–turned–warlord who ran the Lord's Resistance Army, a gang of rape-for-fun, kill-for-kicks zombies. Basic training was simple in that army. They kidnapped children, made them watch a few torture-mutilations, pointed at the bodies, and gave the children a choice: Join us, or join them. Kony started in Uganda, but was now based in the south of Sudan, where he was getting paid to make sure the region stayed destabilized. The

World Court issued a warrant for his arrest. They didn't say who was going to serve it on him.

It sure wasn't going to be the UN — they probably figured their "condemnation" of the use of child soldiers would fix everything. Just like their "oil for food" program had in Iraq. That monument to impotence still thinks that you can hand out food to warlords, and count on them to distribute it . . . after the boss's son gets his cut, of course. Or that a good, stern admonition will deter missile launches. What's their next move: calling for a boycott of genocide?

Besides, Kony can always make a deal. Call off his army of psychotic children, hand over some weapons, go in front of some "Truth and Reconciliation" committee, admit every crime known to humanity, be told he did bad things . . . and be forgiven. Just like going on *Oprah*. Only, instead of some door prize, you get to keep the fortune you've stashed away in a nice "safe" country.

A "reverend" in Illinois was arrested for "disciplining" a twelve-year-old girl. Supposedly, he applied this discipline with a piece of wood, while her mother waited outside the punishment chamber. The mother told the police her daughter had accused a man of sexually abusing her, so she took her for "counseling." This reverend told the mother he'd been a police officer, so he could always tell when a child was lying about sexual abuse, and the "rod" would bring out the truth. The mother thought this was a great idea. When the child wouldn't recant after a month of ritual beatings, it just meant she was stubborn. But when the cops arrested the perpetrator, the mother suddenly got very upset. The holy man begged her not to tell anyone about the fun he'd been having, but her "concern" forced her to tell the cops about that, too. After all, nobody was going to beat *her* for "false allegations." Poor woman — she actually had to change churches after that; the congregation was very upset with her betrayal.

A massacre of women and children by combat troops was reported in Iraq. An investigation is in progress. If someone actually did this, they better pray Big Christian is still in the White House by the time they're found guilty, so he can do the patriotic thing before he leaves office, like Nixon did for Calley, back in the day.

The ACLU was suing some town that passed an ordinance saying registered sex offenders couldn't come within a thousand feet of children's playgrounds. Un-fucking-constitutional! I guess camouflage is a civil right now. Just like the right to videotape.

Harder to tell who's stupider: wet-brains who don't realize that laws like that don't keep freaks away from *private* playgrounds — check out any McDonald's lately? — or imbeciles who believe laws like that actually protect kids.

You know why we hate you? Not because you don't know what we know, but because, even if you did, you wouldn't give a damn.

So I'm sitting here, waiting to commit extortion, and planning a lot worse. I'm what you'd call a career criminal. That's why I'll never be you. And I'm proud of it.

◆

When a Maybach 62 — the chauffeur-only version, in a shade of blue I've never seen in real life — pulled to the curb, I felt a slight drop in tension. The tank-on-wheels may have been fitted with bulletproof glass and armor-plated doors, but it was no getaway driver's car.

The man behind the wheel never left the car. The rear door popped open. The man who climbed out of the backseat was tall, with thick dark hair, worn longer than I would have guessed. His hands were empty.

He looked at me. I nodded. He stepped through the opening in the wrought iron that surrounded the patio and made his way toward me, covering the distance as effortlessly as a shark in a swimming pool.

I stood up as he approached, offered my hand.

He took it. Gave me a "nothing to prove" grip. His hand was dry.

We sat. He had a good-looking, professionally toned face, milk-chocolate eyes, strong chin.

A waiter appeared.

"A drink to start?" I asked Reedy.

"Black," he said to the waiter, holding up two fingers.

"Gordon's," I told him. "Cold, no ice."

The waiter disappeared.

"You know my name. . . ."

"Mine's Gardener," I told him. "A family name."

He made a question out of his expression.

"My family's been in the business for generations. Each one passes on what it learned to the next. Me, I'm the very, very best. I'm such a good gardener that I can do magic tricks with flowers. My specialty is the rose."

"What's so — ?"

"I can create a whole rosebush without a

single thorn. Not by hand-clipping each one off, like some do. I can actually make a rosebush that no thorn can *ever* grow on."

"That does sound like tricky work," he said, as the waiter appeared with our drinks.

"You ready, order?"

"I'll let you know," I told him.

He bowed slightly, disappeared again.

"I heard you might be interested in my services," I said. "But, you know how it is, you find the perfect gardener, you *don't* tell your friends . . . because you don't want him poached, right? So my business doesn't rely on word-of-mouth. I know I have to show each new client what I'm capable of, and I can't expect former clients to be references."

"That sounds like a very difficult business plan to execute," he said, relaxed and casual.

"Not if you have my kind of portfolio."

"Talk isn't a portfolio," he said, glancing at his watch.

"Talking to you on your private cell — was that the kind of 'talk' you meant?"

"Is that it?"

"Not even close. Mr. LeBrock still work for you? Or did you fire him after DrepTech went under?"

"I have no idea —"

"DrepTech's not your problem, is it? Not

even check number 2078. Problem is the credit card LeBrock used to book his flight. And his hotel. And . . . well, you understand, I'm sure. Since you still own the real-estate investment company you set up. Sole owner. Then and now."

He stared at me for a long few seconds.

"And then there's that tape."

"Tape?"

"Good play," I complimented him. "And you're right, either way. Even with the original in your hands, you wouldn't be clear, not for an absolute certainty."

"I don't see where you're going with all this," he said, lowering his voice just a notch.

"The statute of limitations on anything *he* did, that's run out decades ago. He's not at risk. But even if he decided to just . . . disappear from your lives — all three of you, I'm talking about now — you couldn't ever be sure he hadn't left something behind. That's the only reason he's still walking around."

He looked down at his hands, then back up at me.

"But there's a way out. A permanent way. It's so magical, only a true expert could get it done. Am I boring you?"

His eyes burned violence. I smiled. Not a friendly smile — the smile you give another convict who just threatened you.

"What if she was alive? What if he was sent to take her to the hospital, only he decided to have some fun with her instead, and ended up with a corpse on his hands? That does *this*," I said, crossing and re-crossing my wrists to show black turning into white. "No matter what *anyone* might have done back then — all three of you, I mean — the statute has run. Criminal *and* civil."

He kept watching me. His drink as untouched as mine.

"That's my portfolio. His confession. Videotaped in real time. Not under duress. Too much detail for it to be anything but the stone truth. A guilty man, apologizing to innocent boys he put through hell all these years. I mean, they *knew* they hadn't done . . . what happened. But they had trusted the wrong man to help. The wrong man, because he wronged *them*."

"Why would such a person ever . . . ?"

"Why would any of you care? Nobody's ever going to see this confession unless he left a package behind. And if he did — which I can't imagine: who could he ever trust with it, and who'd ever trust *him*, anyway? — the confession ends any problem. Stops it dead in its tracks. Kills it, you might say."

"It's still talk" was all he said, but his voice was wound as tight as a garrote.

"When I said 'real time,' that's what I meant. You bring the price. And whoever you want to protect it. I bring you the show. *Live*. I come alone, and I walk away alone. Me with the price; you with the tape."

"And the — ?"

"He does what a lot of people do when guilt gets too much to bear, is my guess."

"What would an exercise like this cost?"

"Six."

"You can't mean —"

"That's only two apiece. Not one of you would miss it. And all three of you are going to want to be there when it goes down, anyway. See it for yourselves."

"I could probably —"

"Stop it. I'm the best at what I do, but I'm not going up against a master outside my field. This isn't negotiating; this is a specific price for a specific service."

"How long is the offer — ?"

"Why insult me? I haven't insulted you. You want me to explain the enormous expenses involved at my end? Want me to *justify* the price? What I said is not an 'offer.' You want the service or you don't."

"I'd have to reach out . . ."

"Yeah, you would," I said, paper in my

eyes to cover the scissors in his . . . so I could drop the rock if he tried to cut the paper. "Because I'm not selling you something for six that you couldn't sell the others for three each. I didn't just come to you because you're the smartest, or the most successful. You were born May 17, 1959. Ask your lawyer what that means in this state."

His eyes told me he'd already had that conversation.

"You already know I don't work alone," I said. "So please don't be stupid. You're a businessman. This is business. If my phone doesn't ring within five days, don't try dialing that number again. It'll be disconnected. And so will I."

He nodded. Not "I agree," but "I understand."

The Maybach's rear door swung open by itself. He stepped inside, and then he was gone.

◆

I didn't look over my shoulder to watch the car move off, I looked across to Michelle. She flipped up her veil, put on a pair of sunglasses. I got up and walked into the restaurant, carrying my drink with me.

I carried that drink all the way through the interior, heading toward the restrooms. I passed a Chinese kid wearing a white kitchen worker's uniform. He nodded at me, took the drink from my hand.

A door closed behind me, a door nobody but me could pass through. It was made up of the same group that were leaning casually against the walls of the basement I found by going down the steps inside a beaded curtain. I didn't recognize any of the faces, but the gold silk shirts, buttoned to the throat, the fingertip-length black leather jackets, and the glossy high pompadours were as distinctive as Crip blue or Blood red.

One of them stepped forward. I followed him down a dim corridor. He rapped twice on a door — I guessed it was a door; I couldn't actually see it until it opened.

Now we were in a tunnel. A short one. At the other end was the basement of an apartment building. We walked up the stairs to the lobby. By the time I rolled out into the street, I was an elderly man in a wheelchair, with a tired-looking Chinese woman in a nurse's uniform pushing me down the block.

"Motherfucker's *good,*" the Prof said, late that night. "You only gave him a narrow slot, but he got it filled. Must have had a whole team in place, ready to roll."

"One by one," I said, looking around the table.

"The two they had in front were real spooks," the Prof started off. "Shadow men. They floated in soon as the man's car moved out."

"They try and get inside?"

"Not for two hours," he said, impressed. "They watched you go in and just went gray, you know? Part of the scenery."

"I was gone before that," Michelle said.

"Me also," Clarence said. "I hung around after my sister left, for another few minutes. Kept looking at my watch, like I was waiting for something. Then I reached in my pocket and opened my cell phone, like I was taking a call. Then I split."

Max stood up. Walked to the wall, drew a box on a piece of posterboard, made a little fence around the front, so we'd know he meant the restaurant.

He held up two fingers, pointed to the front door. Arranged his face into an expression of total puzzlement, showing us what the two shadows encountered. Then he took the black marker and made a pair of dots behind the building, pointed to his eyes, made the gesture of a door opening. So they had men in place *behind* the restaurant, too. If they were waiting for me to step out that way, they'd be there a long time.

I thought Max was done, but he used another board to draw a cube, pointed at the first drawing and shook his head to make sure we understood he wasn't talking about the same building, then added a stick figure of a man . . . on the roof. He made his hands into binoculars.

I made the sign of a man holding a rifle.

Max shook his head "no." This had been all about surveillance, not a hit.

"Reedy's got a deal with the feds?" I said, aloud.

"No," the Prof said.

We all looked his way.

"They — the ones I saw, anyway — they moved too good. If you blinked, you couldn't be sure they were even there. If the government spooks had men that good, they wouldn't be using them up on a favor for a friend."

"They don't seem to be using them for much else," Michelle said.

"You not lying, girl. But these men . . . I

370

can't explain it exactly, but they were the kind of guys who wouldn't work for no government salary. Maybe they did once — they were no kids — but they got that . . . neutral thing going."

"Freelancers?" I said.

"The less they shout, the less I doubt, son."

I looked over at Max. He made a "this close" gesture to show me he hadn't caught the glint of binoculars — he'd been on that roof himself. The Mongol pointed at the Prof, nodded several times. Total agreement.

"They wouldn't have gone inside without orders," I said. "Breaking cover like that, it would be against everything they believe in. So he didn't have any more people close enough. Otherwise, they hold their positions, and he sends in new faces."

"You set up a meet with him, he'll have all the time in the world, Schoolboy. No way he does the payphone shuffle with six mil in a suitcase."

"I told him, if he brought the price, he could bring whatever he wanted to protect it."

"So what's to stop them from just taking —"

"I got that part figured," I assured them

371

all. "He already knows I didn't turn into the Invisible Man on him without major help. And I told him I don't work alone, anyway. He's not going to risk a firefight over money. And when he sees what I'm going to deliver, he's not going to worry about ever being tapped again."

"He's going to call, baby?" Michelle asked. Not anxious, just asking for me to set the odds.

"Sure as Satan, honey," I told her. "He's got five days, but we can't count on him using them all. We've got to put it all in place, starting right now."

◆

This time, when I finished bribing the dogs, the orca-blotched female came over and sat next to me. I risked patting her wedge head, hoping the old stud didn't decide to go pit bull–istic on me for invading his turf twice in a row. He watched, but let it slide.

It was too early to actually do it yet. But I felt the pull. So I walked around to the back of the two-pump gas station and rapped nine times, regularly spaced.

The door opened. The man inside was short, with legs like tree stumps and a chest you could project movies on. Looked like a double-wide trailer that had been crushed to half-height. He was some kind of Latino, crossbred with who-knows-what. A businessman whose business you didn't want to know. I always called him Jester, after the image blue-tattooed on one of his python biceps.

We had been just two businessmen, doing business the way it's done here. Goods for services. Cash, not conversation. Just enough talk to make the deal; just enough respect to keep to it.

That had all changed one afternoon. I was out back, under the Plymouth, checking a fitting on the transmission cooler. Jester was inside the enclosure with me: grooming his dogs, crooning to them in a language I understood, even though I couldn't tell you a single word. The beasts were chained to separate thick steel posts, just in case some strange dog wandered through the open gate.

We heard the music before they showed, the throbbing of the mega-bass speakers turning the whole scene into a movie soundtrack. A bad movie. A blinged-out Escalade with spinner twankie-deuces pulled in, and a trio of gold-roped gangstahs stepped out.

"Hey, bro!" the leader said. I could tell he

was the leader from the way the other two flanked him, posing. Probably even choreographed their drive-bys. "Word is, you got the baddest fucking pit in the whole city. Now, see this, I'm putting together a *major* match. Got a place the size of a fucking *arena,* babe. We doing it tournament-style, like K-1."

Jester said nothing. I couldn't see his face, but I knew it was wearing the kind of expression only being Inside can bring. I saw his feet shift, though. Slightly, but just enough.

I stayed where I was, exchanging the socket wrench I'd been holding for my short-barreled .357.

The leader took Jester's silence for something it wasn't. "Look, man," he said, confidence flowing like an unfurling ribbon through his Suge Knight–wannabe's voice, "here's how it gonna go: Forty dogs enter; one dog leaves. Got it? No entry fee. And for the winner? A hundred grand, cash money. Your dog *that* good? Or was what I heard not the word?"

"Oh," Jester said, like he was having trouble with English. "You want to fight my dog?"

"*Sí, sí,*" the gangstah said, mockingly. His boys laughed on cue.

"Bueno!" Jester said. "He's right over there, *maricón.* You just walk back to that cage" — meaning the chain-linked spot where I'd parked my Plymouth — "you step in, I unhook my dog, you can fight him all you want."

The gangstah was even dumber than his blue-and-white crocodile shoes. "No, you fucking taco —"

I slid out from under the Plymouth, took up a position behind the rear fender just as Jester snatched the gangstah's throat in one hand, holding him off the ground like he was a can of spray paint, ready to write a message. The other two backed away, then whipped out their shiny semi-autos. Still posing, but lost without a script.

"Put down the pieces," I said, from cover. "Put them down, and everybody gets to live."

It went quiet enough for them to hear my .357 being cocked.

"Vito!" I yelled over to my imaginary confederate behind them. "Hold your fire. These guys just didn't know the score." I addressed the punks with the pistols.

"Whoever shoots, dies," I said, very calm. "You come here, you show no respect. One more stupid move and you niggers are all dog food."

The leader made a frantic gesture. The chrome pistols went to the concrete. Gently. I stepped out of the shadows — not enough for them to see my face, but they couldn't miss the .357. It was all they were looking at, anyway.

Jester dropped the leader like a sack of smelly garbage, took a step back. The pits were both snarling in fury, *ramming* themselves against the chains, threatening to snap the steel with their combined power.

"This place is protected, understand?" I said, in my best *Sopranos* voice. "It belongs to us. You didn't know before; now you do. Next fucking yom we see *close* to this joint, it's gonna take him *days* to die. We got your plate, we'll have your name in an hour. We got your pictures, too. You're on the list now. You want to keep breathing, stay the fuck *away.*"

When they left, smoking the tires, Jester turned to me. His face said, "I could have handled it."

My face said, "I know you could."

That was a few years ago; before the orca pup had been born.

Tonight, I asked him, "That little female, the black one with the white spots?"

"Yeah?"

"I really like her. Any chance you might

consider letting me buy her from you?"

He crossed his arms over his chest. Not threatening, thinking.

"I got to ask Nova about it first, *ese.*"

"Nova?"

"El jefe," he said, pointing at the huge stud.

"Why d'you name him Nova?" I asked, frankly curious.

"Is short for 'Casanova,' " Jester said, grinning. Then his face turned cold. "You know I never fight my dog."

"Fuck, no. But I figure *someone* did — he's half scar tissue, that old guy. Maybe you, uh, 'rescued' him. A man who does something like that, I'd admire him for it."

He gave me a long look. Not challenging, searching. "I think maybe you the right man for Rosita."

"Thank you," I said, respectfully. Thinking, *I have to ask Pansy, too.*

Then I walked home, alone.

◆

"Watch this," I told Thornton.

I took a chair in front of the videocam we had set on a tripod. The boom mikes were already in place, invisible to the viewer.

I faced the camera squarely. "My name is

Wesley," I said, hearing the iceman's voice come out of my mouth. "You think I'm gone, don't you, suckers? Bang!

"You like the stuff I mailed you? All true, right? You checked it out. That's what you blue boys do, check things out. *After* some snitch tips you. You know how many men I killed? You ever solve *one* of them?

"So you're saying, maybe he made this tape before he blew himself up. Maybe he's just fucking with us. You know, like the way we fucked with him when he was just a little kid. You know who I mean. All of you, you know.

"I hate you. I hate you all. So here's your personal nightmare, pigs. Ask your Bronx boys where Fernando Quinones is. Nobody's seen him around lately. Big-time politician like him, missing. Been all over the papers. You're never going to find him. The people who paid me didn't want him found, but they had to be sure I did my work. So I brought them the pieces. I hear there's certain Cuban restaurants in the South Bronx you don't want to order from for the next few weeks. Nothing with meat in it, anyway.

"I had to go away for a while. Not because of you clowns. For a job. A big job. Out of the country. Took me a long time to plan it out, get everything in place. But I got it done.

"And now I'm back. With a long list. Watch your backs, pigs. You got a lot of men locked up, but you never found their money."

Claw clicked off the camera. He reached over and rewound the tape we had made.

"Here," I said, handing it to Thornton.

"What am I supposed to do with this?"

"Just stick it in the player, make sure everything works."

"I believe —"

"Do it," Claw said.

Thornton inserted the cassette, hit "play."

And there I was, confessing to a murder.

"Rewind it," I told him. "Then pop it out."

He did it.

"Now take it with you."

"Huh?!?"

"Take it with you," I repeated. "Stick it in any machine you want. And play it again."

"Why? What's all this — ?"

"It's all about showing you how we've got you covered," I explained, bringing him under the partnership blanket that he needed to feel around his shoulders if he was going to go all the way we needed him to. "You hit 'play' and that tape is going to be nothing but static."

"But I just saw —"

"What you just saw cost us fifty grand. It records anything perfectly. Plays it back perfectly, too. *Once.* That activates the software. It's all digital — for every frame it plays, it goes back and wipes it. Not 'erase,' *wipe.* Like a computer doing a total over-write, understand? Instead of data, or images, or whatever, you get random-generated ones and zeros. It can't be recovered, can't be repaired. It is fucking *gone.*"

His mouth dropped open, but no sound came out.

"I just told you my real name. And con-fessed to a murder that just happened, too — check it out for yourself. I put it on tape. Would I give it to you and let you walk out of here with it if I wasn't absolutely sure it would work?"

"How do I know this isn't a bluff? Or some kind of test?"

"You know it's not a bluff because you *are* going to take it. And you *are* going to see for yourself. And, once you see for yourself, you know this is no test.

"Because then you'll know what it *really* is. It's us, protecting you. I already told Claw what you're going to say on the tape we're going to make. He knows it's all a shuck, total fraud. But we need to deliver them *something* to make all this money happen. And the only thing they'll take is you, on tape, saying what we worked out. What we rehearsed."

"So they'd have to play it . . ."

"To be sure we delivered, exactly!" I congratulated him. "But when they try to play it again . . ."

"They're fucked!"

"No," I said, very seriously. "They're not. You're in the Philippines, with your half-mil, and you're not coming back. Sure, they don't have a tape, but, for real, you're no threat to them anymore. They'll get what they paid for, even if it wasn't in the way they expected. And they got something else, too."

"What?"

"They'll get the *message*," I said, dialing up the freak's rheostat. "You've got *people.* People who know things. People who know how to get things *done.* You know what that spells, Thorn. Pro*tec*tion! They'll know you're not a threat to them because we'll *tell* them. And we'll tell them something else: they fuck with you, they fuck with us. And there's no way they want to do that."

I watched the freak swell with the surge of power flowing through him. I knew what turned his crank, even if he didn't.

When he left — with the tape — Claw and I exchanged the slightest of nods. A prison-yard gesture: the shot-caller giving the okay to take someone down.

◆

"Let me tell it," the Prof commanded, silencing us all. We were gathered in Gateman's back room. The mirror on the wall separating the wheelchair-bound shooter's living quarters from the flophouse desk he supposedly manned around the clock was a see-through, just in case someone wandered in, looking for a room. For the first few years, Gateman had expected his PO to drop by, but he'd given that up after a while.

Anyway, he was finally off that paper. The plea deal Davidson had worked out for him last time ended up being a Man Two, which translated to almost eight in, because Gate was a predicate felon. He'd done the time the way you're supposed to do it.

By the time he was out of Processing and rolling onto the yard, the word was out about his last time in court. The judge had offered to cut the deal lower, all the way down to a simple assault beef: "In consideration of three factors, sir: one, the Court agrees with your counsel that your justification defense might well have, at a minimum, cast a significant shadow of reasonable doubt; two, your physical handicap; and, three, an equitable cooperation agreement, to be negotiated between —"

Gateman cut the judge off at the knees, his voice booming through the crowded court. "You got that whole 'handicapped' thing wrong, Judge. Just because a man's in a wheelchair don't mean he can't stand up. Cooperate *this,* you miserable whore."

Gateman never lacked for friends Inside. Old-school cons made it a point to go over and shake his hand, as clear a message as if they had Day-Glo-ed it on those big gray walls.

The Prof held center stage. On his feet, ready to preach, the way he used to do. "Back down home, son, they said I had the spirit in me when I was just a little boy. They got that right, in church. But they never came to my house.

"Okay, now," he said, "here's how it goes, people. My boy" — nodding in my direction — "he figures this guy Reedy tried to follow him once, he'd try it again. But last time he did? Flop City. So what's the man gonna do now? That's right!" he said as if anyone had spoken. "Gonna send someone back to the vanishing point. No ghosts this time, though. Gotta be someone who can speak the language. No teams, this scene. One guy. Thai?"

Max nodded.

"Anyway, he strolls in, sits at a table. Asks the waiter who comes over if any of his friends have been in lately. Only he's not speaking Thai, he's speaking . . . Chinese?"

Max nodded again, making a patting-something-down gesture: Cantonese, not Mandarin. Not a language you learn in college.

"These 'friends,' he's talking about *Max's* friends. You know, the boys with the . . . Anyway, he figures, *I* figure, that someone's gonna make a call, bring them all. Then he's gonna negotiate. Had fifty large in this little leather bag he brought with him.

"Call goes to Mama's. So, when the boys show, they got Max in tow."

"Oh," Michelle said. Not to rhyme, just to show she was part of the congregation.

"That's right!" the Prof said, again. "Man thinks he's looking at gang boys. Shooters, sure. He's relaxed behind that. All he was packing was the money. Not even a blade. Kind of man, he's walked into guns before. But when he got to the roof — the part you can't see from across the street, because of that old water tank they never took down — there was Max."

"You saw this?" I asked him. Wondering why Max was letting the Prof do all the talking.

"These eyes don't lie," the little man fired back. "I was on the spot. In fact, my son took us all there."

Clarence nodded. Apparently, he'd been left at the curb. Not because he was being disrespected — in case the visitor had brought friends.

"I was in the corner. Bundle of rags. Both barrels cocked, ready to drop if anyone came to bop.

"Now listen, people," he exhorted us. "This guy, he showed a *picture* of Burke. Big, clear picture. Close-up. Looks just like him, except for his hair and . . . something around his eyes."

"That was me," Michelle said, proudly.

"It was still a *nice* picture, sweet girl. Whatever those boys use, it's the best. So, anyway, he shows the picture around. Opens his bag, shows the cash, too. The boys all give him the 'never seen him' routine. But then one of them screws up, blows the role. Pulls his iron, says, 'You don't come back.' "

"This guy they sent, he was *fast*. I mean, the kind of fast you got to wonder if you even saw what you think you did. He flashes his foot, the gun goes flying, and the boy who pulled it, he's going to need steel pins in his wrist. The Thai guy, he's back to where he was, still holding Burke's picture, like he never moved."

"Fuck!" Gateman said. "Didn't they all — ?"

"No," the Prof cut him off. "They stepped right off. You know why? Because, all of a sudden, Max the Silent was just . . . *there.* And when the life-taking, widow-making silent wind of death walks, these boys know the show: step aside or die.

"But the guy with the moves, you could tell he's not from around here. An import.

"Max points. You don't have to know no sign language to read what's he's saying. And then the Thai fucking *jumps* him.

"Max lets him come. Like watching a breeze rush a rock. The Thai lands a kick to Max's leg, below the knee, then he grabs Max behind the neck and fires a triple knee-strike: thigh, chest, head. Only the last one never gets there."

"Jesus!" I blurted out. I'd seen Max go against a Muay Thai fighter before. He had blocked the long-distance strikes, feinted a slip, and let the other guy get in close, where he'd want to be for the climbing knee-

386

strikes that they specialize in. Max had stabbed a nerve on the Muay Thai man's left side. In a split-second pause, the Mongol drove his blue-knuckled fist to the guy's sternum. Stopped his heart.

"So he never came out?" Gateman asked, way ahead of me.

"Sure, he did!" the Prof scoffed. "He disappears, what kind of message is that? Maybe a dozen guys ventilated him. That'd be okay with his boss. The guy he sent was good, *real* good, but he was just cannon fodder. So he walked right out the front door. After he came to."

"Max choked him out?"

"Bingo!" the little man congratulated me. "When the Thai comes to, he's back in the same booth he started from. *With* his bag of cash. He walks out the front door and walks a few blocks. Makes a call from a cell phone. Probably for the pickup.

"Don't know what story he told, people, but I guarantee you this: no way it made whoever sent him sleep easier that night."

Thornton was telling me and Claw how the tape I'd made had disappeared when he'd tried to play it. This was the third time he told us, and he was still slack-jawed with amazement.

"Enough," I told him. "If you're not ready to do it now, then you're —"

The Mole's phone-bomb rang. I stepped out of the concrete box to take the call, said, "What?" when I was far enough away.

"We can do it this Friday." Reedy.

"Which means — ?" I pressed him.

"All three."

"With the — ?"

"Yes, yes," he said, annoyed at the trivia. "You're going to bring what you said you had to show us. We're going to authenticate it — we'll have our appraiser on the premises, as agreed — and, should it prove to be all you promised, the transaction will be completed on the spot."

"Friday's fine. Where and when?"

The silence that came back over the satellite connection was the sound of a boxer who'd been warned about your jab and never saw the hook coming.

"You want *us* to pick the site?"

"Why not?" I said, with an innocence as real as Russian democracy. "You already know you're dealing with more than just me, so why should you get all stupid when we're so close?"

"Why indeed?" he agreed. "I admit, this is

a little unexpected. You understand, there is a need for privacy, so it can't be at my —"

"Call me back with the time and place," I told him, and cut him off.

◆

"Three days," the Prof said, solemnly.

"You want me to make sure he —"

"No!" I cut off Claw, sharply. "I told you we were doing this my way. No threats. And *absolutely* no rehearsals. This has got to be live. And come across that way. Besides, he doesn't need any practice; he's got this one down pat."

"I know," the guy I'd been calling "the cancer-man" in my head ever since we first spoke said. "Your man" — he meant the Mole, who hadn't said a word all the time he was working inside the concrete box — "has got it perfect. All I have to do is wait for this one to ring" — he held up a cell phone with a band of red duct tape across the back — "to let me know that we're coming through, and this one" — this time, the tape was yellow — "to tell me that we're done. I don't *answer* either one; I just make sure it's ringing."

He looked to me for confirmation. I nodded.

"Couldn't you use someone else? For my part, I mean?"

"Why?"

"You're not going in bareback. I know you've got a crew, but me and that big guy" — nobody who'd ever watched Gigi work ever called him "fat" — "showed you we can do work, right?"

"Thanks," I said, meaning it. "But without you right there, in the room, the maggot could always get stupid. He couldn't pull this off if he was scared. He needs you right there with him. Needs you to believe that the whole thing is a scam. He needs your . . . approval, I guess is the only way to say it. He needs to be *with* someone, feel like he's part of something. Sure, Inside, he paid. But that was for protection, not membership. Now he's *earning*, see? Contributing. That's your job, your piece of this: you've got to let this freak feel your *respect*, understand? He's *showing* you something, and you're going to admire how slick he pulls it off."

Claw said nothing for a minute.

"You can do this," Michelle told him, using her spell-caster's eyes. "Then you can do that other thing you have to do."

"I can see it in you," the Prof said, softly.

"What?"

"You're going to kick its ass," the little man said. "I can see that in a man. You think I don't have the sight, you ask Silver about the night I was right."

Claw stuck out his hand.

"If it had been a different place —"

The Prof took his hand. "You'd be with us," he said. "I know this, too. I do *now,* anyway."

"Can you get this whole thing ready on time?"

"For the kind of money you're talking, I could get it done tonight," Gigi assured me. "But what's that ramp thing you want out back for?"

"Wheelchair access," I said.

"Your car, mahn? Your *own* car?"

"It'll be a different color. With dead-end plates."

"Still, Burke. How many cars — ?"

"You know a faster one? Or a better corner-carver?"

"No, mahn. Your machine is the work of a magician."

"Yeah. And what we might need is a disappearing act."

◆

"That is *heavy* matériel," the man I knew as Yitzhak said. He wasn't talking weight; he was talking cost.

"Did I lie to you?" Meaning: the last time we dealt with each other.

"You did not."

"There's plenty of them out there for sale. I came to you because I believe you are a man of honor. You won't cheat me on the price, but that isn't what I'm worried about."

"You have to know it is going to work."

"That's it," I confirmed. "The SCUDs were duds."

"And they came from . . . Yes, I understand. It is none of my business, but . . ."

"What?"

He looked at me for a long moment. "I understand you have . . . friends. Some of those friends, they consider us, what our people do, a disgrace."

"Because you're not out hunting Nazis?"

"Because we are businessmen."

"Plenty of businessmen —"

"What? Write checks, and call themselves

freedom fighters? You don't know everything that we do," he said, hurt, but making it sound like an accusation.

"Like you said: Business. Not *my* business."

"You come back here," he said, consulting a massive wristwatch — if you weighed it, the measurement would be twelve ounces to a pound — "in twenty-four hours."

◆

They were waiting when I pulled up. Two men, standing outside their car, so I could see Yitzhak hadn't come alone.

I had. I followed their hand signals, backed the Plymouth in so our cars were trunk-to-trunk. Mine was already lined with quilts, covering the fuel cell and the relocated battery.

Yitzhak offered his hand. A signal to the man next to him. The man wasn't wearing a uniform, but everything about him screamed "military."

No introductions.

"We have an Igla," the man said, meaning whatever was in the trunk of Yitzhak's car. "You have used one?"

"I don't even know what it is."

He exchanged a look with Yitzhak, then

turned to face me again.

"It is also called an SA-16 Gimlet," he said, as if that would explain anything. "This is perhaps twenty-five years old. I say 'old,' although it has never been used. But it has been properly maintained. It is as good now as it was the day it was made. I have a model with me. In case . . ."

"Please," I said, respectfully.

He removed a tube of metal, pulled on the underside with both hands, and hoisted it to his shoulder. "It is not so heavy — maybe twenty kilos — for what it can do. But you understand, it must be aimed at *least* ten meters off the ground to be effective. More is better."

I nodded. He went through a lot of stuff about "target acquisition" and "passive infrared."

He watched my face as he spoke. "Unless you are experienced, this is not what you want," he finally said. "An RPG would be much more effective. And much cheaper." He never glanced at Yitzhak — this guy was all about the work.

"We're not looking at an armored car," I told him.

"A helicopter?"

"Maybe," I said. Then, realizing he'd take that for craftiness, I explained: "It's just for backup. The people we . . . might have a dispute with, they have access to one."

"Altitude?" the military guy said. Not so much a question as data-gathering.

"I don't know," I said. "But low, real low."

"No, no, no!" he said, disgusted. "The surface-to-air you asked for, it requires an experienced hand."

"I can —"

"What? Practice, you think? On what? Where? *With* what?"

I just stood there, listening to him put my lame idea through the Cuisinart of his professional's mind.

"The SAM is a heat-seeker," he finally said. "*It* acquires the target, not the operator. But an RPG, it's just a shoulder-fired rocket. Like a tiny bazooka — does that help you understand?"

"I think so."

"It weighs less than *half* of the Igla. And you aim it like a rifle. Your eye finds the target, hot or cold."

"Yeah, but —"

"Yes." He sighed, almost bored. "It *will* bring down a bird, if it comes in low enough. And that's even without our modifications."

I said nothing. I already felt like an idiot; I wasn't going to make it worse.

"I never understand him, either," Yitzhak said, kindly.

"The warhead, that is custom work," the unnamed man said, as matter-of-factly as a hardware-store guy explaining a power drill. "The one we have, it will totally destroy whatever it hits. And burn whatever is left."

"That does sound better," I admitted.

"It *is* actually cheaper," Yitzhak reminded me.

"What do I have to — ?"

"I have it with us," the military man said.

◆

"The building is in Upper Westchester," Reedy said. "I own it. By midnight, it will be completely empty, except for invitees. I'm giving you the address in advance, so you can put anyone you want in place. Good faith."

"Good faith," I echoed the lie.

◆

"You know I can drive," Michelle said, just a fingernail's distance from the detonator to her temper.

"We've already got —"

"I'm not saying I'll *be* the driver. I'm saying I can drive. Things happen. You could need me."

"My sister —"

"You don't say a *word* to me." She wheeled on Clarence. "I was doing work before you were —" Michelle cut herself off. She wasn't afraid of dying, but she'd *rather* die than admit she was older than Clarence.

"Sweetheart, you too pretty to be —"

"Spare me," she sneered at the Prof. "Only one man gets to pat me on the ass, and he couldn't honey-talk a woman if his life depended on it."

"You're in on the sin," the little man said, surrendering on behalf of us all.

◆

"Really should have a rifleman for this, boss. That kind of distance . . ."

"We don't know the distance yet, Gate. May not *be* any distance, if they play it square."

"What's the odds?"

"Fifty-fifty."

"You looked over the scene?"

"Not me personally, but it was done," I said, showing him the aerial photos.

"I don't like that long alley, boss. You got high ground on both sides."

"Cleared ground," I said. "They put anyone up there, they're still going to be there when the cops show up. Nobody'll have to read them their rights, either."

◆

It was a three-story building, looked like the management office for what had once been an industrial park, now in the process of being converted to condos. Land in this part of the country is more valuable than any business conducted on it.

The place looked deserted. Only the third floor had lights showing.

Clarence pulled up to the front door. I stepped out of my Plymouth. Gigi's panel van was close by, a probably still-fuming Michelle sitting next to the monster. Gateman was checking through the gun-slit openings in the steel plates lining the van, spinning freely in his wheelchair.

Max was in the shadows, somewhere. I didn't know where the Blood Shadows were, either. Or the Prof.

I pulled back on the unlocked doors, saw the elevator lights were out, and started up the stairs. My mind started to take me places I didn't want to go: *Maybe the only threat they see is me. If that's so, I'm about to solve their problem. In fact, I guess I already did.* So I went back to that place I found every time I had to walk into an enemy's darkness. Some people have faith. Me, I had the born-to-lose career criminal's mantra: *Fuck it!*

◆

The conference room was big enough for a twenty-person table, with plenty of space surrounding it. The double doors were standing open. Behind the table, facing me, were three men. Reedy was in the middle, Bender to his left, Henricks on his right. Three rich, privileged, glossy lumps of necrotic flesh.

Behind them: a huge pane of glass, black night for a curtain. As I stepped forward, I deliberately scanned the men in the corners, and along the walls. I'd seen them all before. In Africa. Not these same men, but from the same tribe.

Wolfe had once called me a mercenary trying to pass for a patriot. She wasn't talking about national loyalty.

I knew what I was. What I'd done. I'd told Wolfe I was back to being myself.

I wasn't lying when I'd said that. And now I was back in the same swamp, wondering if

I could find my way home.

I took off the shoulder strap to the canvas pouch I had slung over one shoulder, put the pouch on the desk across from the three men facing me.

None of the hired guns moved.

I put the briefcase I'd been carrying on the table, too.

"Want to do it?" I asked, starting to pull my jacket off.

Reedy waved it off. His silent gesture said it all: if I was wired, it wasn't going to do me any good — nobody on their side was going to speak out loud.

"This," I said, taking out the Mole's phone, "is the transmitter. The signal is cellular, not cyber. Scrambled at both ends. I have to dial in the encryption codes for it to work. When the connect is made, you'll be able to see it all, live, on this screen.

"That's what's in here," I told them, pointing at the briefcase. "Just a magnifier, so you can all watch at once — the pickup screen's pretty small, but the sound is adjustable. There's also a couple of tripods to set the whole thing up, so you don't need to hand-hold it. What you're going to see could take a while."

Reedy nodded assent. They all slid their chairs back so I had room to set up the apparatus.

"There's something I have to show you first," I told them, holding up a quarter-inch-thick stack of paper, my back deliberately to the hired guns. "Now's not the time, but soon, if everything goes the way it's supposed to. Ready?"

When I got the silent nod, I punched in the number of the phone Claw would be holding, the one with the red tape on the back. Then I added a string of numbers, fake-dialing the nonexistent encryption.

I stepped back. And the magnified screen popped into life.

I moved back to the door. Not to be closer to it — I was sure the staircase would be blanketed by then — but to watch their faces.

Reedy stayed flat. Maybe his eyes narrowed a little. Henricks was a beefy slab. But Bender's complexion picked up a greenish hue, and his mouth was dry enough so that he broke ranks and took a drink of something from the iced glass on his left.

The voice that came over the micro-speakers was as clear as if Thornton was in the room.

My name is Thornton, Percival K. Thornton. Back in the day, I went by "Thorn." Now, I go by "Terminal." Because that's me, now: terminal. I'm just about done. But there's something I have to do first.

One night in August of 1975, a girl was killed. Her name was Melissa. Melissa Turnbridge. They never caught who did it. I don't think they ever had any real suspects. That's the part I can't fix — the wrong I can't make right.

But there's one part of it I *can* fix, and that's why I'm doing this. There's someone — or maybe even more than one; I'm not saying — who've been blaming themselves for what happened. More than thirty years of carrying that around. Not the fear of the knock on the door — that's never going to happen, not now. But there's something worse. Something I found out for myself. The guilt.

The speaker took an audible breath. Then:

Here's the truth. The truth the cops never knew. The one they may *never* know — that part's not up to me. Melissa was my girlfriend. Yeah, I know what you're thinking. How could a grown man have a thirteen-year-old girlfriend?

It's not what you think. You didn't know her; I did. You've heard about "natural-born killers," right? I didn't believe there was any such thing until I went to prison. Then I saw it for myself. They weren't abused as kids; that's all bullshit. They were just born to be what they are, same as a rattlesnake.

Slimeball probably believes what he just said, I thought. "Natural-born" is how people always account for what they don't understand . . . or don't want to.

Well, that was her, Melissa. Not a born killer, a born whore. And not just a whore, a dirty little slut who loved what she did. Loved it. Not the money — oh, she liked money, but she already had so much, from her parents and all, that it didn't have much of a jolt for her. For her, money was like . . . tribute or something. The only thing that really got that little cunt wet was power. *That's* what made her come, making people crawl.

Before her, I was a normal guy. Better than normal. I was a good-looking man — ask anyone who knew me back then. I had a sweet ride, my own place, plenty of spending money. All the pussy anyone could ever want, and I never paid a dime for any of it.

Melissa came on to me, not the other way around. What did I want with some junior-high kid? I'm just sitting in my car, near the school, when she jumps in. Before I could say a word, she pulls up her skirt, right to her panties. "Turn left at the light," she tells me. I'm, like, in a trance. This is broad daylight, okay? And suddenly we're in this . . . forestlike place. And she's kneeling on the front seat, sucking my cock. Not just sucking it: she's got her fingernail under my balls, twirling her tongue, making all these noises. I've had — this was years later — five-hundred-dollar-an-hour hookers, and none of them could do it like Melissa. Like I said, a natural.

This is all happening, and I'm, like, frozen. And I don't mean my cock. I couldn't move. She reaches back and pulls her skirt up, so I can watch her ass wiggle. I explode in her mouth. She makes these "yum, yum" sounds, like she just had a bowl of ice cream. Licks her lips. Tells me, don't worry about anything — where we are, it's on her property. Not her father's, hers, the way she says it.

I'm dead. I know I'm dead, but I can't do anything about it. She reaches in her purse, takes out a tube of something. "You'll need this, for next time," she says. "Your cock's so big, it won't fit, otherwise."

I already know there's never going to be any next time with this one. All I want to do is get out of there. But she can *see* this. "Tomorrow, we can use the cabin," she says. Not asking me, telling me.

It gets worse after that. I was never in charge. Not for a minute. Once she made me . . . get down on my knees and . . . It was . . . degrading. She made me say things. Do things. She even took pictures of me, and I couldn't stop her.

I hated her more every day. But she held the whip. From the very first time, she kept telling me what was going to happen to me if she told her daddy. That's what she called him. She knew more about the law than any lawyer. "Where do you think I learned all this?" I remember her saying. "I've been in charge since I was nine years old."

She never thought I had the balls to stop her. I don't think she was afraid of anything. She was like some devil-girl.

Well, she was wrong. Maybe I didn't have the balls to kill her, but I had one thing nobody ever gave me credit for: brains. Not school brains, street brains.

Once she made me into a . . . It doesn't matter, but that's when I started. I knew it would take time, and I'd have to be careful. But I also knew where I had to look for what I needed.

These three spineless little nothings. Always hung out together . . . if you call circle-jerking hanging out. They had nothing going for them but money. Only, where we lived, just about everyone had money, so that didn't get them anything. A guy like me, a guy they thought

405

had it all, they fucking worshiped me.

So when I invited them over one day — they knew who I was, knew I dealt to some of the older guys, so they weren't surprised to see my car around the school — it was like they died and went to heaven.

I started them slow. First, just talk. Advice, like.

I showed them stuff. Cards, dice. Let them hear me place a few bets. Like a big brother.

The marijuana mellowed them, but I didn't want them too mellow.

It was the tapes that got them going. I started them off on lightweight porn, so I could see if they had the taste. For all I knew, they could have been queer.

By the time I was up to the heavy stuff — you had to know where to get hard S&M in those days, not like now — that's all they wanted to see. The more the girls had to take it, the more those punks liked it. Because, on the tapes, the *girls* liked it, see?

In the stuff I showed them, no matter what got done to them, the bitches always begged for more. Fuck them in the ass, come all over their faces, make them eat shit — they'd love you for it.

It was like I showed the little punks a special secret. The girls who were always blowing them off, what they *really* wanted was a *man* to make them take it. That arrogant stuff was just a front — inside, they're all the same.

That's when I started feeding Melissa into the picture. Got them to see her for the fuck-princess she could be if she was only handled right. By the right guys.

I got them into keeping a journal. Just a fantasy thing. Told them all men did that, planned out what they were going to do to a certain bitch to teach her a few lessons. Showed them a couple of mine, in fact.

I kept working on them, waiting for everything to come together. When they were ready, totally committed, I even had the place for them to do it. I knew the house would be empty, because the owners were paying me to keep an eye on it while they were on some cruise. They were planning on doing all this redecorating when they got back, so the front rooms were right down to the bare floor, no furniture. I'm the one who put the rug there . . . and the plastic underneath.

The plan was perfect. I knew where Melissa would be that night. Summertime, she could stay out until . . . Ah, for all I knew, she didn't even have a curfew. I sure as hell knew I wasn't the first guy she had turned into a . . .

Anyway, the reason I knew where she'd be was she thought she was going to meet me.

That bitch had a mouth on her like a thousand razors, but she didn't have any physical strength. Besides, I had these punks so pumped up on what studs they were going to turn into after doing the job on her. I mean, they were absolutely convinced she'd take it every way they gave it to her, then she'd be their girlfriend — all three of them — forever. Just to make sure, I had them all a little wired on speed. They thought they could do anything.

He paused for a second. Reached out of camera view for something. I heard the distinct sound of exhaled cigarette smoke. I knew what this was all about. What Thornton was all about. Power. He could smoke; Claw couldn't — not without revealing his presence. And Claw really needed a smoke. That's the reason we'd never rehearsed; it would have detracted from the freak's perfect-truth performance.

The docs say these things can kill you. Well, they won't kill me. You'll see.

Anyway, I'm just kicking back, waiting for those stupid little tools to show up with the photos I told them to take. I knew Melissa wouldn't go to the cops about other kids, but those pictures would be my proof, in case she ever went to them about me. Like she was always saying she might do, every time I tried to . . . make her stop.

And then it went haywire. The stupid punks run into my house, babbling about how they killed her. They didn't mean to — Christ, they must of said that a million times — but it happened. So I did what I had to do — if anything at the scene connected back to those wimps, they'd be spilling their guts to the cops in ten seconds. And I'd be in it.

Only thing is, when I get there, she's not dead. Not fucking close to it. Oh, she's beat up pretty good, bleeding a little bit. Maybe she even was unconscious for a while. Must of been, actually, since she was still there when I showed up. That's probably why they thought they'd croaked her.

But there she is. Just been tied up, gang-fucked, pissed on . . . and she's threatening *me!*

That's when I knew how it had to end. I punched her right in the mouth — man, I had been wanting to do that for so long — and that's when she knew, too. I could see it in her eyes. The one thing I'd never thought I'd see there: fear. Because she knew it was finally going to happen. She'd gone too far.

She didn't even try and fight when I used the handcuffs and the gag. I wrapped her in the rug and the plastic, and I drove her out to this spot I know.

And that's where I showed her what happens to any cunt who abuses me like she had.

I know the cops never released any of the crime-scene photos. At least, not to the public. So these pathetic little punks — the ones who've been thinking they're "killers" for all these years — they never saw what the body looked like when it was dug up. If they had, they would have known the truth.

What I really wanted was to carve my initials in her ass after I finished with her, but I knew I couldn't do that. But I did burn a sign into her. With cigarettes. She probably died while I was finishing — I could hear her trying to scream through the gag — but it doesn't matter. Because I had to make sure.

Nothing was ever in the papers about exactly how she died, but I know. I'm the *only* one who knows. Because it was me who beat her face in until those dirty whore-cunt eyes of hers were gone. Then I turned her over and used the same bat to open her skull, right down to the white stuff.

That was the real last laugh. She thought I didn't have any brains, so I beat hers in.

I slid some of the paper across the slick surface of the table. It landed in front of Reedy. The autopsy photos. A perfect match to everything Thornton had just confessed to.

"Copies of the police files," I said. "The

originals are still in their evidence locker. In storage. Cold-cased. The seals are intact." I was just a messenger, describing the contents of the package I was handing over to its rightful owner.

Reedy couldn't help himself. "How could you possibly — ?"

"Trade secret," I told him. And then Thornton came back on:

I can't say I'm proud of what I did. That's not why I'm making this statement, or whatever you want to call it, now. That filthy whore made me into what I ended up being. Nothing. That's what I ended up being. I was on the fast track, and she turned me into a loser.

Those kids I used? I ended up blackmailing them. Right up to the time anyone sees this, they're always going to believe that they're killers. I told them that I had a tape . . . an audiotape. There never was any tape; it was all a bluff. But if you're scared enough, if you feel guilty enough — or if you're afraid of being caught — that bluff is always good for . . . for whatever you want.

Where do you think I learned that trick? That's right. Sweet little Melissa. She was the expert. Far as I'm concerned, I did the world a favor by taking her out. What I'm doing now isn't for her. She's probably in hell right this minute, sucking the Devil's cock, saying, "Oh, that tastes so good, Daddy!" No, this is for the people I really wronged.

What good is an apology now? Especially from a man who's terminal? I'm not going to pay for what I did. But I don't want anyone else to, either.

I have to be back in the hospital in another couple of hours. Next time I leave, I'll be in a box. A little box.

I'm sorry about a lot of things. But what I'm sorriest about most is that I'll never be able to watch that dirty little cunt die again. I still have the Polaroids I took. I'm going to burn them before I go back to the hospital, bring the ashes with me. In my will, I tell them to cremate me. And scatter my ashes with the ones from those pictures I took of her that night. So we can be together, forever.

That's all I have to say.

The speakers went silent, but you could still see Thornton's image on the screen. Lighting another cigarette, leaning back in his chair, like he'd just had a *real* good one, from a *really* experienced whore.

"Well?" was all I said.

Reedy made a crooking motion with his left forefinger. One of the mercs stepped over, handed me a big, soft-sided suitcase.

"Want to count it?"

"No," I said. "I want to add to it."

"What?" Reedy snapped, both hands grasping the Mole's special phone, as if I was going to try and snatch it back from him.

"I brought you what I promised," I said, hands open at my sides. "Walked into the lion's den to do it. Am I lying?"

All three shook their heads "no." Reedy handled it nicely; Henricks went at it a little harder. Bender looked like one of those bobble-head dolls.

"You can keep that phone," I said. "The whole thing has been captured. You can transfer it to video. Right now, if you want; I'll wait."

Reedy made another signal. One of the mercs — I knew he was a tech, because he wasn't carrying — immediately ran over. He examined the phone, nodded. He moved rapidly back to a bank of equipment, plugged a thin cable into the phone, the other end into an adaptor, into which he plugged a much thicker cable, leading to a computer screen.

"Just press '22' on the phone," I said.

The tech did it.

"When it's rewound, the screen will flash

413

red. Just hit '23' and you can transfer."

It took a few minutes, but there was Thornton, on the tech's computer screen, the terminal man, doing his thing.

"You can keep these, too," I said, tossing the rest of the police-file photocopies over to Reedy.

"So the extra money would be for what exactly?"

"Remember what Thornton called his statement?"

"An apology?" Reedy said, angry at something, but I couldn't tell what — he had a lot of choices.

"A dying declaration," I said. "To be legal, it has to meet two criteria. You know what they are?"

"Why don't you tell us?"

"Sure," I said. "One, it can't be made under duress. Like, if someone had him wired to a source of electricity, and he was reading off a script, knowing one slip and he was going to feel *real* pain. Over and over, until he got it right. If a man did that, and later changed his story, well, it wouldn't pass the first test."

"And the second?"

"A dying declaration is only good if the person not only *believes* they're dying, but . . ."

Reedy nodded again. Another merc opened another suitcase. There was a lot more in there than the six I'd asked for. He counted it out, pointed at the over-the-shoulder canvas bag I'd used to bring in the Mole's cell phone. I opened it — showed him it was empty — and he shoveled in the money.

"There's one more thing," I said. "I've played this straight, right down the line. I hope you did, but I can't be sure. You had me followed before. At least twice. I can't have that."

"Nobody move," Reedy ordered.

"Yeah, that's very nice," I told him. "But it won't do. That phone you're holding? Keep holding it. You let me walk clear, no trail, no trace; I keep walking. And you never see me again."

"Agreed."

"Right. And when I'm *sure,* I'll call you . . . on that phone. You pick it up, say whatever you want, just so I recognize your voice. Then, I'll say, 'Okay.' And then we're done. I'll take care of the rest of what you just paid me for. If you've got any sense at all, you'll leave me free to do just that."

"We have a deal," Reedy said.

I turned and walked out the door.

On the way down the staircase, I passed a man dressed all in black. Not breathing.

I guess the guy they'd stationed on the next landing never heard his partner go — he looked like he'd never seen it coming, either.

As I walked out the front door, Clarence pulled up in my Roadrunner. Max would already be gone, along with the Shadows. The loudest sound was the blood pounding in my ears.

Clarence handed me a cell phone. I motioned for him to get rolling, and I dialed the Mole's device.

"Already?" Reedy answered, no surprise in his voice that his staircase assassins had failed. "You see? I'm a man of my word, too."

I punched in "88."

The top of the building exploded into a raging fireball — the mercs must have been packing something heavier than the firearms I'd seen.

The Plymouth blasted down the narrow corridor like it was trying for a ten-second quarter. I spotted a black blotch against the wall just ahead, screamed: "Stop!"

The Plymouth's four-piston calipers

locked like an anchor in asphalt. I was out the door while it was still skidding.

"Prof!" I screamed. The little man was lying with his back to the wall. His right thigh was torn so badly I couldn't see anything but blood.

I knelt next to him as Clarence ran up, pistol at the ready.

"Get that car out of here, quick!" the Prof gasped. "Too big a target."

"Prof —"

"I was inside, 'cross the way," the little man said. He twisted his head at the building across from Reedy's headquarters. It was just one story higher than the one I'd just left — the windows said it was some kind of factory, not for the executive class. "I was on full ghost, but the motherfuckers peeped me anyway. Must have had an electronic eye somewhere. I thought I'd got away clean, but they got a sniper on the top floor. Left corner window."

Pain flashed across his face. "They got ten, twelve men on that floor. Full gear. Probably be coming down this way any second." A warrior's grin drove the pain from his eyes. "If they got the balls — I fed them some lead before I fled. Now go!"

"We will not —"

"You *hush,* boy!" the Prof snapped at

417

Clarence. "I'm done, but I can buy you time to get gone."

"Father . . ."

The Prof's eyelids fluttered. I took over. "Get the car around the corner, where the sniper can't see it," I snapped at Clarence. "Pop the trunk. Then get back behind the wheel. I've got this."

The Prof's eyes came back to life. A bubble of blood was in his mouth from where he'd bitten into his lip to revive himself. "Do what I tell you, boy!" he barked, his iron voice too full of love to be disobeyed.

A piece of the wall just above us came off. Never heard a shot — the shooter must be using a suppressor.

"Cocksucker ain't no Wesley," the little man sneered. "I been laying here like a fucking bull's-eye; he already missed twice."

I leaned close, needing to catch every word, but desperate to get to my car.

"Honor thy father," he whispered. "Call my name, son. My true name. Say it! Say it *loud,* so those whores know who's gonna bar their door."

"John Henry!" I screamed, with all my strength. The war cry pulled the Prof back from the brink — I could see the blaze of golden fire flare in his all-seeing brown eyes.

"Fetch me my hammer, son!" the little man commanded. "Time for me to drive some steel for real."

I was frozen — trapped between the two most compelling forces of my life.

"Get gone, Schoolboy," he assured me. "I'll be waiting when you show up. Me and that hound of yours."

I kissed him. Another shot ripped the wall. I pulled a fistful of spare 12-gauge double 0's from the Prof's side pocket, dropped them by his side. Found his scattergun a few feet away, placed it reverently in his right hand . . . and ran for the corner.

◆

The trunk was open, but Clarence wasn't behind the wheel. He was on one knee, his pistol out, a rabid dog on a gossamer leash. I'd told him to get around the corner, but that was as far as he was going.

I grabbed the RPG, shouldered it, shouted, "Get ready to fly!" . . . and ran back the way I'd come.

The Prof was still down, but his sawed-off was up. Waiting. The concrete was dark next to him, a spreading stain.

He never saw me as I dropped to one knee, sighted, and let loose at the sniper's roost, screaming *"Die!"* inside my heart, like I'd been doing since I was a kid. I could actually feel my hate raging inside that whistling warhead.

Yitzhak's man hadn't been lying. I was still staring at what was left of the top corner of the building when the armored van wheeled up broadside, a string of killer wasps flying out of the gun slits, a buzzing fog of death for whoever wanted to come down that alley toward us.

Gateman kept blasting, emptying clip after clip, covering Gigi as the giant lumbered out, so wrapped in Kevlar he looked like a moving boulder.

He scooped up the unconscious Prof, draping some layers of bullet-blanket over him. The back doors opened. Gigi laid him down, ran around to the front door. Michelle was already in motion. She jumped into the back. I could see Gateman already had the tourniquet out just before the doors closed. I knew the morphine was next.

I left the RPG where it was and sprinted down the alley. I stole a quick look over my shoulder. The alley was empty.

Couldn't face John Henry, could you, punks? My father's too much man for every fucking one of you! I was sobbing with pride, moving faster than that rocket had.

As I turned the corner, I yelled, "We got him! He's in the van!" as I dove into the passenger's seat.

Clarence had the Plymouth on full-jet as I speed-dialed Claw's last phone . . . the one with the yellow tape.

"Count it," I told Claw, three days later.

"I don't need to."

"I *want* you to."

He gave me an unreadable look, then opened the duffel bag, stacked the banded cash on the table in my booth at Mama's. Took him a long time to count — he knew I wanted him to touch every bill.

"There's an extra —"

"— share," I finished for him. "The guy who was supposed to get it, he won't be needing it."

"That's the fucking truth," the AB man said, grimly. "I did it plenty of times before. Inside, I mean — never on the street. Did it because I had to. I always stayed away from guys who *liked* doing it. But this time . . ."

"I know," I said. I held out my hand. He grasped it with the claw he'd used on Thornton. "You're going to make it," I told him. "The Prof knows."

"Is *he* going to?"

"We do not know yet, mahn," Clarence said. "My father is in a place where he is getting the best of everything, but we could not get him there immediately. We cannot visit. Every day, we wait. Every day, we pray."

He didn't mention that it was going to take a big chunk out of our piece to cover the freight for this one. And cost a few doctors their licenses if they got caught.

"I pray for him, too," Claw said.

Max bowed. Meaning: we didn't care who or what Claw was praying to — we believed that he was.

Mama came over to my booth. Handed Claw a Barnard mug.

"What's this?" he asked. It wasn't a food question.

"Old Chinese medicine," Mama told him, her black-ice eyes unblinking. "Kill bad things inside."

Claw held her eyes as he drank it down.

"Sure cure," Mama said. "Need two cups."

"May I please have the — ?"

"When you come back," she said. And walked away.

"All we can do is wait?" Michelle said, floodlighting the truth none of us wanted to speak aloud.

"If my father does not come back to us —"

"He's got the best," I cut Clarence off. Meaning: there's some things you can't get revenge for, and if the Prof didn't come back to us, it wouldn't be due to malpractice. The sniper who'd shot our father was already nothing but tissue samples.

"Maybe the Mole has something," Michelle said, hopefully. "Something special."

"Couldn't hurt to go ask, honey," I told her.

I finally said the first prayer of my life that didn't ask for death. I couldn't know if it would mean anything, but I had to say it. I would never disgrace my father by begging. But I could be a man and still say what I'd been saying ever since I could remember: "You owe me this."

Only, this time, I didn't curse whoever I was talking to.

ABOUT THE AUTHOR

Andrew Vachss has been a federal investigator in sexually transmitted diseases, a social-services caseworker, and a labor organizer, and has directed a maximum-security prison for "aggressive-violent" youth. Now a lawyer in private practice, he represents children and youths exclusively. He is the author of numerous novels, including the Burke series, two collections of short stories, and a wide variety of other material including song lyrics, graphic novels, essays, and a "children's book for adults." His books have been translated into twenty languages, and his work has appeared in *Parade, Antaeus, Esquire, Playboy, The New York Times,* and many other forums. A native New Yorker, he now divides his time between the city of his birth and the Pacific Northwest.

The dedicated Web site for Vachss and his work is www.vachss.com.

The employees of Thorndike Press hope you have enjoyed this Large Print book. All our Thorndike and Wheeler Large Print titles are designed for easy reading, and all our books are made to last. Other Thorndike Press Large Print books are available at your library, through selected bookstores, or directly from us.

For information about titles, please call:
(800) 223-1244

or visit our Web site at:
www.gale.com/thorndike
www.gale.com/wheeler

To share your comments, please write:
Publisher
Thorndike Press
295 Kennedy Memorial Drive
Waterville, ME 04901

MAI

3-11-08

GAYLORD FG